I0785216

HANK

USA TODAY BESTSELLING AUTHOR

PJ FIALA

RT
ROLLING THUNDER
PUBLISHING INC

DEDICATION

I've had so many wonderful people come into my life and I want you all to know how much I appreciate it. From each and every reader who takes the time out of their days to read my stories and leave reviews, thank you. My beautiful, smart and fun Road Queens, who play games with me, post fun memes, keep the conversation rolling and help me create these captivating characters, places, businesses and more.

To my family, my greatest blessing and unwavering support system. Your love, encouragement, and sacrifices have made this dream possible. And to my husband and best friend, Gene—thank you for standing beside me every step of the way. Your belief in me, your patience, and your love are the foundation of everything I do. Words will never be enough to express how much you mean to me, but I will spend my life showing you.

***

To our veterans and all those currently serving in the armed forces, police, fire departments, and as EMTs—your courage, dedication, and sacrifices do not go unnoticed. Thank you for your unwavering commitment to protecting and serving. It is with heartfelt gratitude and deep respect that I honor you here. You are the true heroes, and your contributions inspire every word on these pages.

DESCRIPTION

She came to heal. He came to win. Neither expected a collision that could change everything.

Brie Spencer escapes to Copper Moon with nothing but a suitcase, a paintbrush, and a heart still shattered from the night her sister died. The peaceful mountain town is supposed to be her sanctuary, a place to grieve, paint, and maybe start breathing again.

Hank James has one goal—win the Copper Moon Cup. After years of close calls and busted dreams, this season feels different. He's poured everything into his bike, and nothing will stop him now.

Until Brie steps into his path—literally.

One wrong turn. One unexpected crash. Suddenly, their lives are entangled in ways neither saw coming. As sparks fly and wounds surface, Brie and Hank must decide if they're willing to risk their hearts on a second chance neither of them were looking for.

***

📖 The Copper Moon series is complete!
USA Today bestselling author PJ Fiala brings you ex-

military heroes, thrilling suspense, and unforgettable romance. No cliffhangers. No cheating. Just page-turning action and a guaranteed happily-ever-after.

🚀 Grab it now and dive in!

***

Looking for stories filled with heart-pounding suspense, steamy romance, and unforgettable characters? Sign up for my newsletter and get a **FREE book** to dive into right away!

It's easy:

1️⃣ Sign up below.

2️⃣ Confirm your email (we like to keep things legit and bot-free 😊).

3️⃣ Start enjoying your free read and exclusive updates, sneak peeks, and special offers!

📚 Love awaits—don't miss your chance to join the adventure!

https://www.pjfiala.com/subscribe/

The road sign emerged from the darkness like a promise: "Copper Moon Beach 5 Miles". Its reflective letters caught his headlights. Hank's chest expanded with the first full breath he'd taken in two hours. His fingers flexed on the steering wheel, joints stiff from gripping too tightly for too long.

"Only a few more minutes." The words came out rough, his throat dry from the recycled air and silence.

Brian shifted in the passenger seat, his massive frame cramped even with the seat pushed all the way back. A soft snore escaped before he settled again. In the back, Colby muttered something unintelligible, probably giving orders in his sleep like he did at the firehouse. The acrid smell of cold French fries mixed with Brian's cologne, something expensive he'd probably charmed off some woman, had been Hank's only company since they'd crossed the Kentucky state line.

His right thigh burned, the familiar ache spreading up into his hip. Thirteen hours behind the wheel was pushing it, but he'd wanted to drive. Needed to. The closer they got to Copper Moon, the more his body hummed with anticipation, and something else. Fear maybe. Or the weight of knowing everything rode on this weekend.

The truck crested Miller's Hill, and Hank's breath caught. This was the moment. His father's voice echoed in his memory: "Watch now, son. Nothing prettier than Copper Moon at night."

He reached over, his calloused fingers finding Brian's shoulder. The muscle beneath was solid as rock, even relaxed. "Hey, you're gonna miss it."

"Hmm." Brian's hand came up, scrubbing at his face. His tactical watch caught the dashboard light, 0058 hours. Old habits. "What..." A yawn cut him off, arms stretching until his knuckles brushed the roof.

"Buddy. Wake up, we're here." Hank rolled his shoulders, vertebrae popping in sequence. The sound made him feel older than forty-three. His neck protested as he turned it side to side, but the pain faded as Miller's Hill delivered its promise.

Brian straightened, suddenly alert, that SEAL training never really left. "Holy shit."

"Yeah." Hank's voice came out reverent.

The bay spread before them like hammered copper, the full moon painting the water in shades of rust and gold. Each wave caught the light differently, creating a living canvas that shifted and breathed. The town below looked like a jewelry box, windows dark but edged in copper light, the marina's masts cutting dark lines through the glow.

"Colby, get up, time to go to work." Brian's voice held mischief.

The reaction was immediate and violent. Colby shot upright, hand reaching for something that wasn't there, eyes wild. "What? Holy crap, don't fuck with me like that, ya jack asses."

Their laughter filled the truck, but it died as they descended into town. Main Street was empty, shop windows reflecting the copper light like mirrors. The Copper Moon Resort sat at the end of the road, directly across from the beach. Hank's chest tightened. Tomorrow, this sleepy paradise would transform into controlled chaos, with motorcycles, mechanics, racers, and thousands of spectators. Tomorrow, everything would change.

Tonight, it was theirs.

He pulled the truck and trailer to the far end of the hotel parking lot, noting the empty spaces. By tomorrow afternoon, there wouldn't be room to walk between vehicles. His hands trembled slightly as he killed the engine. Exhaustion or anticipation, he couldn't tell anymore.

"Okay, guys, let's check in and see if we can get a few hours of shut-eye." He pushed open the driver's door, the humid beach air hitting him like a physical presence. Salt, seaweed, and something else, possibility, maybe. "I'm getting up early to warm Julie up before we start timing her."

Brian stretched again, his back cracking loud enough to echo. "Every time you call the bike Julie, it freaks me out just a little."

"Thirty years, Brian. Thirty years you've known about Julie, and you're still not used to it?" Hank's fingers found his right thigh, massaging the knot that had formed during the drive. The muscle spasmed once before releasing.

Colby climbed out, steadying himself against the truck. "You should be used to it by now." He looked toward the water, visible between buildings. "Place hasn't changed much."

"Some things shouldn't change." Hank grabbed his duffel from the truck bed, the weight of it familiar. Everything he needed was in that bag: racing leathers, tools, and the photo of his grandfather with the original Julie. The bike was named after his grandmother, the only woman who could make the old man smile like that.

They walked toward the hotel entrance, Hank's limp more pronounced now that he thought no one was watching. But Colby noticed, Colby always noticed. His friend fell into step beside him, close enough to catch him if the leg gave out but not so close as to wound his pride.

The lobby hit them with aggressive air conditioning and the smell of lemon cleaner trying to mask something floral. Fresh flowers, birds of paradise, and something purple Hank didn't recognize, sat in crystal vases. But it was the cookies that made his stomach growl. Chocolate chip, fresh enough that he could see the steam rising.

"Damn, those cookies smell good." Brian's stomach joined the chorus, growling loud enough to echo.

"You're a garbage can, Brian. You haven't stopped eating since we left Kentucky," Colby griped, but there was affection in it.

"Don't worry about it, I'm a growing boy." Brian's whole demeanor shifted, shoulders squaring, that megawatt smile clicking into place.

Hank followed his friend's gaze to the reception desk. The girl behind it couldn't have been more than twenty-five, with blonde hair piled in a messy bun that probably took an hour to look that effortless. Pretty in that beach town way, sun-kissed and glowing. She noticed Brian immediately. They always did.

"Here we go," Colby muttered.

Hank stepped ahead of Brian, cutting off his approach.

The girl's eyes tracked Brian even as she addressed Hank. "Hi, welcome to the Copper Moon Resort. Do you have a reservation?"

"Hank James." He pulled the folded confirmation from his back pocket, the paper soft from his nervous handling during the drive. But she was already typing, pink-polished nails clicking against keys.

The printer hummed to life. She swiped two key cards, stopped, and looked directly at Brian. The blush started at her chest, visible above her resort polo shirt. "How many keys do you need?"

Brian moved in for the kill, all six-foot-four of him leaning against the counter. His biceps flexed, accidentally on purpose, showing off the tail end of his SEAL trident tattoo. The temperature in the room seemed to rise ten degrees. "Three, darlin', unless you'd like to make yourself one too."

Her hand fluttered to her throat, fingers playing with a small necklace there. The key card machine beeped three times while she tried to remember how to breathe.

She spread a map on the counter with shaking hands, using a pink highlighter to mark their route. "You're in building C, room 247. It's a suite with a view of the beach." Her voice cracked slightly. "I'm April. I'm here until eight if you need... anything."

"Thank you." Hank grabbed two key cards and the paperwork, leaving one for Romeo. "See you in the room, Brian."

Colby laughed as they walked back to the truck. "I watch him do his thing all the time, and I'm still amazed by it. It's damned effortless for that son-of-a-bitch to get laid."

"Natural talent." Hank hefted his bag, trying not to

favor his right side. "Though at our age, you'd think he'd slow down."

"Brian? Slow down? The day he slows down is the day they put him in the ground." Colby grabbed his own gear, tactical bag perfectly organized. "You okay? That leg's bothering you."

"I'm fine."

"Bullshit. But we'll pretend I believe you." Colby held the door as they entered the hotel. "Big day tomorrow."

"Yeah." Hank's free hand found the key card in his pocket, running his thumb along the edge. "Everything changes tomorrow."

They found their room, a decent suite with three beds and a balcony overlooking the beach. Brian would get the pull-out when he finally finished his hunt. Hank chose the bed nearest the balcony door, needing to hear the water. Colby took the one with the best sight lines to the door, always tactical, always ready.

Hank sat on his bed, unlacing his boots slowly. His fingers found the scar tissue along his thigh, pressing into the damaged muscle. Tomorrow, he'd need to be at one hundred percent. Tomorrow, thirty years of family history would ride on his shoulders.

"Hey." Colby's voice was quiet. "We're gonna do this. Your grandpa would be proud."

"Yeah." Hank lay back, still fully clothed except for his boots. The sound of waves carried through the glass door. "He would be."

Within minutes, exhaustion won. But just before sleep took him, Hank could have sworn he smelled copper on the ocean breeze, like the moon itself was blessing their arrival.

Tomorrow, everything would change.

Tonight, he just needed to believe they were ready for it.

CHAPTER
TWO

The grandfather clock in the hotel lobby chimed half past two as Bree Spencer pushed through the heavy glass doors, her travel-weary body aching from the long drive. The warm air of the Copper Moon Resort enveloped her like a gentle embrace, carrying with it the mingled scents of lavender from the fresh flower arrangements and something sweet, freshly baked goods that made her empty stomach clench with hunger.

"Hi, my name is Bree Spencer." Her voice came out raspier than intended, throat dry from hours of highway driving. She cleared it softly before continuing. "My friend, Blake Donaldson, booked a room for me here."

The pretty blonde clerk behind the reception desk looked up from her computer screen, her fingers pausing mid-type. Under the soft amber lighting of the lobby, her features seemed almost ethereal, with bright blue eyes that sparkled with genuine warmth and a messy bun that somehow looked both effortless and charming, with wisps of golden hair framing her face. A blue ballpoint pen tucked behind her ear completed the picture of organized chaos that seemed to suit the late hour perfectly.

As the clerk's fingers danced across the keyboard, searching for the reservation, Bree allowed herself a moment to truly take in her surroundings. The lobby was a study in understated elegance, earth-toned furniture arranged in intimate conversation areas, plush armchairs that looked like they could swallow a person whole, and those magnificent flower arrangements that dotted every surface. Fresh roses, lilies, and what looked like locally sourced wildflowers created splashes of color against the muted backdrop.

The soft clicking of keys filled the silence before the clerk looked up, studying Bree with those perceptive blue eyes. "Stiff from traveling?" The question was accompanied by a sympathetic smile as Bree rolled her shoulders, producing an audible crack that echoed in the quiet lobby.

"Yeah." Bree managed a self-deprecating laugh, her hand automatically going to massage the knot at the base of her skull. "I'm not used to it. I'm sort of a homebody, to be honest. This is the farthest I've driven by myself in... well, ever."

The admission hung between them for a moment, carrying more weight than Bree had intended to share with a stranger.

"I am too. A homebody, I mean." The clerk's voice brightened, as if finding a kindred spirit at this ungodly hour was a small miracle. "We have enough action here in the summer that I prefer to stay home when I can. But working the night shift, I hear hundreds of accents each year from all over. It's like traveling without ever leaving town."

Her enthusiasm was infectious, and Bree found herself

genuinely smiling for the first time in what felt like weeks. "Wow. When Blake told me to come here, he didn't say it was such a lively place." She paused, looking toward the front doors where moonlight transformed the water beyond into a canvas of liquid copper. "He said the beach would be great for getting my creative juices flowing and that it was beautiful here. But now I'm wondering just how much he left out."

The moonlit water held her transfixed for a moment; it was achingly beautiful, the kind of scene that made her fingers itch for a paintbrush, even through her exhaustion.

"Oh, he left out plenty if he didn't mention race week," the clerk, whose name tag read April, said with a knowing chuckle. "This is one of our biggest weeks of the year. The whole town transforms. But don't worry, there are still quiet spots if you know where to look."

As if on cue, Bree's stomach let out a prolonged, embarrassingly loud growl that seemed to echo off the lobby's high ceiling. The sound was so unexpected and so thoroughly undignified that both women froze for a moment before bursting into laughter.

Bree's hand flew to her belly, her cheeks flushing pink. "Oh God, I'm so sorry. I guess it's been longer than I thought since I've eaten. I was so focused on just getting here that I forgot to stop for dinner."

"I've got just the thing for you." April's eyes lit up with the enthusiasm of someone who took genuine pleasure in small acts of kindness. She practically bounced on her toes as she disappeared through a doorway behind the desk marked "Employees Only."

The brief solitude allowed Bree a moment to sag against the counter, the polished wood cool against her palms. She was here. She'd actually done it, driven all those miles alone, pushed through the fear and uncertainty, and arrived at this place Blake had promised would help her heal.

Mere seconds later, April reappeared, carrying something that made Bree's mouth water instantly. The chocolate chip cookie was enormous, easily the size of her palm, and still warm enough that wisps of steam rose from its surface. The chocolate chips glistened, not quite fully set, promising that perfect balance of crispy edges and gooey center.

"Our cook is getting ready for breakfast and comes in at one o'clock in the morning to start baking," April explained. "This is literally fresh from the oven, maybe five minutes old. Martha makes the best chocolate chip cookies on the eastern seaboard, and I'll fight anyone who says otherwise."

The aroma hit Bree full force: butter, vanilla, dark chocolate, and something else, something that reminded her of home, of better times, of her sister's kitchen on Sunday mornings. Her stomach responded with another audible complaint, and this time her blush deepened to crimson.

"My name is April, by the way," the clerk said, extending her hand across the counter. "April Morrison. Nice to meet you officially."

"Bree." She shook April's hand, noting the firm grip and the calluses that suggested this woman did more than just work the desk. "Oh, but you know that already. Sorry, I'm hungry and tired, so I guess I'm not thinking clearly. My brain feels like it's running on fumes."

She picked up the still-warm cookie and inhaled deeply. The first bite was transcendent, the perfect combination of textures and temperatures, the chocolate melting on her tongue, the slight saltiness enhancing the sweetness. It was, quite possibly, the best thing she'd eaten in months.

"No need to apologize," April said gently, seeming to sense the deeper exhaustion beneath Bree's travel weariness. "Three a.m. arrivals are always a little disoriented. It's like being in a different dimension, not quite night, not quite morning, somewhere in between. That's why we keep the cookies coming. Martha says sugar and chocolate can cure almost anything, at least temporarily."

Bree gathered her key card and paperwork, the cookie already half-devoured despite her best efforts at restraint. "Thank you, April. Not just for the cookie, but for being so welcoming. I'm sure I'll be seeing you around while I'm here."

"I work nights all week, midnight to eight, so I'm your girl if you need anything during the vampire hours." April's smile was warm and genuine, the kind that reached her eyes and crinkled the corners. "And Bree? Welcome to Copper Moon Beach. Something tells me this place is exactly what you need right now, even if you don't know it yet."

As Bree headed toward her car to retrieve her luggage, April's words echoed in her mind. The night air was thick with salt and possibility, the sound of waves a distant whisper beneath the hum of crickets and night birds. She paused, looking out at the moon-painted water once more. The copper moon that gave this place its name hung low and full, casting its unique light over everything, transforming the ordinary into something magical.

Her artist's eye caught the play of shadows and light, the way the moon's reflection created a pathway across the water that seemed to lead directly to the horizon. Tomorrow, she promised herself, she would paint this. She would capture this moment of arrival, of transition, of stepping from one life into something unknown.

The handle of her suitcase was cool against her palm as she pulled it from the trunk, the wheels clicking rhythmically against the pavement as she made her way back to the lobby. Through the windows, she could see April back at her computer, probably preparing for the next late-night arrival. But the woman looked up as Bree passed, offering a small wave that somehow felt like a promise of friendship.

In her room, 208, ocean view, Blake had splurged; Bree didn't even bother to fully unpack. She kicked off her shoes, letting them land wherever they fell, and collapsed onto the bed fully clothed. The last thing she saw before exhaustion claimed her was the copper moon through her window, watching over her like a benevolent guardian.

For the first time in a year, since that horrible day when the doctor had delivered the diagnosis that would change everything, Bree fell asleep without crying. The half-eaten cookie sat on her nightstand, a sweet reminder that even in the darkest hours, kindness could be found in the most unexpected places.

Tomorrow would bring new challenges, she knew. Tomorrow she would have to face the blank canvas, the grief that painting sometimes brought to the surface, and the reality of being alone in a strange place. But tonight, with her belly finally quiet and the taste of chocolate still lingering on her tongue, she could rest.

The sound of the waves through her cracked window became a lullaby, and somewhere in that space between waking and sleeping, Bree could have sworn she heard her sister's voice on the salt breeze: "You're going to be okay, Bree. You're finally going to be okay."

CHAPTER
THREE

The first tendrils of dawn were painting the sky in shades of coral and gold when Bree Spencer's eyes fluttered open. She lay there for a moment, disoriented by the unfamiliar ceiling, the weight of the hotel comforter, the sound of waves that had replaced the suburban traffic she was accustomed to. The digital clock on the nightstand glowed 5:17 a.m., and despite having only slept for two hours, she felt more rested than she had in months.

Perhaps it was the sea air, or maybe it was the lingering sweetness of April's cookie still coating her tongue, but something had shifted in the night. The crushing weight that had been her constant companion for the past year felt lighter somehow, as if the salt breeze had begun to erode its edges.

Sitting up, Bree stretched, her spine creating a satisfying series of pops that echoed in the quiet room. She padded to the window on bare feet, the plush carpet soft between her toes. Her fingers found the heavy curtains, and she pulled them back slowly, squinting in anticipation of the brightness.

The sunrise hit her like a physical force, all that copper and crimson light reflecting off the water in a display that made her artist's heart leap. She had to close her eyes against the intensity, seeing spots dance behind her eyelids like tiny fireworks. When she opened them again, more carefully this time, starting from the windowsill and gradually lifting her gaze, what she saw took her breath away.

The beach stretched out before her, pristine and perfect. Someone had raked it during the night, creating neat parallel lines in the sand that looked like an enormous zen garden. The water was a living canvas of light, each wave capped with copper foam that sparkled like scattered pennies. Not a soul moved on the beach; even the seabirds seemed to be sleeping in. The entire town looked drowsy and peaceful, as if it hadn't quite decided whether to wake up yet.

"Bryn," she whispered, her breath fogging the glass slightly. "I see why you loved it here. It's absolutely beautiful."

The tears came then, but they were different from the bitter, angry tears she'd been crying for months. These were soft, almost grateful. Her sister had tried to tell her about this place, had shared stories from her honeymoon here with Charlie, describing the way the morning light transformed everything it touched. Bree had thought it was just newlywed romanticism, the tendency to see the world through rose-colored glasses when you're drunk on love and possibility. But standing here now, she understood it was simply the truth.

She swiped at her eyes with the back of her hand and turned toward the bathroom, suddenly eager to get outside and capture this light. Her fingers were already itching for a brush, her mind automatically mixing colors: burnt sienna with a touch of cadmium orange, perhaps a hint of gold ochre for the highlights on the water.

She dressed quickly but carefully, choosing cream-colored capri pants that Bryn had bought for her last birthday and a soft-blue sleeveless button-up blouse that had been Bryn's. The clothes still smelled faintly of her sister's favorite fabric softener, a small comfort she wasn't ready to wash away. She unpacked the items she'd been too exhausted to unpack last night. She heard her mother's voice: "A cluttered space means a cluttered mind, girls." It brought a smile to her lips.

Stepping out of her room, she made her way to the elevator, then through the lobby, where April was still at her post, looking remarkably fresh for someone who'd been working all night. They exchanged waves, April's smile bright despite the early hour.

Outside, the morning air wrapped around her like a cool, salty embrace. She popped the trunk of her car with the key fob, the electronic chirp seeming too loud in the morning quiet. Her painting supplies were organized in the trunk with the same meticulous care she applied to every-thing: canvas in protective sleeves, her paint tote with each tube in its designated spot, her easel folded neatly and compact.

She gathered her supplies, the familiar weight of them comforting in her arms, and headed across the road toward the beach. Her leather sandals made soft whisking sounds against the pavement, then transitioned to a gentle swoosh as she stepped onto the sand. The breeze played with her newly shortened hair, the bob cut swaying and tickling her neck in a way she still wasn't used to. She'd cut it three weeks after the funeral, needing to change something, anything, to mark the transition from before to after.

Looking down the beach, she noticed something odd. The meticulously raked section ended abruptly, giving way to smooth, hard-packed sand that looked almost like concrete. The texture difference was striking; soft and groomed on one side, compressed and worn on the other. The morning waves rolled up the hard-packed section, their foam fingers reaching only a few feet before retreating back to the sea.

Her artist's eye was drawn to a rock formation ahead, its top worn flat by centuries of wind and weather. "Perfect," she whispered, already envisioning how she'd set up her easel there, using the natural platform to steady her supplies.

The beach sounds created a symphony around her: waves lapping in rhythm, birds beginning their morning songs, the distant croak of frogs from some hidden marsh. This was what Bryn had tried to describe, this sense of being held by nature, of being part of something both ancient and immediate.

Then she heard it: a sharp, mechanical roar that shattered the morning peace like a hammer through glass. An engine revving, growing louder, angrier. She turned back toward the road, frowning, waiting to see what kind of person would destroy such perfect quiet at this ungodly hour. The sound grew closer, the pitch changing as gears shifted, but she saw nothing on the road. No car, no truck, nothing.

Shaking her head at the invisible disturbance, she continued toward the rocks. She was just stepping onto the hard-packed sand, navigating around the far edge of the formation, when she saw him.

Time seemed to slow, the way it does in dreams or accidents. A motorcycle was bearing down on her, its rider leaning into the speed, the machine itself a blur of chrome and color. She had perhaps a second to process what was happening: the bike was on the beach, not the road; it was racing directly toward her; she was in its path.

She squealed, a high, frightened sound she'd never made before, and dove sideways. Her painting supplies flew from her arms as she hit the sand hard, rolling twice before coming to a stop. She could feel sand in her mouth, in her hair, coating one side of her face like gritty makeup.

The motorcycle's brakes screamed in protest, the back wheel sliding sideways, leaving a dark scar in the pristine sand. The rider fought for control, his body language speaking of barely contained disaster. Finally, impossibly, he brought the machine to a stop some thirty yards away.

But even as Bree pushed herself up on her elbows, spitting sand and trying to process what had just happened, she saw her canvas. The wind, aided by the motorcycle's passage, had caught it like a sail. It tumbled end over end down the beach, directly toward the rider who was now turning his bike around.

"No, no, no," she whispered, watching in horror as the inevitable unfolded.

The rider, his attention divided between controlling the bike and looking at her, didn't see the canvas until it was too late. It hit him square in the chest just as he accelerated. His hands came off the handlebars instinctively, trying to bat it away. The motorcycle, suddenly without guidance, lurched sideways and went down hard, sliding several feet before coming to rest on its side.

The sound of metal on sand was horrible, a grinding scrape that made her teeth ache. But worse was the stream of profanity that followed. The rider ripped his helmet off and hurled it at the ground, where it bounced twice before rolling to a stop. His curses were creative, extensive, and loud enough that she was certain they could hear him back at the hotel.

Despite everything, despite nearly being run over, despite being covered in sand and having her peaceful morning shattered, Bree found herself running toward him. "Are you okay?" she called out, her voice high and worried.

The man turned to look at her for the first time, really look at her, and she felt the full force of his anger like a physical blow. His eyes were dark, furious, his jaw clenched so tightly she could see the muscles jumping beneath the skin. He planted his hands on his hips in a stance that screamed confrontation.

She stopped short, suddenly uncertain. "I'm so sorry. Are you hurt?"

"You're *sorry*?" His voice was rough, gravelly, as if he'd been gargling sand. "That's all you have to say? I could have been killed. What the hell are you doing, throwing this shit around the beach?" He gestured wildly at her scattered supplies. "And why in the hell did you step in front of me? For crying out loud, you must have heard me coming."

The sympathy she'd been feeling evaporated like morning dew under his harsh tone. Being scolded like a misbehaving child flipped a switch in her that she didn't know existed. Her own hands found her hips, mirroring his stance, her chin lifting in defiance.

"I'll have you know, Mr. Mayor," she said, her voice dripping with sarcasm as she made exaggerated air quotes around the title, "that I wasn't throwing 'shit' around the beach. I was trying to paint, which is a perfectly reasonable thing to do at sunrise on a public beach. And while we're at it, why didn't you honk your horn or something when you saw me so I would get out of the way?"

"Really? What?" He raked both hands through his dark hair, leaving it standing in frustrated spikes. When he raised his voice, she could hear the frustration giving way to incredulity. "I was racing. And it's a racing bike. It doesn't have a horn." He slammed his hands back on his hips, his stance widening as he stared her down. "And what would you call that?" He pointed at her broken canvas, now twisted and torn beyond repair. "And why in the hell did you call me Mr. Mayor?"

Despite their height difference, she was maybe five-four to his six feet, Bree refused to be intimidated. She tilted her head back, meeting his glare with one of her own, noting absently that his eyes weren't black as she'd first thought but a deep brown with flecks of gold, like tiger's eye stones.

She tossed her head, trying unsuccessfully to get her sand-coated hair out of her face. "I called you, Mr. Mayor, because you act like you own this beach. I don't know your name, and frankly, you're being an ass."

Something shifted in his expression at her words, a flicker of what might have been amusement quickly suppressed. He stepped closer, close enough that she could smell motor oil and leather and something else, something warm and masculine that made her stomach do an unexpected flip. They were nose to chest now, and she had to crane her neck back at an uncomfortable angle to maintain eye contact, but she'd be damned if she'd back down first.

"My name, Miss Sassy Pants," he said, his voice dropping to something almost intimate, "is Hank. I act like I run this place because any fool can see how clean this beach is, and you don't throw trash on a beach." His voice rose again on the last words. "And you made me dump Julie. Do you even know how much time and effort I have to put in to get Julie ready for this week?"

Bree's mind went completely blank for a moment. She looked around the beach, searching for another person, this Julie he was so concerned about. When she saw no one, her confusion gave way to a different kind of concern. The man was clearly unhinged. Crazy equaled trouble in her world, trouble she didn't need.

She took a strategic step backward, trying for a placating tone. "Well, Hank, I'll let you get back to Julie." Despite her best efforts, a smirk tugged at her lips, and then a giggle escaped, high and slightly hysterical.

His expression darkened to something approaching thunderous. "You're laughing at the fact that Julie might be damaged?"

She watched, fascinated despite herself, as he turned to his motorcycle. With a couple of grunts and an impressive display of strength, he hauled the machine upright. The kickstand went down with a metallic snap, and he leaned the bike over onto it before pulling off his leather gloves with sharp, angry movements.

Then something changed. His hands, she noticed, became gentle as they moved over the motorcycle, checking for damage with the tenderness of a parent examining a hurt child. He brushed sand from the sections that weren't hot from the engine, his touch reverent, loving even. He shook his head slowly from side to side, and she could hear him murmuring something under his breath.

Understanding dawned slowly, and with it came a mix of emotions she couldn't quite sort out. "Wait," she said, her brows drawing together in confusion. "Julie is... your... bike?"

He didn't answer immediately. Instead, he walked

slowly around the motorcycle, his fingers touching gauges, checking cables, and examining every inch of painted surface that had come into contact with the sand. His inspection was thorough, methodical, and filled with obvious concern.

When he finally spoke, his voice had lost its angry edge, replaced by something that sounded like pride mixed with deep affection. "I'll have you know, this here is a 1942 Crocker. It was my grandpa's bike, then my dad's. Now it's mine. This year, Julie is going to help me win the Copper Moon Cup. She's all I have, and she's the most important thing in the world to me."

The words hung between them, heavy with meaning she couldn't quite grasp. Bree's lips pressed into a thin line as she processed this information. The morning breeze picked up, carrying with it the faint smell of fish and salt water, swirling her sandy hair across her face again.

"What's the Copper Moon Cup?" she asked, genuinely curious now.

Hank straightened from his inspection and looked at her, really looked at her, as if seeing her for the first time. He shook his head slowly, a gesture that seemed to encompass disbelief, frustration, and something that might have been amusement.

"Do you mean to tell me," he said, walking toward her with measured steps, "that you're here in Copper Moon this week, race week, and you don't know what the Cup is?"

Heat bloomed in her cheeks, a blush she could feel spreading down her neck. "My friend, Blake, made the reservation for me here. He told me Copper Moon would be good for me."

A smirk tugged at one corner of Hank's mouth, transforming his face from angry to almost roguish. "So your boyfriend made a reservation for you, but didn't tell you that the race for the Cup was going on? And how long ago did he make this reservation?"

"He's not my boyfriend," she said quickly, perhaps too quickly. "We're friends. And he made the reservation last week. What difference does that make?"

"He famous or something?" The question came out sharp, and she saw his jaw tick with tension. There was something else in his tone now, something that sounded almost like... annoyance? Jealousy?

She winced at his tone, bending to retrieve her broken canvas, which had blown back toward them on the breeze. The canvas was ruined, torn in three places with a tire track across its center. "He manages bands and knows a lot of people all over the place. One of his bands plays in this area a lot."

"A musician," Hank muttered, the words barely audible but clearly dismissive.

"He's not... never mind, it doesn't matter." She examined the tattered canvas, mourning its loss for a moment before looking back up at him. "I'm sorry about your... Julie." A soft smile curved her lips at the name, finding it endearing despite everything.

Hank moved around the bike again, giving it one more visual inspection. His tone had shifted to something more practical, almost concerned. "Be more careful around here. Today, all the other teams will be showing up, and bikes will be running up and down the beach to test conditions. Not a good place to be throwing your stuff down."

He took a few steps toward her, and that's when she noticed it: a slight hitch in his gait, the way he seemed to favor his right leg.

"Are you injured? You're limping."

His response was curt, defensive. "I'm fine."

He looked toward the hotel then, and she followed his gaze to see two men approaching across the beach. One was massive, all blonde hair and bulging muscles, built like a Viking warrior. The other was leaner, sandy-haired, moving with the controlled grace of someone accustomed to physical work.

Hank bent to retrieve his helmet, his fingers roughly brushing at the scuffs the impact had left on its shiny black surface. There was something in his movements now, a tension that hadn't been there before, as if the approaching men brought complications he wasn't ready to deal with.

Bree found herself studying his hands as he worked on the helmet. They were rough, calloused, with small scars across the knuckles and what looked like old burns on one thumb. Working hands. Hands that knew machinery and labor and, apparently, how to gentle a vintage motorcycle like a skittish horse.

His temper had cooled completely now, replaced by what looked like genuine concern, though whether for his bike or the situation in general, she couldn't tell. As he raised his head to watch the approaching men, a furrow appeared between his brows, deepening the worry lines that suggested this wasn't his first stress-inducing week.

His posture stiffened, shoulders squaring as if preparing for battle. He pulled off his leather jacket in one fluid motion, laying it carefully across the motorcycle's seat. The gray T-shirt he wore underneath stretched across his back and chest in a way that made her mouth go dry. He was lean but muscled, his body speaking of strength earned through use rather than a gym. The shirt tapered down to a narrow waist before tucking into jeans that... well, jeans that fit him exceptionally well.

She was staring at his backside, she realized with a start. And it was, objectively speaking, a mighty fine backside.

He turned and caught her looking. Their eyes met, and the knowing grin that spread across his face made her cheeks flare so hot she was surprised her hair didn't catch fire. His eyebrows rose, disappearing beneath that touchable lock of dark hair that had flopped forward over his forehead.

"Okay. Well, I'm going then," she said quickly, her voice pitched higher than normal. She turned and started walking toward her scattered painting supplies, needing distance, needing to think, needing to stop noticing how well those jeans fit.

But as she walked, something that had been nagging at the back of her mind suddenly surfaced. Something about the way he held himself, the set of his shoulders, even the way he'd swung his leg over the motorcycle. It was familiar in a way that had nothing to do with their morning encounter.

She stopped and turned back toward him. "Are you Hank James?"

He froze in the middle of checking something on the bike, his whole body going still before he straightened slowly. "Yeah. How do you know that?"

For the first time since their collision, she smiled, a real, genuine smile that transformed her face. She took a couple of steps back toward him, the morning suddenly feeling full of possibility rather than disaster.

"I think we went to high school together. I'm Bree Spencer. I was a sophomore when you were a senior. You played football, as I recall. Quarterback, right? You threw the winning touchdown at homecoming."

Something shifted in his expression as he studied her, his eyes moving over her face as if trying to reconcile the woman before him with a memory from decades past. He brushed his hands together absently, a nervous gesture that seemed at odds with his earlier confidence.

"You have a sister?" he said finally. "Bryn, I think."

The name hit her like a physical blow, the way it always did when spoken by someone who'd known her sister in the before times. Her smile turned wistful, tinged with a sadness that had become her constant companion.

"Yeah. I did." She rubbed her hands nervously on her hips, a self-soothing gesture she'd developed over the past year, and bit her lower lip before continuing. "She died last year."

She watched his face transform, the curiosity replaced by something softer, more genuine. His lips twitched, then turned down into a frown of genuine sympathy. "I'm sorry. As I recall, she was very sweet. She dated my friend Charlie."

"She married him, too," Bree said, finding comfort in talking about the life her sister had built. "They have two kids, Bobby and Carly. Twenty-two and twenty now. They look just like her."

"That must be hard for Charlie." There was understanding in his voice now, the kind that suggested personal experience with loss. "I lost touch with most of the folks back home."

"Yeah. Me too." The words came out softer than intended, carrying the weight of all the relationships that had fallen away after Bryn's death, all the people who didn't know what to say to her anymore.

She busied herself with picking up her wooden easel, needing something to do with her hands, needing to move past this moment of unexpected connection. The easel had survived the morning's chaos intact, its worn wood smooth under her fingers.

She looked back at Hank just as his friends arrived, close enough now that she could see their faces. The blonde one had bright blue eyes and dimples, the kind of face that probably had been getting him out of trouble since kindergarten. The sandy-haired one looked more serious, his expression already suspicious as he looked between her and Hank.

"Sorry our reintroduction was... abrupt," she said, attempting a smile. "Good luck with the race."

She nodded at the other two men as she began walking toward the hotel, her arms full of salvaged art supplies. She could feel Hank's eyes on her as she walked, could feel the weight of his gaze like a physical touch. Unable to resist, she bent forward to pick up her paint case from where it had landed, taking perhaps a bit longer than necessary, aware that her capri pants were probably providing quite a view.

When she straightened and glanced back, she caught him looking. His expression was unreadable, but there was something in his eyes, a heat that made her stomach flutter in a way it hadn't in a very long time.

Behind him, the beach was coming alive with the morning sun, the copper light turning everything it touched into something magical. She could hear his friends approaching, could hear the questions that would surely come. But for just a moment longer, it was just the two of them, standing on a beach at sunrise, connected by shared history and an almost-accident that had somehow become something else entirely.

She thought about the broken canvas in her hand,

about how she'd planned to paint the sunrise, to capture the peace and beauty of Copper Moon Beach. Instead, she'd nearly been run over by a man on a motorcycle named Julie, a man she'd known in another lifetime, in the before times when her sister was alive, and the future seemed certain.

Maybe Blake had known exactly what he was doing when he sent her here. Maybe Copper Moon Beach, with its copper light and racing motorcycles and men who named their bikes after women, was exactly what she needed. Not peace, perhaps, but something else. Something that made her feel alive in a way she'd forgotten was possible.

As she walked back toward the hotel, she could hear Hank's friends reaching him, could hear the low rumble of male voices discussing the morning's events. She didn't look back again, but she knew, with a certainty that surprised her, that this wasn't over.

This was just the beginning.

CHAPTER

FOUR

Hank stared at the empty racetrack, his mind replaying yesterday's practice runs. Julie had performed flawlessly, but he couldn't shake the feeling that it wasn't enough. Not yet.

"Hey, daydreamer!" Brian's voice cut through his thoughts. "You planning to stand there all morning, or are you actually going to help us prep?"

Hank turned to find Brian and Colby approaching, matching grins on their faces. They'd been his crew for three years now, and he knew that look. They were about to give him hell.

"I'm thinking," Hank said.

"Thinking?" Colby laughed. "Is that what we're calling it now? Because from where I'm standing, it looked more like mooning over a certain blonde from the beach."

Heat crept up Hank's neck. "I wasn't..."

"Oh, he's blushing," Brian announced loudly enough that a few nearby teams turned to look. "Guys, our fearless driver is blushing."

"Will you two knock it off?" Hank grabbed a wrench

from the toolbox, more for something to do with his hands than any actual need for it. "I just met her yesterday."

"Uh-huh." Brian crossed his arms. "And you just happened to nearly get yourself killed staring at her instead of watching where you were going."

Colby leaned against the trailer. "Not that we're complaining. Anyone who can make you forget about racing for five whole minutes must be something special."

"I didn't forget about racing."

Both men burst out laughing.

"Hank," Brian said, wiping his eyes, "you literally walked into traffic. For a woman. You, the guy who won't even take a coffee break during prep."

"It wasn't like that."

"See?" Colby gestured at him. "He's already defensive. This is serious."

Before Hank could respond, the sound of engines roaring to life echoed across the facility. Not the steady, controlled rumble of teams doing maintenance checks, but something louder. Aggressive.

Showy.

The three of them turned toward the entrance just as a convoy of vehicles rolled in. Five gleaming black trucks, each one sporting oversized tires and custom paint jobs that screamed money. The lead truck had flames painted along its sides, and mounted on its roof was a speaker system blasting heavy metal loud enough to rattle windows.

"Oh hell," Brian muttered. "They're back."

Team Red Dragon had arrived.

The convoy made a slow, deliberate circle of the parking area, ensuring every team saw them. The music pounded, the engines revved unnecessarily, and the driver of the lead truck laid on the horn in a pattern that sounded almost like a battle cry.

Other teams stopped what they were doing to watch. Some shook their heads in disgust. Others made rude gestures. Nobody looked happy to see them.

"I was hoping they wouldn't come back this year," Colby said quietly.

Hank's jaw tightened as the trucks finally parked, taking up twice the space they needed. The music cut off, and the doors opened in synchronized choreography. Six men stepped out, all wearing matching red and black racing suits with a dragon logo embroidered across their backs. They moved with the swagger of men who expected everyone to watch them.

And unfortunately, everyone was.

The team's driver, Marcus Steele, was the last to emerge. He pulled off his sunglasses with practiced flair and surveyed the facility like a king inspecting his domain. His gaze swept across the other teams, lingering just long enough on each one to make it clear he didn't consider any of them competition.

When his eyes landed on Hank, his smile turned predatory.

"Well, well," Marcus called out, his voice carrying across the parking lot. "If it isn't Hank James. Still driving that ancient rust bucket, I see."

Brian's hand clamped down on Hank's shoulder before he could take a step forward.

"Not worth it," Brian murmured. "You know that's what he wants."

Hank forced himself to breathe slowly, to keep his hands relaxed at his sides instead of curled into fists. Brian was right. Marcus thrived on getting under people's skin. Reacting would only make things worse.

"Ignore him," Colby added. "We've got work to do."

But ignoring Team Red Dragon was easier said than done. They set up their pit area with military precision, unloading equipment that looked brand new and expensive. Everything was top-of-the-line, from their tools to their tires to the massive trailer that probably cost more than Hank's entire operation combined.

"How does a team like that even exist?" Colby asked, not bothering to hide his bitterness. "It's like they're playing a different sport."

"Money," Brian said flatly. "Lots and lots of money."

Hank had heard the stories. Team Red Dragon was backed by some tech billionaire who'd decided competitive racing would be a fun hobby. They'd only been on the circuit for two years, but they'd already made a reputation for themselves, and not a good one.

Last year, they'd swept through the regionals and made it all the way to the championship. They'd won by a narrow margin, but there had been whispers. Accusations of tampering with other teams' vehicles. Suspicious mechanical failures during critical races. Nothing proven, nothing concrete, but enough smoke to make everyone suspicious of fire.

The racing federation had investigated and found nothing. Or rather, they'd found nothing they could prove. Team Red Dragon had walked away with their trophy and their reputation intact, at least officially.

Unofficially, everyone knew something had been off.

"You think they'll try the same crap this year?" Brian asked.

"Probably," Hank said. "But we'll be ready this time."

He hoped that was true. Last year, he'd been too focused on his own performance to pay attention to the politics and dirty tricks. This year, he couldn't afford that luxury. Not when so much was riding on this championship.

Across the lot, Marcus was holding court with his team, laughing loudly at something one of them said. When he caught Hank looking, he raised his hand in a mocking salute.

Hank turned away.

"Come on," he said to Brian and Colby. "Let's get back to work. We've got a championship to win, and they're not going to intimidate us out of it."

But as he walked back to Julie, he couldn't shake the weight that had settled in his chest. Team Red Dragon had resources he couldn't match, connections he didn't have, and apparently no qualms about bending or breaking rules to get what they wanted.

His dream of winning the championship, of proving himself, of escaping the shadows of his past, had just gotten a lot more complicated.

FIVE

Bree stood on her balcony, coffee mug cradled in both hands, watching the organized chaos unfold below. The racetrack stretched out beyond the hotel grounds, and even from this distance, she could see teams swarming around their vehicles like bees around a hive.

She'd woken to the sound of engines and voices, the peaceful morning she'd imagined shattered before she'd even opened her eyes. When she'd stepped onto the balcony, confused and still half-asleep, she'd realized what Blake had conveniently forgotten to mention.

The Copper Moon Cup was this weekend.

Her quiet retreat had turned into the epicenter of what appeared to be a major racing event, and she didn't know whether to laugh or cry at the irony.

A flash of movement caught her eye. Three men stood around a vintage motorcycle, their body language speaking of easy camaraderie and shared purpose. Even from here, she recognized the tallest one. The set of his shoulders, the way he moved with deliberate economy, the dark hair that needed a trim.

Hank.

Her stomach did an unexpected flip.

She'd thought about him more than she cared to admit since yesterday. The quiet intensity in his eyes when he'd made sure she was okay. The careful way he'd responded to her.

Now she watched him crouch beside the motorcycle, running his hand along something she couldn't see from this distance. One of his friends, the one with the ball cap, said something that made the other laugh, but Hank just shook his head, focused entirely on the bike.

She should go inside. Stop staring at a man she'd met once, briefly, under embarrassing circumstances. She had coffee to drink, breakfast to eat, and a day to plan that didn't involve watching strangers work.

Except he wasn't quite a stranger anymore, was he?

Bree took a sip of coffee, annoyed with herself. She'd come here to heal, to find the peace Bryn had always described when she talked about Copper Moon. She hadn't come here to develop an inconvenient fascination with a man who probably hadn't thought about her once since yesterday.

Hank straightened, wiping his hands on his jeans, and said something to his friends. They nodded, and all three turned toward a convoy of black trucks that had just pulled into the lot. Even from her balcony, Bree could feel the shift in atmosphere. The playful energy around Hank's team vanished, replaced by something harder.

Tense.

The new team piled out of their trucks with theatrical precision, all matching uniforms and swagger. The leader, a man with dark hair and sunglasses despite the early hour, surveyed the lot like he owned it.

When his gaze landed on Hank, Bree's hands tightened on her mug.

She couldn't hear what was said, but she saw Hank's friend grab his shoulder, saw the careful way Hank kept his hands loose at his sides. The other team's leader said something else, laughed, and turned away.

Hank stood there for a moment, his jaw tight, before his friends pulled him back toward their bike.

Bree's chest ached with an emotion she couldn't quite name. Something about the way Hank had held himself, controlled and contained, reminded her of the way he'd been yesterday. Careful. Guarded. Like a man who'd learned the hard way not to let people see too much.

Her stomach growled, loud enough to break through her thoughts. She glanced at her watch and realized she'd been standing here for nearly thirty minutes, watching Hank work and ignoring her own needs.

Classic.

She drained the last of her coffee and headed inside. A shower, fresh clothes, and breakfast would help clear her head. Maybe then she could figure out why Blake had sent her to Copper Moon during the biggest event of the season, and why she wasn't as annoyed about it as she should be.

The hotel restaurant was packed.

Bree stood in the doorway, taking in the full tables, the harried waitstaff, the buzz of conversation that filled every corner of the space. Apparently, everyone associated with the race had decided to have breakfast at the same time.

She almost turned around. The room felt too full, too loud, too much like the chaos she'd been trying to escape.

But her stomach growled again, and she'd already checked; room service was backed up for at least an hour.

"Table for one?" The hostess appeared at her elbow, looking frazzled but determined.

"Yes, please."

The hostess scanned the room, her expression growing increasingly hopeless. "It's going to be at least a twenty-minute wait. Unless," she paused, "you'd be willing to share? We have a woman at a table for four who said she wouldn't mind company."

Bree hesitated. She'd come to Copper Moon to be alone, to process her grief without having to make small talk with strangers. But the alternative was going hungry or hiding in her room, and neither option appealed.

"That's fine," she said.

The hostess led her through the crowded restaurant to a table near the windows. A woman sat alone, her sleek black hair pulled back in a low ponytail, her attention focused on her phone. She looked up as they approached, and her face broke into a warm smile.

"Thank you for sharing your table," the hostess said. "This is..."

"Bree," Bree supplied. "Bree Spencer."

"Carmen Reyes." The woman gestured to the empty chair across from her. "Please, sit. I was starting to feel like I was taking up too much real estate."

Bree settled into the chair, grateful for the woman's easy manner. Carmen had the kind of confidence that put people at ease, the kind that came from being comfortable in her own skin.

"Are you here for the race?" Carmen asked, setting her phone aside.

"Accidentally," Bree said, then laughed at how ridiculous it sounded. "A friend suggested I come to Copper Moon for some peace and quiet. He forgot to mention it was race weekend."

Carmen's laugh was rich and genuine. "Peace and quiet during race week. Oh honey, that's like looking for silence at a rock concert."

"I'm starting to realize that."

A waitress appeared, harried but smiling, and took their orders. Bree asked for an omelet and toast; Carmen ordered the breakfast special with enough food for two people.

"Stress eating," Carmen explained when the waitress left. "My sister's working the race, and I'm a nervous wreck about it."

"Working as in racing?"

"Heidi's the one who handles all the Red Dragons' design work," Carmen added, rolling her eyes. "She's brilliant with engines and aesthetics, but she's also... intense. Race week makes her impossible to live with."

Bree smiled. "Sounds like sisters."

"You'll meet her sooner or later," Carmen said. "Trust me, she'll make sure of it."

Carmen took a sip of her coffee. "What about you? What brings you to Copper Moon, besides the accidental timing?"

Bree traced the rim of her water glass, considering how much to share. Something about Carmen's open expression and the genuine interest in her eyes made the truth easier to say.

"My sister used to come here. She passed away a year ago, and I thought," she paused, searching for the right words, "I thought maybe being here would help me feel close to her again."

Carmen's expression softened. "I'm so sorry. A year is nothing, really. Not when it comes to grief."

"No," Bree agreed quietly. "It's not."

They sat in comfortable silence for a moment, the noise of the restaurant fading into background static. It was strange how loss could create an instant connection between strangers, how shared pain could build bridges faster than any small talk.

"What was her name?" Carmen asked.

"Bryn. She was," Bree's voice caught, "she was my best friend. My anchor. I don't really know who I am without her."

Carmen reached across the table and squeezed Bree's hand. "You're you. That doesn't change just because she's gone. It just," she paused, "it just takes time to remember that."

The waitress returned with their food, breaking the moment, but the warmth of Carmen's words stayed with Bree as they began to eat. They talked about other things then: Carmen's work as a physical therapist, Bree's painting, the beauty of Copper Moon in early summer.

"So you paint?" Carmen asked, spearing a piece of sausage. "What kind of art?"

"Landscapes, mostly. Some abstract pieces when I'm feeling emotional." Bree smiled. "Bryn used to say my paintings were like windows into how I was feeling. Happy paintings when life was good, stormy ones when things were hard."

"Have you painted since she died?"

"Not really. I've tried a few times, but," Bree shrugged, "nothing comes out right."

"Maybe that's okay," Carmen said. "Maybe you're not

supposed to paint right now. Maybe you're supposed to just be."

Bree looked out the window, watching the morning sun climb higher in the sky. Below, teams were still working on their vehicles, preparing for whatever came next. She couldn't see Hank's team from here, but she knew they were out there somewhere.

"My therapist said something similar," Bree admitted. "That I needed to stop trying to force myself through grief and just let it be what it is."

"Smart therapist."

"She also said I needed to get out of my house, stop isolating myself." Bree laughed softly. "I'm not sure she meant come to a racing event, but here I am."

"Here you are," Carmen echoed. "And maybe this is exactly what you need. Not quiet, not isolation, but life. Noise. People doing things they're passionate about. Energy."

Bree thought about that as she finished her omelet. Maybe Carmen was right. Maybe peace didn't have to mean silence. Maybe it could mean being in a place Bryn had loved, surrounded by people who were fully alive, fully engaged in something that mattered to them.

Maybe peace could mean watching a man with careful hands work on a vintage motorcycle, feeling her heart skip for the first time in months, and not feeling guilty about it.

"You know what?" Bree said, setting down her fork. "I think you might be onto something."

Carmen grinned. "I usually am. Now, tell me more about this friend who sent you here without warning you about race week. That seems like something we need to discuss."

Bree laughed, and for the first time since arriving in Copper Moon, felt something in her chest loosen. Not heal, exactly, but shift. Making room for something new alongside the grief.

Hope, maybe.

Or at least, possibility.

They finished breakfast, talking about Blake's question-able planning skills, Carmen's sister's racing team, and the best places in Copper Moon to find actual quiet when you needed it. By the time they paid their bills and stood to leave, Bree felt lighter than she had in months.

She glanced across the room and saw Hank and his friends sitting at a table. Their eyes met, and she smiled. Her heart beat rapidly in her chest when he stood and strolled toward her. She swallowed when he stopped at their table. "Hi."

"I think that's my cue," the woman said, standing smoothly. She touched Bree's shoulder as she passed. "I'll be at the counter. Take your time."

CHAPTER
SIX

The café smelled like coffee, bacon, and possibility. Hank pushed through the door with Brian and Colby right behind him, their voices still carrying the energy of the morning's work. They'd spent three hours fine-tuning Julie's engine, adjusting the carburetor until she purred like a contented cat, and now his hands were clean, but his shirt still carried the faint scent of motor oil.

He was hungry, wired on adrenaline, and ready for a meal that didn't come from a vending machine.

"Table by the window," Brian called out, already heading that direction without waiting for consensus.

The café was packed, as it had been every morning since they'd arrived in Copper Moon. Local families mixed with racing teams, everyone drawn to what was apparently the best breakfast spot in town. The walls were covered with vintage photographs of past races, and a glass case near the register displayed trophies from decades of Copper Moon Cups.

Hank followed Brian toward the window table, his

mind still half on Julie's performance metrics, when he saw her.

Bree sat two tables over, her blonde hair catching the morning sunlight that streamed through the windows. She was laughing at something the dark-haired woman across from her said, her whole face lit up with genuine amusement, and the sound hit him square in the chest.

He stopped walking.

"Hank?" Colby's voice came from somewhere behind him. "You coming?"

He couldn't move. Couldn't look away. Bree's laughter faded into a soft, warm smile, and she tucked her hair behind her ear in a gesture that seemed unconscious. Natural. The kind of detail a man noticed when he was paying far too much attention.

"Oh, this is good," Brian said, his voice gleeful. "Colby, look at his face."

"I'm looking." Colby moved to stand beside Hank, following his gaze. "That's the woman from yesterday, isn't it? The one he nearly killed?"

"I didn't nearly kill her," Hank corrected automatically. "I swerved just in time."

"Right," Brian drawled. "After you knocked her down."

Hank forced himself to move, to follow them to the table, but his attention kept drifting back to Bree. She wore a light blue sundress today, something simple and feminine that made her look like she belonged in a painting. Her hands moved as she talked, graceful and expressive, and he found himself wondering what she was saying that made her friend smile like that.

"Earth to Hank," Brian said once they were seated. "You want to order, or are you just going to stare at her all morning?"

"I'm not staring."

"You're absolutely staring," Colby said, picking up his menu. "And she's going to notice if you keep doing it."

Hank grabbed his own menu, determined to focus on breakfast options instead of the woman two tables over. Eggs. Bacon. Toast. Simple. Easy. Except his eyes kept sliding past the laminated pages toward Bree, noting the way she sipped her coffee, and how her expression shifted from amusement to something more thoughtful.

The waitress appeared, and they ordered. Hank asked for the special without even knowing what it was, his mind too occupied to care about food.

"So," Brian said the moment the waitress left, "are you going to talk to her, or just pine from a distance like some tragic hero?"

"I'm not pining."

"He's totally pining," Brian told Colby.

"Definitely pining," Colby agreed. "Look at him. I've never seen Hank look at anyone like that."

"Can you two shut up?" Hank shifted in his chair, trying to get comfortable and failing. "I barely know her."

"Which is why you should go talk to her." Brian leaned forward, his expression turning serious despite the teasing tone. "Come on, Hank. When's the last time you looked at a woman like that? When's the last time you let yourself be interested in anything besides Julie and the race?"

Never, Hank thought. Or at least not since the fire, not since his life had narrowed down to survival and purpose and dreams that felt just out of reach.

"She's looking over here," Colby said quietly.

Hank's head came up before he could stop himself, and his eyes found Bree's across the café. She'd been mid-conversation with her friend, but her gaze had drifted toward their table, and now their eyes met.

The connection was immediate. Electric. Like touching a live wire.

She didn't look away. Didn't blush or pretend she hadn't been looking. Instead, a small smile curved her lips, tentative and a little surprised, as if she hadn't expected to see him here either.

Hank's chest tightened.

"Go," Brian said. "Before you lose your nerve."

"I don't have the nerve to lose."

"Then go before I drag you over there myself."

Hank stood before he could talk himself out of it. His legs carried him across the café on autopilot, weaving between tables while his brain scrambled to figure out what he was going to say. He'd faced enemy fire with more composure than this.

Bree's friend noticed him first. She glanced up, took in his approach and the way Bree was watching him, and her smile turned knowing.

"I think that's my cue," the woman said, standing smoothly. She touched Bree's shoulder as she passed. "I'll be at the counter. Take your time."

Then she was gone, and Hank was standing beside Bree's table with no backup plan and no idea what to say next.

"Hi," he managed.

"Hi." Bree's smile widened, genuine and warm. "Fancy meeting you here."

"Yeah, I," he gestured vaguely toward his own table, "breakfast."

"Me too." Her eyes sparkled with amusement. "Apparently, it's the place to be in Copper Moon."

"So I'm learning." He shifted his weight, suddenly aware of how public this was, how many people might be watching. "How are you today?"

"Fine. Only my pride is bruised." She tilted her head, studying him. "How's your conscience?"

"Still guilty."

"Don't be." She gestured to the empty chair across from her. "Do you want to sit?"

He should say no. Should go back to his table, where Brian and Colby were undoubtedly watching this entire interaction and planning new ways to torture him about it. But he found himself pulling out the chair and sitting before he'd consciously made the decision.

"I really am sorry about yesterday," he said. "I wasn't paying attention."

"To be fair, neither was I." She traced the rim of her coffee cup. "My friend Carmen says I have a habit of getting lost in my own head."

"Carmen, that's," he nodded toward the counter where the dark-haired woman was now chatting with the cashier, "your friend?"

"I met her this morning, actually. We shared a table at the hotel because the restaurant was packed." Bree's expression softened. "She's nice. Easy to talk to."

"Unlike me?"

"I didn't say that." But her smile suggested she was teasing. "Though you do have a habit of nearly killing people and then brooding about it."

"I don't brood."

"You absolutely brood. You have the posture for it. Very," she waved her hand, "stoic and intense."

Hank felt his lips twitch despite himself. "Stoic and intense?"

"It's not a criticism. It's," she paused, "actually kind of attractive, if I'm being honest."

The words hung between them, unexpected and charged. Bree's cheeks flushed pink, as if she hadn't meant to say that out loud, but she didn't take it back.

"You ride like a bat out of hell," she added quickly, clearly trying to redirect. "Is that a racing thing, or just your natural state?"

"A little of both." He relaxed slightly, grateful for the change in subject. "Though yesterday I was just distracted."

"By?"

You, he thought. By green eyes and blonde hair and the way you looked standing on that beach like you belonged there.

"The race," he said instead. "Big week coming up."

"The Copper Moon Cup." She nodded. "My friend Blake failed to mention it was happening this weekend when he booked my trip."

"You didn't come for the race?"

"I came for peace and quiet." Her laugh was soft and self-deprecating. "Shows what I know about planning."

"To be fair, Copper Moon is usually quiet. Just not this week."

"So everyone keeps telling me." She took a sip of her coffee. "That bike you were working on this morning, is that the one you're racing?"

He shouldn't be surprised she'd seen him. The hotel overlooked the track, and he'd been out there since dawn. Still, knowing she'd been watching sent an unexpected warmth through his chest.

"Julie," he said. "1942 Crocker. She belonged to my grandfather."

"Julie." Bree's expression softened. "That's right. You named her after someone?"

"My grandmother. She was," he paused, "the reason my grandfather started racing in the first place. He wanted to impress her."

"Did it work?"

"They were married for fifty-three years, so I'd say yes."

Bree smiled, but something in her eyes shifted. A shadow passed across her face, there and gone so quickly he almost missed it. Grief, he realized. The kind that surfaced unexpectedly, triggered by stories of long marriages and lifelong love.

"Your sister," he said quietly. "Bryn. I remember her from high school. She was," he searched for the right words, "hard to forget."

Bree's eyes widened slightly. "You knew Bryn?"

"Not well. But enough to know she was the kind of person who made everyone around her better." He held her gaze, letting her see he meant it. "I'm sorry for your loss."

"Thank you." Her voice came out rough, and she cleared her throat. "She loved Copper Moon. Talked about it all the time. I thought," she paused, "I thought being here might help me feel close to her again."

"Is it working?"

"I don't know yet." She smiled, but it didn't quite reach her eyes. "This morning I've been thinking about her a lot, contemplating on why I'm here, this week of all weeks, and what I should do about it."

"That makes sense." He meant it. "What do you paint?"

"Landscapes, mostly. Nothing professional, just," she shrugged, "something I've always done."

"You should keep doing it. Especially if it helps."

They sat in comfortable silence for a moment, the noise

of the café fading into background static. Hank couldn't remember the last time he'd felt this settled around someone new, this willing to just be present without needing to fill every second with words.

"Are you all right?" he asked finally. "After yesterday, I mean. Really, all right?"

"I'm fine. Promise." She studied him with those too-perceptive green eyes. "Are you?"

The question caught him off guard. Most people didn't ask if he was all right. They saw what they wanted to see: a former Marine, a racer, someone who had his life together enough to chase a championship. They didn't see the nights he couldn't sleep, the phantom pain in his leg, the weight of knowing this race was his last shot at something better.

"I'm good," he said, because it was easier than the truth.

Bree's expression suggested she didn't quite believe him, but she didn't push. Instead, she changed the subject.

"So what happens next? With the race, I mean."

"Qualifying rounds start tomorrow. Then eliminations, then the final on Sunday."

"And you're confident? With Julie?"

"As confident as I can be." He thought about Team Red Dragon, about Marcus Steele's predatory smile, about all the ways this could go wrong. "It's a good bike. We've done everything we can to prepare."

"But?"

"But there are always variables you can't control."

She nodded like she understood. Maybe she did. Loss taught you that lesson better than anything else.

The waitress appeared at his table across the café, setting down plates of food, and Colby caught his eye with a pointed look.

"I should go," Hank gestured toward his friends, "they're waiting."

"Of course." But she looked almost disappointed. "Thanks for coming over."

He stood, then hesitated. The words came out before he'd fully thought them through.

"We're going to the pier for lunch later. The guys and I. If you wanted to join us."

Bree's eyebrows rose. "Is this a peace offering? For yesterday?"

"Maybe." He allowed himself a small smile. "We can take my truck."

She bit her lower lip, considering, and Hank found himself holding his breath waiting for her answer. When had he started caring so much about whether a woman he barely knew wanted to have lunch with him?

"I'll think about it," she said finally.

It wasn't a yes, but it wasn't a no either. Hank would take it.

"Think hard," he said, then walked back to his table before he could say something stupid.

Brian and Colby were grinning like idiots when he sat down.

"Smooth," Brian said. "Real smooth."

"Shut up."

"Did she say yes?" Colby asked.

"She said she'd think about it."

"That's basically a yes," Brian declared. "In girl speak, 'I'll think about it' means 'yes, but I don't want to seem too eager.'"

"How would you know?" Colby asked. "When's the last time you talked to a woman?"

"I talk to women all the time."

"Your sister doesn't count."

While they bickered, Hank let his gaze drift back to Bree's table. She was talking to Carmen again, but even from across the café, he could feel the moment she glanced his way. Their eyes met, and she smiled.

Just a small curve of her lips, nothing dramatic, but it hit him like a punch to the chest.

"You're doomed," Colby said quietly, following his gaze. "Completely and utterly doomed."

Hank picked up his fork and focused on his breakfast, ignoring the knowing looks from his friends.

The problem was, Colby was probably right.

CHAPTER

SEVEN

The morning light painted Copper Moon Beach in shades of honey and rose, the kind of palette that made Bree's fingers twitch for her brushes. She'd set up her portable easel on the balcony of her room, her canvas angled to catch both the water and the distant race-track where Hank had been working since dawn.

She told herself she was painting the landscape. The way the sun gilded the waves, the weathered pier jutting into the lake like an old friend refusing to leave. But her brush kept drifting toward the track, toward the small figure bent over a vintage motorcycle, his movements precise and purposeful even from this distance.

The breeze carried the scent of fresh air and motor oil, an oddly appealing combination that reminded her of yesterday's near disaster on the beach. Her cheeks warmed at the memory of Hank standing over her, all concern and quiet intensity, those dark eyes studying her like she mattered.

"You're being ridiculous," she murmured to her canvas, mixing cerulean blue with a touch of burnt sienna. "You came here to paint. To heal. Not to moon over some brooding motorcycle racer you just met."

But even as she said it, her gaze drifted back to the track.

A gull cried overhead, sharp and insistent, and for a moment Bree could have sworn she heard Bryn's laugh on the wind. Her sister had always loved the beach, had talked endlessly about Copper Moon after her visits here. The way the light changed throughout the day. The sound of the waves at night. The feeling that anything was possible when you stood at the edge of the water.

"I miss you," Bree whispered. "God, Brynie, I miss you so much."

The paint on her palette blurred slightly. She blinked hard, refusing to let tears fall. She'd promised herself she wouldn't cry today. Wouldn't let the grief swallow her whole the way it had for months after the funeral.

Instead, she focused on the canvas, letting her brush move with muscle memory rather than conscious thought. Bryn had always said that painting was Bree's way of processing the world, of making sense of things too big for words. Maybe that's what she needed now. To paint her way through the loss, through the loneliness, through the terrifying prospect of a future without her sister's laughter.

The motorcycle's engine roared to life on the track, a deep purr that seemed to vibrate through the morning air. Bree looked up in time to see Hank guide Julie around the first turn, his body moving with the bike like they were one creature. Even from here, she could see the concentration in his posture, the way he leaned into the curve with absolute trust.

It was beautiful. Dangerous and reckless and absolutely beautiful.

She added a slash of crimson to her canvas, then another, building the shape of the motorcycle against the pale morning light. The painting was becoming something she hadn't intended; not just a landscape, but a moment. A feeling. The strange pull she felt watching Hank race, the way her heart seemed to speed up in time with Julie's engine.

"You'd like him," she told Bryn's memory. "He's stubborn and serious, and he named his motorcycle after his grandmother. You always said I needed someone who wasn't afraid of commitment."

The wind picked up, warm and salt-sweet, and Bree felt something shift inside her chest. Not grief, exactly. More like permission. Like Bryn was standing beside her on this balcony, giving her that knowing smile she used to wear whenever Bree tried to deny she was interested in someone.

Live, she imagined her sister saying. *Stop hiding and live.*

Bree set down her brush and simply watched as Hank completed another lap, this one faster than the last. The sun caught the chrome of Julie's pipes, sending splinters of light across the track. He was good; even her untrained eye could see that. The way he handled the turns, the confidence in his movements. This wasn't just a hobby for him. This was everything.

The thought should have scared her. She'd learned the hard way what it felt like to lose someone who meant everything. But watching Hank race, seeing the pure joy in the way he moved, Bree felt something unfurl inside her. Something that had been closed tight since the day the doctor had sat them down in that sterile office and explained that Bryn's time was running out.

Hope, maybe. Or possibility. Or just the simple pleasure of watching someone do what they loved.

Hank brought Julie to a stop near the trailer, and even from her balcony, Bree could see him looking up toward the hotel. Toward her room specifically, as if he'd known all along that she was there.

Their eyes met across the distance.

Her heart did something complicated in her chest, a flutter and squeeze that made her breath catch. She should look away. Should go back to her painting and pretend she hadn't spent the last hour watching him like some lovesick teenager. But she couldn't make herself move.

Hank raised one hand in a wave, slow and deliberate, and Bree found herself waving back before she'd consciously decided to.

He pointed to the hotel, then made a drinking motion. Universal sign language for want to grab a drink?

Bree glanced at her canvas, at the half-finished painting that captured this morning better than any photograph could. Then she looked back at Hank, still waiting patiently for her answer, and felt herself smile.

She nodded.

The grin that broke across his face was worth every ounce of uncertainty churning in her stomach. He held up ten fingers, then pointed toward the hotel bar, and Bree nodded again before disappearing into her room.

Her hands shook slightly as she cleaned her brushes, her mind already racing ahead. This was just a drink. Nothing serious. Two people getting to know each other in a town neither of them called home. It didn't have to mean anything.

But as she changed out of her paint-splattered shirt and ran a brush through her hair, Bree couldn't quite convince herself that was true.

Fifteen minutes later, she found Hank waiting in the

hotel bar, freshly showered and wearing a clean t-shirt that did absolutely nothing to hide the breadth of his shoulders. He stood when he saw her, that old-fashioned courtesy that made her pulse skip.

"You came," he said, and there was genuine surprise in his voice.

"You invited me." She slid into the seat across from him, hyper-aware of how small the table was, how close their knees were to touching. "Though I have to say, two p.m. is early for a drink."

"Coffee, actually." He gestured to the two cups already waiting. "I figured we'd start civilized."

"How very restrained of you."

His lips twitched. "I have my moments."

They fell into easy conversation, the kind that felt effortless despite having known each other for less than two days. Hank asked about her painting, and Bree found herself telling him things she hadn't shared with anyone since Bryn died. How color felt like language sometimes, more honest than words. How the beach made her want to paint things she'd never attempted before.

"You were watching me this morning," Hank said, his dark eyes steady on hers. It wasn't a question.

Bree's cheeks warmed. "You were hard to miss. You and Julie put on quite a show."

"She's running well. Better than I hoped, actually." He traced the rim of his coffee cup, a gesture she was beginning to recognize as his tell when he was thinking hard about something. "The qualifying rounds start tomorrow. If we make it through, we have a real shot at the championship."

"When you make it through," Bree corrected. "You looked pretty confident out there."

"Confident and prepared aren't the same as guaranteed." His expression darkened slightly. "There's another team; Red Dragon Racing. They've won the Cup three years running, and their lead rider doesn't like competition."

Before Bree could respond, the bar door swung open hard enough to bang against the wall. Three men strode in wearing matching red and black racing leathers, their presence immediately commanding attention. The one in front was tall and lean, with sharp features and an uglier expression.

"Well, well," the man drawled, his gaze landing on Hank with obvious malice. "If it isn't the has-been Marine and his grandfather's hand-me-down bike."

Bree felt Hank go still across from her, that particular kind of stillness that preceded violence. But when he spoke, his voice was perfectly calm.

"Marcus. Nice to see you've maintained your winning personality."

"Save the pleasantries, James." Marcus moved closer, his friends flanking him like well-trained dogs. "We both know you don't stand a chance tomorrow. That antique you're riding might look pretty, but she'll fall apart the second you push her hard."

"Julie's tougher than she looks."

"Maybe." Marcus's smile was sharp and cold. "But are you? Word is you've still got a limp from Afghanistan. Hard to race when your body can't keep up."

Bree's hands clenched in her lap, anger flaring hot and immediate. How dare this man talk to Hank like that? How dare he weaponize war wounds like they were ammunition? Hank was a Marine. He is all that embodies a hero.

But Hank simply stood, his movements controlled and deliberate. He was taller than Marcus by at least two inches, and when he stepped closer, the other man actually took a step back.

"The track will answer your questions tomorrow," Hank said quietly. "Until then, you might want to work on your trash talk. This amateur hour routine is getting old."

Marcus's face flushed red, but before he could respond, the bartender cleared his throat loudly.

"Gentlemen. This is a family establishment. Take the pissing contest outside."

For a long moment, nobody moved. Then Marcus sneered, spat something crude under his breath, and stalked out with his entourage trailing behind.

The bar seemed to exhale collectively.

Hank sat back down, his jaw tight but his hands steady as he reached for his coffee. "Sorry about that. Marcus likes to play mind games before races. Thinks it gives him an edge."

"Does it work?" Bree asked, surprised by how fierce her voice sounded.

"Not on me." Hank met her eyes, and something in his expression made her stomach flip. "I learned a long time ago that the only opinion that matters is my own."

"Good." She meant it. "Because that man is clearly an ass, and anything he says is suspect at best."

Hank's smile was slow and genuine, reaching his eyes in a way that transformed his entire face. "You defending my honor, Spencer?"

"Someone has to." She took a sip of her coffee, trying to ignore how much she'd wanted to throw something at Marcus's smug face. "Besides, I've seen you ride. You're going to crush him tomorrow."

"I appreciate the vote of confidence."

"It's not confidence. It's observation." Bree leaned

forward, surprising herself with her intensity. "That man talks like someone who's afraid. And fear causes people to make mistakes."

Hank studied her for a long moment, something shifting in his expression. When he spoke, his voice was softer. "You're something else, you know that?"

"Is that good or bad?"

"Very good." He reached across the table, his fingers brushing hers in a touch so light it might have been accidental. Except it wasn't, and they both knew it. "Want to get out of here? I know a place on the beach where the tourists don't go."

Bree should say no. Should go back to her room and her painting and the safety of keeping her distance. But Bryn's voice echoed in her head again; *live, stop hiding and live.*

"Yes," she said. "I'd like that."

As they left the bar together, Bree caught sight of Marcus outside, watching them with cold calculation. A shiver ran down her spine, but Hank's hand found the small of her back, steady and warm, and the fear dissolved into something else entirely.

Tomorrow would bring the race and whatever games Marcus wanted to play. But right now, walking into the sunshine with Hank beside her, Bree felt more alive than she had in a year.

And maybe, just maybe, that was enough.

Hank watched Bree's sandals sink into the softer sand as the boardwalk ended and the narrow path opened up between the dunes.

"This is where people usually turn around," he said. "They see the sign and decide it's too much effort."

Her gaze flicked to the weathered post half-buried in the dune. *Protected dunes, no motorized vehicles beyond this point.*

"Is this you telling me we're breaking the law?" she asked.

"More like bending it. No bikes out here, just feet." He tipped his head toward the path. "Come on. It's worth it."

She hesitated only a second, then stepped beside him. The wind muffled the sounds from town; each yard they walked stole more of the noise. The low crash of waves and the whisper of grass along the dunes were all that remained after the engines, shouting, and clatter of tools faded.

Her shoulders dropped, just a bit.

"You come out here a lot?" Bree asked.

"When I need to get out of my own head." He adjusted

his pace to match hers. Her legs were shorter, and the sand fought every step. "Brian and Colby call it my disappearing act."

"Do they know where you go?"

"Brian does. Colby pretends he doesn't, but he's tracked me once or twice."

She smiled at that. "Good friends."

"The best."

The path curved, then opened onto a pocket of beach framed by two low rock outcroppings. The sand here lay untouched, no tire tracks, no footprints. A length of driftwood sat far enough from the waterline to stay dry, bleached silver by sun and time.

Bree stopped dead.

"Oh," she breathed.

That one syllable hit him harder than any compliment he had ever gotten about his riding. Her eyes had gone wide, that soft green lifting to take in the curve of the rocks, the sweep of open water, the way the shoreline hooked around to make a half-circle of quiet.

"Nobody comes this far," he said. "Tourists stop back there where the chairs are. Locals stake out the pier or the public access lot. This little corner gets forgotten."

She turned slowly, as if memorizing every angle. "This is perfect."

"That was the idea." He nodded toward the driftwood. "You can set up there, stay out of the wind, still see everything."

Bree walked to the log and brushed sand from the top with her palm. "You've been keeping this spot to yourself all week, and you just decided to share?"

"I figured you earned it after surviving that confrontation with Marcus."

Her mouth twisted. "Is he always like that?"

"Pretty much." Hank shrugged. "He thinks if he rattles everybody, they'll make mistakes."

"Does it work on you?"

He sank onto the driftwood, elbows on his knees. The sand under his boots shifted, giving a little, the way his leg liked. "Used to. Not anymore."

She stayed standing, arms folded loosely at her middle, hair lifting in the breeze. "You were very calm back there."

"Bartender would have thrown us out otherwise."

"That is not what I meant." She shook her head. "He went right for your leg. Your service. He wanted blood."

"Yeah." Hank watched the water roll in toward the rocks and break apart, clean and predictable. "Guys like Marcus, they have one move. If you let it work once, they keep using it."

"And you just decided not to let it work."

"Something like that."

Bree looked at him for a long moment, then eased onto the driftwood beside him. She left a polite few inches between them, but he could feel the heat of her body along his arm.

"I'm not used to men shrugging off that kind of thing," she said. "My brother-in-law, Charlie, would still be pacing and planning comebacks."

"He has kids. Different pressure." Hank nudged a small shell with the toe of his boot. "Besides, I'm used to people staring at the limp. Since I've finished with therapy and was told there wasn't anything more that could be done for me, I've learned to live with it. It's part of who I am."

Her gaze dipped automatically to his right leg, then back up. "Is it still painful?"

"Depends on the day." He rolled his ankle once, easing a

tight pull in the muscle. "Shrapnel took out more than they could fix. The docs did what they could. The rest is just noise I work around."

"Noise." She tasted the word, thoughtful. "And racing quiets it?"

"Sometimes." He glanced at her. "Sometimes it turns it up. But out there, at least I know what I'm fighting."

Bree rested her hands on her thighs, fingers laced loosely. "I get that."

He waited. She didn't look like she was sure she wanted to explain, but she did it anyway.

"After Bryn died, everyone kept telling me to keep painting," she said. "Like it was a faucet I could turn on to feel better. 'Do what you love, Bree, it will help.'" Her voice softened into imitation. "Only every time I picked up a brush, all I could see was the hospital room. Her hands. The way she looked at me when she asked me to be okay."

His chest tightened.

"I started avoiding my studio," she continued. "I told myself I would go in tomorrow, then the next day. Then I just stopped saying anything about it at all."

"How long?" he asked quietly.

She blew out a breath. "Almost a year. The stuff I did try to paint was... wrong. Muddy. Like I was painting with fog instead of color."

He thought of the sunrise outside her window, of her on the balcony that morning, brush moving in small, sure strokes. "The canvas you had up there today did not look wrong."

"It surprised me." She traced a small knot in the wood between them. "I was just blocking in shapes at first. When I looked back at it, there you were. You and Julie on the track. I did not mean to put you in it."

He tilted his head. "Is that good or bad?"

"It is something," she said. "Which is more than I have had in months."

He let that sit for a moment. The wind shifted, bringing the faintest hint of salt and sunblock from farther down the beach. Out here, it was softer, less crowded.

"You know," he said, "my granddad used to say the only bad laps were the ones you did not run."

She looked over, the hint of a smile tugging at her mouth. "Is everything a racing metaphor with you?"

"Not everything. Sometimes I talk about coffee. Or torque."

That pulled a quiet laugh from her. The sound threaded under his skin, warm and light.

"What would he think?" she asked. "Your grandfather. About you racing Julie in the Cup."

Hank pictured the old man, wearing an oil-stained ball cap, and hands as nicked up as Hank's were now. "He would tell me to keep my line clean and not let any yahoo push me around on the straightaway." His throat tightened unexpectedly. "And he would be proud. Even if I came in last. He cared more about the run than the trophy. He and my father worked so hard to bring this Cup home. But they did it with honesty and hard work."

Bree's hand found his forearm, light as a bird landing. "Your dad?"

"He likes the trophies." The answer came with a wry edge he didn't bother to hide. "He wants that Cup on the mantel. Says the James men have been chasing it long enough."

She rubbed her thumb once along his skin, absent and soothing. "And what do you want?"

He had been answering that question for months

without really hearing himself. The Cup. Redemption. A way out. The words had worn grooves in his brain.

Right now, with her beside him and the track blessedly out of sight, the answer felt different.

"I want to know I was not done at forty-two," he said. "That the leg, the discharge, all of it did not write the last chapter for me."

She did not look away. "You really think one race decides that?"

"No." He let out a breath. "I think I decided that. I just attached it to the race because it gave me something to aim at."

Bree studied him, her expression open and clear in a way that made him feel too seen.

"For what it's worth," she said, "you do not look done."

His mouth tugged. "No?"

"You look tired." Her eyes softened, taking in the lines at the corners, the shadows from long nights. "You look like someone who has carried more than his share for a long time. But you also look very alive when you are on that bike."

He swallowed. The way she said it, like she had watched him closely enough to notice the difference, landed deep.

"Bryn would have liked you," she added. "She always had a thing for men who fixed things. She used to say the way a man treated an engine told you everything you needed to know about his heart."

"Smart woman," he said.

"The smartest." Her hand slipped away from his arm, leaving a faint warmth behind. "She and Charlie spent their honeymoon here. They came back a few times with friends. She would bring me seashells and say I needed to stop painting other people's scenery and come see this place for myself."

"Why didn't you?"

She looked out over the water, lashes low. "Life. Work. Excuses. I told myself I would go next year. There is always a next year until there isn't."

He knew that one in his bones.

"Blake said Copper Moon would shake me loose," she said. "I thought he meant... quiet mornings, long walks, that kind of thing."

"Instead, you got pit crews and exhaust fumes." Hank tipped one shoulder. "He wasn't wrong, though."

"No," she admitted. "He wasn't."

They sat there, side by side, while the waves rolled in and out in their steady rhythm. A kid's laugh drifted faintly from the far end of the public beach, then faded again. Here, the silence settled softly rather than heavily.

Bree nudged his knee with hers. "So this is your hideout."

"Yeah."

"And you just handed it to me."

"It seemed like you needed it more today." He looked at her profile, the stubborn line of her jaw, the freckles across her nose that the sun had brought out. "You did say you came here to paint."

Her mouth curved. "I did."

"Bring your easel tomorrow," he said. "Come early. Before the rest of the teams finish breakfast and turn the place into a circus."

"While you are on the track," she guessed.

"While I am on the track," he confirmed. "You can paint without worrying about stray motorcycles."

"I do like that part of the plan." She angled toward him a little. "You're sure you don't mind?"

"If I minded, I would have taken the long way around and lost you in the dunes."

Her eyes sparked. "You couldn't lose me if you tried, James."

"That sounds like a challenge."

"It might be." She rose from the driftwood and brushed sand from the back of her jeans. "Come on. If I stay here any longer without a canvas, I will start sketching in the sand like a kid."

He pushed to his feet, careful with the shift of weight. The leg gave him one quick protest he ignored. "You ever do that? When you were younger?"

"Draw in the sand?" She started along the waterline, walking where the tide had packed the ground firm. "Bryn and I used to fill the whole driveway with chalk. Our mother hated it. The neighbors loved it. Kids we barely knew would come over just to scribble." Her smile went soft. "Bryn always drew suns. Big, bright, impossible-to-miss suns."

"And you?"

"I drew houses." She looked up at him from the corner of her eye. "And trees. And one unforgettable portrait of our dog that looked more like a meatloaf."

He laughed. "Poor dog."

"She was offended. Refused to sit for me after that."

They walked in easy silence for a few strides. The water swept up to kiss Bree's toes; she stepped out of reach on instinct, then went back to the firmer line with a quiet huff.

"You okay out here?" he asked. "You are not a fan of getting wet, I take it."

"I like water. I don't like unexpected cold feet." She wriggled her toes in her sandals. "You?"

"Spent enough time being wet and cold deployed. I pick my battles now."

That earned him another of those small, true smiles. "So racing on a wet track is out."

"Not my favorite." He shaded his eyes to glance up the beach, where the hotel roofline was just visible above the dunes. "We should head back. I told the guys I wouldn't be gone all day."

She slowed, then stopped altogether. "Hank?"

"Yeah?"

"Thank you. For this." She swept a hand around, taking in the little stretch of empty beach. "For not trying to fix anything. Just... showing me a place where I can breathe."

He shifted closer, drawn in before he could think better of it. "Some things don't need fixing, Bree. They just need space."

Her throat worked. For a heartbeat, neither of them moved.

A gull cried overhead, cutting the tension, and she cleared her throat. "If I paint out here tomorrow, you aren't allowed to sneak up on me."

He lifted his right hand like he was taking an oath. "No sneaking."

"Good. Because I would hate to accidentally knock you off your feet with a canvas."

"Now that," he said, "I would like to avoid."

They started back toward the path. The sand grew softer again, grabbing at her sandals. She stumbled once on a hidden dip; his hand shot out, fingers closing around her waist.

For a second, he held her there. Her hands landed on his

chest, eyes wide, breath caught. The world narrowed to the warm press of her body against his and the faint tremor under his palm.

"Got you," he said quietly.

"I noticed."

Neither of them moved away.

Her fingers curled slightly in his shirt, bunching the cotton. Color climbed her neck. "You can let go now."

"Right." He eased his grip, but his hand dragged along her waist before he forced it back to his side. "Sorry."

"Don't be." She stepped past him, voice lighter than the flush on her cheeks. "It would have been very dramatic if I'd face-planted."

He fell into step beside her again. The distance between them had shrunk somehow, close enough that their arms brushed now and then. When her knuckles bumped his, she didn't pull away. The third time it happened, he turned his hand, rough fingers curling around hers.

She looked down, then up at him.

"Hank."

"If you want me to let go..."

Her hand tightened around his instead. "I'll let you know."

He nodded, something warm and dangerous settling low in his chest.

They walked the rest of the way hand in hand. At the boardwalk, she stopped and looked back at the little hidden stretch of beach, eyes bright and thoughtful.

"I'm going to paint the rocks first," she decided. "Then the water. I'll save the sky for last."

"Why the sky last?"

"Because it changes the most." She smiled up at him. "Like people."

He thought of the man he had been when he rolled into Copper Moon three days ago, carrying nothing but pressure and old ghosts. Then he looked at the woman standing in front of him, paint under her nails, grief in her eyes, hope just starting to show through the cracks.

"Yeah," he said. "Like people."

Back at the hotel steps, he forced himself to release her hand. "I need to go check in with Brian and Colby, make sure they haven't picked a fight with anyone they can't take."

"I should rinse sand out of places it doesn't belong." Her mouth quirked. "If I set up on the balcony later, you'll see me."

"I'll keep an eye out."

She turned to go, then pivoted back and rose on her toes, pressing a light kiss to his cheek. It was brief, soft as a brushstroke, but it landed like a jolt.

"Good luck tomorrow," she said. "Not that you need it."

He touched the spot as she walked inside, fingers resting there like he could hold the warmth a little longer.

For the first time since he'd signed up for this season's circuit, Hank James headed back to the track thinking about something other than the Copper Moon Cup.

He was thinking about a painter with sea-green eyes, and a hidden strip of beach that didn't feel like his alone anymore.

CHAPTER

NINE

H ank tightened the last bolt on Julie's rear set and sat back on his heels. The afternoon sun had climbed high enough that heat baked off the packed sand of the pit area; sweat slid down his spine under his T-shirt. Around him, the controlled chaos of race prep had settled into a steady rhythm. Engines revved, air guns chattered, and someone shouted for a torque wrench.

He liked this part. The checklists, the mechanics, the way everything had a place and a purpose. It kept his mind focused; it kept the noise in his head down to something manageable.

"You keep crawling around on the ground like that, old man, we're going to need a crane to get you up," Brian said.

Hank glanced over his shoulder. Brian leaned against the trailer, water bottle tipped up, sweat darkening his ball cap. Colby sat on a folding chair with a laptop balanced on his knees, logging times and adjustments from the morning runs.

"Keep talking, Viking," Hank said. "I've got a list of jobs with your name on them."

"Make sure one of them is a taste tester when those food trucks open." Brian crumpled his empty bottle and lobbed it toward the trash can. It hit the rim, bounced out, and rolled. "Close enough."

Colby didn't look up from the screen. "You're a disgrace to the Navy. Pick it up."

"You're a disgrace to fun," Brian shot back, but he bent to snag the bottle anyway.

Hank grinned and stood, stretching his back until his spine popped. The familiar ache in his right leg complained, but it was a background grumble now; he could work with that.

He looked automatically toward the hotel. Third-floor balcony, far right. No Bree in sight. He told himself he wasn't disappointed.

"She'll be out there tomorrow," Colby said quietly, still typing. "If she's smart, she'll sleep this afternoon."

Hank frowned. "You watching my balcony now?"

"Not yours," Colby said. "Hers. She's good for you."

Brian snorted. "She's bad for his concentration. Did you see his face at breakfast?"

"I qualified just fine," Hank said. "Julie did exactly what she was supposed to do."

"Julie always does," Colby replied. "You, on the other hand, are human. Try not to forget that."

Hank shook his head, more amused than annoyed. "You two want to run this show without me, feel free. I'll go find a hammock somewhere."

"Liar," Brian said. "You'd last ten minutes before you started worrying we torqued something wrong."

"Because you would," Colby said.

Hank turned away before the grin broke free. He checked the pit again. Tools in place, fuel jugs full, spare tires stacked. The Red Dragons had set up at the far end of the row, their massive hauler a gleaming black contrast to everyone else's trailers.

He tried not to look.

It didn't work.

The Red Dragons' area buzzed with a different kind of energy. Loud music blasted from their speakers. Two of their guys leaned against a truck, beers already in hand, even though qualifying had just ended. Someone spun a rear tire in the air, smoke curling up as rubber burned.

Careless. Sloppy. Exactly like last year.

Hank ground his teeth as Marcus strutted between bikes, sunglasses on despite the glare bouncing off chrome, talking with his hands like some kind of celebrity. The man loved a crowd. Loved making everything a performance.

A flash of blue caught Hank's eye.

His breath hitched.

Bree.

She stood just inside the Red Dragons' tape line, that soft blue sundress from the café swapped for fitted jeans and a pale shirt that made her eyes look almost turquoise from this distance. Her hair was pulled up in a messy knot, sunglasses perched on her head. She held her sketchbook against her chest, fingers tight on the spiral edge.

Carmen stood beside her, talking, one hand moving as if she were explaining something. On Carmen's other side, a woman in fire-engine red shorts, four-inch heels, and tanned legs perched on a stool, crossing and uncrossing those legs like she knew exactly who was watching.

Heidi, Hank guessed.

His chest went tight.

"What the hell," he muttered.

Brian followed his line of sight. "Uh-oh."

"Don't start," Hank said.

"I didn't say anything."

Colby closed the laptop and stood. "You're not really surprised, are you? Carmen's sister works their pit. Of course, she'd drag Bree over there."

"She didn't drag her," Hank said. "Bree's standing there just fine on her own."

And she was. She looked a little unsure, but she wasn't backing away. Marcus stepped closer, shaking Carmen's hand, leaning in to say something. Heidi's laugh cut through the distance, high and breathy, as she tossed her hair over one shoulder.

Bree's mouth tightened.

Good, he thought savagely. She can see for herself what kind of circus that is.

Marcus turned toward Bree. Even from across the pits, Hank saw the way Marcus's gaze swept down her body and back up; saw the way he adjusted his posture, shoulders back, chin up, smile turned on full wattage.

Hank's hands curled into fists.

"Easy," Colby said.

"I'm just watching," Hank replied.

"Your jaw says otherwise," Brian added.

Marcus said something, and Bree shook her head, a small, firm motion. Carmen shifted, putting herself slightly more between them. Heidi swung one long leg, crossing it over the other, and rested her elbow on her knee in a pose that screamed *Look at me*.

Marcus didn't. His attention stayed locked on Bree.

That was enough.

Hank grabbed a rag from the table, wiped his hands, and started walking.

"Here he goes," Brian said quietly behind him.

Colby's sigh followed. "Sam's on duty. If this turns into a thing, at least we know who's going to be writing the report."

Hank ignored them. The distance between the pits felt longer than usual, each step punctuated by the roar of an engine or the clang of a dropped tool. He kept his pace even, his expression neutral. The last thing he needed was to look like he was charging in.

He wasn't her keeper.

He just didn't like seeing her in the middle of a pack of wolves.

By the time he reached the edge of the Red Dragons' taped boundary, he'd smoothed the worst of the heat out of his tone.

Mostly.

He stopped just outside their line. They'd strung red caution tape in a neat rectangle, stakes hammered into the hard-packed sand. A sign on one post read, "Crew Only".

Carmen saw him first. Relief washed over her face, quick and unguarded.

"Hank," she called. "Hey."

Bree turned. Her eyes widened when she saw him; surprise, a flicker of guilt, then something warmer that hit him square in the chest.

Marcus pivoted lazily, then smiled, all teeth.

"Hank James," he said. "What a coincidence. I was just getting to know your friend."

"Yeah," Hank said. "I saw."

He kept his gaze on Bree, not Marcus. "You okay?"

"I'm fine." She brushed a loose strand of hair back from her face. "Carmen brought me over to see the other side of things."

"So she could see how a real team operates," Heidi added.

Up close, Heidi was all sharp angles and shine; glossy black hair, red lipstick, a tank top that showed off toned arms, and a lot of skin. She swung her leg again, the movement deliberate.

Carmen shot her a look. "Heidi."

"What?" Heidi spread her hands. "It's true. Some people like vintage. Some people like winning."

"That must be why you're here watching us," Hank said mildly. "Research."

A few of the Red Dragons' crew snickered. Marcus's smile tightened a fraction of an inch.

Bree pressed her lips together, fighting a smile of her own.

"You're welcome to look around," Marcus said. "We don't have anything to hide."

Except you do, Hank thought, but he didn't say it. Not yet.

He shifted his weight, the ache in his leg reminding him to keep it short. "Bree, Colby's got some telemetry he wanted to show you. Thought you might want the data for painting the lines around the track."

It wasn't entirely a lie. Colby had mentioned something like that. He just hadn't intended to use it as an extraction tool.

Bree hesitated, glancing between him and Carmen. "We were just..."

"She was just about to come with me," Carmen said firmly. "We've got that thing, remember?"

Heidi rolled her eyes. "Oh my God, you two are so dramatic. We're not savages. We're just fast."

"And loud," Carmen said. "And one of you almost took my head off with a flying socket ten minutes ago."

"That wasn't my fault," one of the crew muttered.

Bree shifted her sketchbook under her arm. "I appreciate the tour, Heidi. Marcus. But I should go see what Hank and his team are up to."

Marcus studied her for a second longer than Hank liked. "Suit yourself. The offer stands. You want to ride with a winning team; you know where to find us."

She smiled, polite and distant. "I'm not here to ride with anyone. I'm just here to paint."

Her tone made it clear that was the end of that.

She stepped over the tape line, careful not to catch her foot, and moved to Hank's side. He felt the subtle brush of her shoulder against his arm and had to bite back the urge to slide an arm around her and walk her out of here like they were a unit.

"Carmen?" Bree asked.

Carmen shot her sister another warning look. "I'm right behind you."

Heidi hopped off her stool with exaggerated grace. "Don't be long. We've got fittings to finish."

"Yeah, yeah." Carmen fell into step on Bree's other side. "Don't blow anything up while I'm gone."

They'd barely cleared the tape before Carmen blew out a breath. "Well. That was a lot."

Bree let out a quiet laugh. "You weren't kidding about intense."

"Marcus is a jerk," Carmen said. "Einstein's tolerable. The rest are a hazard to themselves and others."

"Einstein?" Bree asked.

"Nicknamed Einstein," Hank said. "He's their tech guy. Smartest one in the bunch. Knows engines inside out, but he doesn't say much."

They'd reached the safer stretch of sand between pits. Hank slowed his pace a little so they could talk without shouting over every engine.

Bree glanced back over her shoulder toward the Red Dragons' area. "I didn't like the way Marcus looked at me."

"Then you're in good company," Carmen said. "I don't like the way he looks at anybody."

Hank watched her expression closely. "He didn't say anything else?"

"Nothing I couldn't handle." Bree's jaw firmed. "He wanted to know if I was with you. I said I was here on my own."

That stung more than it should have. He nodded anyway. "Probably safer that way."

Her gaze snapped to his. "Safer?"

"He likes to make trouble," Hank said. "If he thinks there's a connection he can exploit, he will."

He didn't say: *He's already thinking about how to use you.* He didn't need to. Bree wasn't stupid.

Her fingers tightened on the sketchbook. "I'm not part of this pissing contest."

"I know." He bumped her shoulder gently. "But you're walking through the middle of it, so you're going to catch some spray."

Carmen snorted. "That's one way to put it."

They reached Hank's pit. Brian looked up, sunglasses pushed on top of his head, gaze flicking from Bree to Hank to Carmen and back like he was cataloging everyone's emotional state.

"You made friends," he said.

"Temporary alliances," Carmen replied. "Don't get excited."

"Too late," Brian said. He offered Bree his chair. "You want a seat?"

"I'm good, thanks." Bree glanced around, taking in the neatly organized tools, the bike on its stand, the calm rhythm of their work area. Her shoulders eased. "This is... very different."

"From the circus down there?" Brian grinned. "We aim for less chaos, more control."

"Chaos is where the accidents happen," Colby added. He'd set the laptop aside and was checking tire pressures again, his movements efficient. "Respect for the machine, respect for the track. Anything else is asking for trouble."

Carmen nodded. "That's what I keep saying. Heidi calls me boring."

"Boring keeps people alive," Hank said.

Bree's gaze drifted past him again, back toward the Red Dragons. Their music had kicked up. One of the crew revved a bike hard, the sound rough and ragged. Another guy tossed a wrench from hand to hand like he was juggling.

Near the edge of their line, a man in a black T-shirt crouched by a frame. He wasn't part of the noise; he was apart from it. Dark hair cut close, lean build, hands moving with precise efficiency as he adjusted something under the seat. He had headphones in, the big over-ear kind that blocked everything else out.

"Is that Einstein?" Bree asked.

Hank followed her line of sight. "Yeah. Nate Eisen. Nobody calls him that to his face, by the way."

"He looks... focused," Bree said.

Focused wasn't the word Hank would have used.

Intense. Controlled. Dangerous in a way Marcus never managed to be.

"Those guys clown around," Hank said, nodding toward the rest of the crew. "He doesn't. In the last hour, every time something weird happens around them, he's been touching the bike."

Carmen looked toward the hotel, then to Bree. "I'm heading back to my room to change for dinner. I'll see you later?"

Bree nodded, "Sure."

Hank watched Carmen walk toward the hotel, avoiding the direction of the Red Dragons. He shook his head slightly, then turned toward the Red Dragons once more.

Brian folded his arms, watching Einstein. "You still think they cheated last year."

"I know they did," Hank said quietly. "Proving it is another thing."

Bree shifted a little closer. "How would someone even cheat at this? I mean, in a way that matters."

Brian leaned a hip against the trailer. "Hidden nitrous, illegal mapping on the fuel injection, modified injectors, traction control tricks. Stuff that gives a burst of power when you need it."

"That sounds... complicated," Bree said.

"Einstein complicated," Colby added.

Bree watched him for another long moment. The way his fingers moved along the frame. The way he checked the same section twice. The quick glance over his shoulder, like he was making sure nobody was too close. He didn't see her; he probably didn't see anything except the machine in front of him.

A little shiver ran through her.

Hank saw it.

"You cold?" he asked.

"A little creeped out," she admitted. "He's so still. Everything around him is chaos, and he's just... zeroed in. It's like watching a surgeon who doesn't care what happens to the patient, only that the cut is clean."

Brian raised his brows. "Remind me not to show you any surgical dramas."

"It's not that," Bree hurried to say. "It's just a feeling."

"You should trust those," Hank said. "They're usually right."

She looked up at him. "What's yours say?"

He thought about lying. About soothing her, telling her everything was fine, that the race was safe, and the worst thing she had to worry about was sunburn.

"They're desperate to keep winning," he said instead. "Desperate men take shortcuts."

Colby blew out a breath. "And shortcuts get people hurt."

"Not if we can help it," Brian said.

He said it lightly, but Hank knew that under all the jokes and flirting, Brian watched everything. People, patterns, angles. The SEAL in him never really clocked out.

Bree hugged her sketchbook closer, then loosened her grip. "Maybe I should come down here tomorrow. Paint from the pits instead of the balcony."

Hank's first instinct was to say no. To tell her to stay in her room with the door locked, to watch from a safe distance where Marcus and his crew couldn't touch her.

But she wasn't a fragile thing to put on a shelf. She was a grown woman who'd survived losing her sister, who'd chosen to come here to try to live again. He didn't get to cage that because it made him feel better.

"You can," he said slowly. "If you want to be in the middle of it."

Her chin tipped. "I don't want to hide in my room. I've done enough of that."

He nodded once. "Then we'll make it safe."

Brian looked at him. "How?"

"We put her here." He gestured to a clear space between the trailer and the cooler. "Back against the wall, out of the main traffic. You or Colby walk her to the bathrooms or the concessions if I can't. No wandering alone. You stay with her if you come down."

Brian didn't argue. "Deal."

Bree blinked. "You're all very sure I need guarding."

"You're new," Brian said. "You don't know which idiots to avoid yet. That's all."

"And Marcus already put a target on you by sniffing around," Brian added. "He likes to poke at anything Hank cares about."

Bree's gaze swung back to Hank. "Do you?"

"Do I what?" he asked.

"Care," she said softly.

The question hung there, suspended between engine noise and gull cries and the distant crash of waves.

He didn't look away. "Yeah. I do."

Her breath shivered out, a tiny hitch he felt more than heard.

"Okay," she said. "Then I'll trust you."

It wasn't just about walking through the pits. They both knew that.

Colby cleared his throat. "On that note, we've got a riders' meeting in twenty. Hank, you need to read the updated grid."

Hank nodded, but his attention stayed on Bree a second longer. "You going back to the hotel?"

Bree glanced toward the hotel. "I probably should. I'll see if Carmen is alright. She loves her sister but hates the drama surrounding her connection with the Red Dragons."

Bree shifted closer. "You'll text me later?"

He hadn't asked for her number yet, but somehow that didn't surprise him. She reached for his phone, fingers brushing his as she took it, entered her number, and handed it back.

"There," she said. "Now you can send me the telemetry or dog pictures or whatever it is race guys share."

He smiled. "Race guys share split times and gear ratios."

"Thrilling."

"I'll throw in a dog picture for you," he added.

"Now we're talking."

On impulse, he reached out and tucked a piece of hair behind her ear. She stilled, eyes locked on his. For a second, the pits, the heat, the smell of fuel, all of it fell away.

He could have kissed her. He wanted to. Her mouth parted on a small inhale, like she'd read the thought.

Not here, he told himself. Not with Marcus watching from across the row and rumors ready to flare.

"I'll see you later," he said instead.

Her smile told him she'd heard all the words he hadn't said. "Later," she agreed.

She turned and headed back toward the path. Heidi was waiting just inside the Red Dragons' area, arms folded, mouth already moving. Bree listened, then answered calmly, her chin up. Heidi's eyes flashed; she tossed her hair and sauntered away, hips swinging as she cut a path directly to Marcus.

She stopped in front of him, pressed a hand to his chest,

and leaned in to say something that made him laugh. She soaked up the attention like the sun, head tipping back, throat exposed, every inch of her body language screaming *Look at me, not at her.*

Marcus obliged, his gaze sliding to Bree once Heidi had his attention, a smirk touching his mouth.

Einstein never looked up.

He stayed crouched by the bike, hands working under the seat, focus locked on whatever he was wiring or adjusting. Only when one of the other crew members walked too close did he lift his head, eyes sharp and cold as he said something that made the guy change direction fast.

Hank filed that away.

"Problem?" Colby asked quietly at his shoulder.

"Not yet," Hank said. "But it's coming."

He could feel it in his bones, in the way the air felt charged, like the seconds before a storm broke.

He rested a hand on Julie's tank, the metal warm under his palm, and let his mind run through tomorrow's grid. His line, his braking points, the spots where someone might try something dirty.

He wasn't just racing for a Cup anymore.

He was racing with a painter on the edge of the track, a woman who trusted him to keep her safe while he chased the last big win of his life.

And as much as the thought scared him, it lit something in him too; something sharp and focused and very, very clear.

TEN

Bree wiped her hands on a small hotel towel and studied her reflection in the bathroom mirror. The steam from her shower had faded, leaving the glass clear, revealing damp hair, a faint flush in her cheeks, and shadows under her eyes that hadn't quite disappeared since Bryn died.

She tilted her head, considered the soft green T-shirt she'd pulled on over faded jeans, and made a face at herself. It wasn't glamorous, but it was clean, and she could move in it. Movement mattered when you spent hours with a sketchbook.

Her phone buzzed on the edge of the sink.

Her pulse jumped before she flipped it over.

A photo filled the screen. Julie from the front, gleaming and ready, Hank kneeling on one knee beside her. He'd taken it from a low angle, so the horizon cut the shot diagonally, the pits and ocean behind him blurred. His mouth was tipped in a half-smile, as if he'd been caught between focusing on the camera and watching something off to the side.

Underneath it, he'd typed, *For reference. In case you want to make me prettier in the painting.*

Her mouth curved. She sank onto the closed toilet lid, thumb hovering over the keyboard.

You're assuming you're the subject, she wrote. *Maybe I'm painting Brian.*

He answered almost immediately. *Brian's hair would take too much paint.*

She laughed out loud, the sound echoing off porcelain and tile.

You're not wrong, she sent. *Are you done for the day?*

Riders' meeting in ten, he replied. *Then we'll tweak gearing and try not to obsess. You headed to the balcony hideout?*

She hesitated. Her sketchbook and pencils sat on the bed, ready. The balcony had the view she loved, the sweep of the track, and the ocean in the same frame.

Before she could answer, a second message appeared.

Wherever you go, stick with Brian or Colby. Promise me.

Warmth and anxiety twisted together under her ribs. He didn't make it a command; he gave her space, but he still wanted her safe.

She typed, *I promise. I'm not wandering into the lion's den.*

There was a knock at her door.

Bree blinked at it, then typed, *Someone's here. Talk later?*

Always, he wrote.

She set the phone aside and crossed the room. When she opened the door, Carmen stood in the hallway, barefoot in worn cutoffs and a black tank top, damp hair pulled back in a low knot. A thin gold chain hung at her throat; her expression was already apologetic.

"Hey," Carmen said. "Got a minute?"

"For you, sure," Bree said. "What's up?"

Carmen glanced toward the elevator, then back. "Heidi's having a moment. A loud, dramatic, potentially wardrobe-related moment. I could use a sane person with eyes who isn't invested in making Marcus look like a god."

Bree blinked. "That's a very specific request."

"It really is." Carmen sighed. "She wants a neutral opinion on the suit designs, and I'm apparently biased because I don't worship at the Red Dragon altar."

You mean you don't drool over men who almost decapitate you with loose tools?" Bree asked.

Carmen snorted. "Exactly. Please come. You'll be my excuse to escape if it goes nuclear. I'll owe you."

Bree thought of Hank's text, of the warning stitched inside the concern. Stick with Brian or Colby. The pits. Needs guarding.

She'd promised.

"Give me thirty seconds," she said.

Carmen nodded and leaned against the doorframe while Bree grabbed her sketchbook and a light hoodie. As she slid her phone into her back pocket, the image of Einstein's bowed head and busy hands flitted through her mind, paired with Hank's quiet certainty that something about the Red Dragons wasn't right.

Maybe seeing them up close wasn't the worst idea.

They walked together down the hallway and took the stairs instead of the elevator. The stairwell smelled faintly of concrete dust and salt air. Carmen moved like someone who'd spent years assessing exits and angles, her hand brushing the railing, her gaze tracking automatically to each landing.

"You sure you're okay being down there?" Carmen asked as they pushed through the ground-floor door into the lobby. "The pits are loud and full of testosterone."

"I survived dealing with Marcus," Bree said. "I think I can handle some engine noise."

Carmen's mouth twisted. "It's not the engines I worry about."

Outside, the late afternoon sun had mellowed, leaving Copper Moon in that soft between-light that painters loved. Long shadows stretched from the trailers and tents; everything looked edged in gold. The crowd that had packed the boardwalk earlier had thinned a little, some people drifting up toward the hotel, others toward their respective hotels.

The pits were still busy.

Engines sounded from different corners, sharply distinct notes like voices in a choir. Wrenches clinked. An air gun rattled in short bursts. The tang of fuel layered over salt and sunscreen.

Carmen wove through the maze of trailers with the ease of someone who'd done it a dozen times. Bree stayed tight to her side, careful not to cross any painted lines without invitation, aware of how many strangers' eyes tracked new movement on autopilot.

They passed Hank's pit. Julie sat on her stand like a coiled spring, gleaming. Colby was hunched over the laptop again, Brian nowhere in sight.

Bree's stride hitched.

Carmen noticed. "Want to stop?" she asked quietly.

"In a minute," Bree said. "If I see him now, I'll be tempted to stay. You said Heidi needed you."

Carmen made a noncommittal sound. "Heidi thinks she needs everyone."

The Red Dragons' setup came into view a moment later. Their hauler loomed behind the pits, glossy black with a stylized red dragon curling along the side. The logo wrapped around the back doors, teeth bared, eyes narrowed.

Music pumped from speakers set on the tailgate of a pickup, some pounding rock song with a driving beat. Two girls in crop tops and cutoffs leaned against the truck, talking to one of the younger crew members, who puffed up visibly with every laugh he earned.

Closer to the bikes, the mood was less playful.

Heidi stood in the center of the taped-off area, holding a glossy red-and-black leather suit up to her body as if she were in a fitting room that had lost its walls. Her jaw was tight, her eyes sharp, and the words coming out of her mouth sounded like they'd been honed on glass.

"It's wrong," she snapped. "The lines are wrong, the shoulders are too wide, and if Marcus leans in the way he rides, the colors are going to warp. It'll look like a cheap knockoff on camera."

The man she was chewing out wore a polo shirt with a small manufacturer logo at the collar and carried a tablet. He looked sweaty and miserable.

"Heidi," he said, patient but clearly tired. "The template is the same as last season's. We adjusted for the new sponsor badge and added side vents like you asked. There's only so much we can alter without compromising impact protection."

"Then you're not trying hard enough," she fired back. "This is the Copper Moon Cup, not some backlot sprint. The suit has to move with him. The dragon's head needs to stay visible through the whole roll, not get swallowed by a seam."

She shook the suit once for emphasis. The light flashed on the embossed dragon scales along the chest and shoulders. Bree had to admit, it was striking.

"Here we go," Carmen murmured. "Storm warning."

Heidi spotted them and homed in. "Finally," she said. "A person with taste. Bree, thank God. Come here."

Bree nearly glanced behind herself to see who else Heidi might mean. "Me?"

"Yes, you," Heidi said. She shoved the suit into Carmen's arms and reached for Bree's hand. "Come stand right here. I need a fresh set of eyes."

Carmen shot Bree a quick apologetic look over the glossy leather, then stepped aside as Heidi pulled Bree into the center of the pits.

Bree felt every gaze that turned their way. Crew members, hangers-on, and one of the riders. Marcus wasn't in sight yet, which made the stage feel even higher, somehow; the actors gathering before the lead.

Heidi held the suit up in front of Bree, squinting, then circled her, muttering under her breath.

"You're close enough to my measurements," Heidi decided. "Turn a little. There. Okay. Pretend you're straddling a bike."

Bree blinked. "I've never straddled a bike in my life."

"That's tragic," a crew member said.

Carmen glared at him. "Watch it."

He lifted both hands and backed up a step.

Heidi made an impatient sound. "Fine. Just imagine you're leaning forward, arms out. Like this." She grabbed Bree's wrist and placed it on an invisible handlebar in the air, then did the same with the other hand. "Perfect. Now, look at the chest."

Bree looked.

The dragon's head sat centered across the chest, its body curling over the ribs, tail wrapping low along the hip. It was beautiful work; the color gradation, the stitching, the subtle stainless accents that would catch the light.

But Heidi was right about one thing. With Bree's arms up, the dragon's eye tipped toward her shoulder instead of the camera line; the lower jaw distorted along where a rib protector seam would sit.

"It pulls," Bree said, surprised at her own certainty. "When you lift your arms, the eye tilts. The snout gets... pinched."

Heidi pointed at her like she'd solved a proof. "Exactly. Thank you."

She turned back on the manufacturer rep. "See? It's wrong."

He sighed. "We can lower the graphic three centimeters and widen the chest panel. Anything more, and the articulation suffers. It's a tradeoff."

"Then we prioritize the shot from the outside of the turns," Heidi said. "Shift the weight of the graphic so it reads clean from the primary camera angle."

The two of them launched into a rapid-fire argument about seams, relief cuts, and camera placement. Carmen slid closer to Bree, still holding the suit.

"Welcome to my life," she said under her breath. "She does this with every set of uniforms. You should've seen the soccer league last spring."

"She cares," Bree said softly.

"She cares about winning the visual," Carmen replied. "Which, to be fair, matters. Just maybe not as much as not blowing a valve at one fifty."

Bree's gaze drifted past them.

Two bikes sat on stands, front wheels off, frame cradled on padded blocks. One of the younger riders tinkered with the chain on a third bike, humming in time with the music.

At the far edge of the taped line, near the hauler, Einstein crouched beside a stripped-down frame.

He'd ditched the over-ear headphones from earlier. Earplugs sat in his ears instead, neon cords trailing. His dark hair stuck slightly to his forehead, damp with sweat. He wore black gloves that fit like a second skin and moved with a precision that made everything else seem clumsy.

Wires snaked along the frame, thin and dark, hugging the angles. Bree hadn't grown up around bikes; most of what she saw looked like a foreign language. But some things were still obvious if you paid attention.

He wasn't working where everyone else had been working.

He was working where no one else seemed to ever touch.

"Is that one Marcus's?" she asked quietly.

Carmen followed her gaze. "Yeah. Main race bike. The spare's over there."

Einstein shifted, blocking Bree's view for a moment. When he leaned back, she saw he'd opened a narrow compartment along the inside of the frame rail, just under where a rider's knee would sit. It wasn't big; the cavity was long and thin, barely more than a channel.

He lifted something from a tray at his side.

It was cylindrical and small, maybe the size of a travel shampoo bottle, but heavier from the way it pulled his glove a fraction lower when he shifted it. The metal caught the light, gleaming dull silver, with a small valve stem at one end and a hose already attached.

Bree frowned.

He turned the cylinder in his hand, checked a tiny gauge attached near the valve; his lips moved, counting. Satisfied, he eased it into the open frame channel, snug, as if it had been built for that exact dimension.

"The Dragons are proud of their tankless design," Carmen said. "Minimalist. All go, no fluff."

"They are?" Bree murmured. "So why does that look like a tank?"

Carmen frowned. "Maybe it's a dampener that will help absorb the vibration of the handlebars."

"It doesn't seem to be mounted where it would absorb anything," Bree said. The words came out before she could second-guess them. "It's hidden."

Heidi's voice climbed, irritated. "I don't care what the old spec says, Elliot, the cameras have moved since then, and if you can't adapt, you're holding us back."

Bree forced her attention away from Einstein for a moment. Heidi had stepped closer to the manufacturer rep, gestures sharp. The rep looked like he'd rather be anywhere else.

"You agreed to the prototype," he said. "If we reprint the suit, the cost goes up, and the sponsor is already at their cap."

"They'll find the money," Heidi said. "If they want their logo on the Cup podium."

Marcus appeared then, walking up from the direction of the timing shack, sunglasses hooked in the collar of his shirt. He took in the scene with a quick sweep of his gaze.

"What's wrong now?" he asked.

Heidi whirled on him. "They butchered the shoulder line. The dragon's going to look like it's sliding off your chest every time you lean. It'll read sloppy."

Marcus looked at Bree, then at Carmen, then at the suit.

He didn't glance once at Einstein.

"That is sloppy," he agreed immediately. "We can't look like amateurs at the biggest race of the season."

"Thank you," Heidi said, throwing her free hand up like she'd won something.

"We can make minor adjustments," the rep said. "But if you expect us to retool the entire run overnight, it's not going to happen."

Heidi launched into a fresh argument, voice climbing. Marcus stepped closer, aligning himself with her, adding his own pressure. Carmen pinched the bridge of her nose.

The argument pulled everyone's focus. The crew looked over. The girls by the truck leaned in. Even the kid with the chain stopped humming to watch the fireworks.

No one watched Einstein.

Except Bree.

He'd finished securing the small cylinder in the frame channel and was threading the hose along a narrow groove, pinning it under the existing wiring so that at a glance, it looked like part of the original loom. His movements were brisk and confident.

She squinted, trying to follow the line. The hose ran up toward the front of the bike, disappearing under the tank, then emerging again near the handlebars. He looped it around a bracket, then connected it to something that looked innocuous: a small pressure switch wired into the horn assembly.

She saw his fingers test it, pressing the horn button once. No sound. He adjusted a screw, pressed again. Still no audible honk.

But the tiny gauge near the cylinder's valve fluttered.

Her skin prickled.

She remembered Brian leaning against Hank's trailer,

listing ways to cheat. Hidden nitrous. Illegal mapping. Tricks that give a burst of power when you need it.

She didn't know what exactly sat inside that little cylinder, but she knew it wasn't stock. She knew the frame hadn't been built to house it, because she'd watched that same frame earlier, empty. She remembered how clean the inside line had looked when one of the other techs had run a cloth along it.

Her mouth went dry.

Einstein worked quickly, securing the frame panel back into place. Once it was closed, you wouldn't know anything lurked under there unless you knew where to press.

He smoothed a hand along the metal, satisfied, then stood and stretched his back. He glanced toward the argument by the suit, rolled his eyes once, and turned to put his tools away.

Bree realized she'd been holding her breath.

Carmen nudged her elbow. "You okay?"

Bree forced her mouth into something like a smile. "Yeah. Just... loud in here."

Carmen accepted that, thankfully. She didn't push. Most people would've asked more questions, poked at her expression, tried to drag out what she was thinking. Carmen simply turned her attention back to the suit fight without a second glance.

Bree breathed out slowly.

Her pulse hadn't steadied. Her hands hadn't either. She pressed her fingers around her sketchbook to mask the tremor and focused on slowing her breath.

She didn't trust her voice enough to speak again just yet.

Einstein moved away from the bike, casual as you please, wiping his gloves on a rag. No one looked at him.

Every gaze in the pit stayed locked on Heidi, flinging her hands, and Marcus lecturing the manufacturer rep.

And that was the problem.

No one noticed what they should've noticed.

Her stomach tightened. She knew enough to know she didn't fully understand what she'd seen — but she also knew enough to understand it was wrong. Something about it felt like too much precision in too quiet a corner.

Bree stepped back, pretending she needed a little more space. Her heart beat too hard, too fast. If she stayed another minute, she was going to telegraph her panic, and Carmen would ask questions Bree couldn't answer.

She needed to get out of here.

She needed Hank.

"Hey," Carmen said, softer now. "You sure you're good?"

Bree nodded quickly. Too quickly.

Carmen's brows knit. "You look like you saw a ghost."

Bree forced a breath. "Just... overwhelmed. This isn't really my world."

Carmen's expression eased with sympathy instead of suspicion. "Yeah, it's a lot the first time. Heidi goes overboard, and Marcus feeds off of an audience. You won't hurt my feelings if you need some air."

That was all Bree needed.

"I think I will," she said. "Fresh air. And quieter company."

Carmen looped a strand of hair behind her ear. "Totally understand. Want me to walk you out?"

Bree almost said yes, but the instinct hit hard and fast: Don't.

Carmen loved her sister fiercely. She wouldn't intentionally hurt Bree, but loyalty was loyalty. If she knew Bree had seen something suspicious, even the smallest detail, she'd have to choose a side — and it wouldn't be Bree's.

"No, I'll be fine," Bree said lightly. "Just need a breather."

Carmen nodded and looked relieved that she wasn't abandoning Heidi in the middle of her meltdown. "Okay. Text me if you want company."

"I will," Bree lied gently.

She eased away from the thrumming chaos, drifting backward until the Red Dragons' pit fell behind her. The music diminished. The voices dropped to murmurs. By the time she reached the open space between trailers, she could finally think.

Her pulse still thrummed like a hummingbird under her ribs.

She didn't fully understand what she'd seen, but she knew — with the same certainty she knew color theory and line weight — that something had been hidden, wired, disguised.

Hank would know the difference between equipment and something meant to tilt the odds.

And he would take her seriously.

She angled toward his pit, scanning instinctively for his height, his shoulders, the way he moved. He wasn't there yet; only Brian and Colby worked quietly at the bench, the air calm and controlled.

Bree paused several steps away, letting her breath settle. She didn't want the panic in her voice when she talked to Hank. She wanted clarity and wanted him to hear the detail, not her fear.

Her heartbeat finally slowed. Just enough.

Across the pits, someone revved an engine, and someone else shouted. Bree barely registered it. The hidden cylinder and the twitch of the gauge when Einstein pressed the horn consumed her thoughts.

This time, when she looked toward Hank's pit, she saw movement.

Hank. Tall. Focused. Eyes scanning automatically for her even before he saw her.

And when he did see her, he started toward her without hesitation.

Relief flooded her so fast her knees almost gave out.

She tightened her grip on the sketchbook and met him halfway.

"Hank," she said, keeping her voice steady by sheer force of will. "I need to tell you something."

And she knew, with complete certainty, he was the only person she could trust with it.

CHAPTER
ELEVEN

Hank came out of the riders' meeting with a headache starting behind his right eye.

Gearing charts, fuel windows, last-minute schedule changes; they all rolled through his brain in tight formation. The late light off the water bounced off the trailers, sharp enough that he had to squint as he stepped back into the pits.

Noise wrapped around him; engines coughing and clearing their throats, an air gun barking in short bursts, Brian's laugh carrying over the clatter for a second before it got swallowed up again.

He checked his phone out of habit.

No new messages from Bree.

He'd texted her during the meeting, thumb moving quicker than his brain had any right to, asking if she was headed to the balcony. Telling her to stick with Brian or Colby. Promise me.

She'd promised.

He slipped the phone into his back pocket and scanned the pits, that automatic sweep he'd never quite shaken.

Bikes, tools, crew, fans leaning over the fences; all the moving parts that turned race weekend into something alive.

His gaze snagged on a splash of red and black.

The Red Dragons' hauler, glossy as ever, their pit taped off like a stage. Music pumped low from a truck, some driving beat that vibrated underfoot. Heidi stood near the center, waving her arms at a man with a tablet. Marcus hovered at her shoulder.

And just off to one side, near the edge of their taped line, stood Bree.

She held her sketchbook to her chest, fingers white-knuckled around the spine. Carmen stood beside her, the two of them a little island of denim and bare legs in all that branded red and black.

Something in Hank's chest pinched.

She was supposed to be with Brian or Colby. She was supposed to be up on that balcony with her pencils and that ocean light she liked so much.

He could hear his own voice from earlier in the week, teasing. This is the lion's den.

It felt a lot less like a joke now.

He watched her for a beat. Her posture was wrong; she wasn't just observing for art reference. Her shoulders were tight, eyes too focused. Not drifting like an artist soaking in color and line, but tracking something. Calculating.

She took a step; then another. Carmen said something, touched her arm; Bree shook her head and peeled away, moving with purpose through the open lane between trailers.

His hurt, stupid as it was, bled out under something heavier.

She looked scared.

Hank started toward her without thinking. The world narrowed down to a corridor of noise and movement with her at the end.

She turned her head slightly. Even from across the pits, he saw the moment she spotted him.

Her face changed. Relief flooded it so fast, it hit him like a physical thing.

They met near the back of his trailer, in the sliver of shade that cut across the gravel. Up close, the tightness around her mouth and the strain in her eyes were impossible to miss.

"Hank," she said, voice low but steady. "I need to tell you something."

He wanted to say a dozen things first; You promised. What were you doing over there? Are you okay?

What came out was, "Come on, honey. Let's get you out of the crowd."

He jerked his chin toward the narrow space between his trailer and the next one. It wasn't much, but it was quieter by a few decibels and out of the line of most cameras and curious eyes.

She followed, fingers flexing restlessly around the edges of her sketchbook. When they were tucked into that little pocket of shadow, engine noise muffled by steel and fiberglass, he leaned one shoulder against the trailer and really looked at her.

Her cheeks were a little pale under the sunburn from earlier. A tiny muscle ticked in her jaw.

"You all right?" he asked. "Anybody bother you?"

"No. I mean, not like that." She took a breath, tried again. "I saw something. I think I saw them cheating."

The word snapped the rest of his focus into place like a safety being flicked off.

Hank's jaw tightened. "Tell me from the beginning. Start with why you were over there."

Guilt flashed in her eyes. "Carmen came to my room. Heidi wanted another opinion on Marcus's suit; she's melting down over the design. Carmen swore it'd be quick." She swallowed. "I know I promised. I thought if I went, it'd just be fabric and attitude. I'm sorry."

He let himself feel the sting and let it go. There wasn't time for that right now.

"Thanks for being honest," he said. "Now talk me through what you saw."

Bree pulled in a slow breath. He watched her do that thing he'd seen on the balcony; sorting through impressions, lining them up like colors on a palette.

"While Heidi was yelling at the manufacturer rep, everyone's attention was over there," she said. "Marcus, the crew, some girls by the truck. Even the kid working on the chain stopped to watch. No one was looking at the bike you'll actually be racing against."

Hank's muscles went tighter. "Marcus's primary bike."

She nodded. "Einstein was at it. He'd switched to earplugs, no big headphones. He opened a compartment along the inside of the frame, just under where the rider's knee would sit. It's not big; long and thin, like it was made for wiring. But I watched other guys wipe that area down. It was empty before."

Hank pictured the Dragons' main bike, the minimalist frame, the way they loved to brag about how clean it was. "Okay."

"He pulled something from a tray. A cylinder." She lifted one hand, thumb and fingers about three inches apart. "About this long. Metal. Dull silver. There was a small valve stem at one end with a hose already attached.

It looked heavy when he shifted it; his glove dipped a little."

"Gauge?" Hank asked.

"Yes." Her eyes lit with the sharp relief of being understood. "A small gauge near the valve. He turned it, counted under his breath, then slid the cylinder into that channel. It fit too perfectly. Like it'd been designed to go there."

Hank's stomach went cold.

"Go on," he said quietly.

"He laid the hose along the frame, pinning it under existing wiring so it looked like part of the loom," she said. "Then he ran it up toward the front of the bike, under the tank. It came out again near the handlebars. He looped it around a bracket and connected it to a small device wired into the horn assembly."

"The horn," Hank repeated. His mind filled in the gaps. "Not the starter, not the kill switch. The horn."

"He pressed the horn button once," she said. "No sound. He adjusted something, pressed again. Still no sound, but the gauge on the cylinder flickered. He looked satisfied; then he closed up the frame so you'd never know anything was there unless you knew exactly where to look. He smoothed his hand over the metal, like he was proud of it."

She stopped, breathing a little harder. "Everyone else was still watching Heidi. No one saw him. Except me."

Hank stared at her for a second, his mind hauling years of mechanical knowledge and a decade of war stories into the same space.

Hidden cylinder. Pressurized. Hosed to the front. Horn-triggered. Gauge jump.

You want a hidden boost? You hide a shot of nitrous. You trigger it off something no marshal will think to check.

His molars ground together.

"Son of a bitch," he muttered.

Bree's fingers curled tighter around the sketchbook. "You think it's nitrous."

"I can't say for sure without looking at it, but it fits," he said. "Pressurized gas, gauge, hose routing; using the horn as a trigger is smart if you're a coward. No one expects the horn to do anything on track, and tech inspectors don't always test buttons if they look wired right. You could hide a short burst in a straight and gain a couple of bike lengths. Easy."

She swallowed. "Is that the kind of cheating Brian was talking about when he listed tricks?"

"Pretty much," Hank said. "And if they're running extra pressure in a frame not meant to hold it, or playing with timing maps to compensate, they could blow the whole thing apart." His voice flattened. "You put unexpected stress on a structure at speed, it doesn't just fail; it shatters."

For a second, he wasn't looking at Copper Moon's pits at all; he was staring down at twisted metal and sand, at the aftermath of somebody else's bad call. Smelling burnt rubber and worse.

He shoved the image away and focused on the woman in front of him.

"You did good, Bree," he said. He kept his tone low and calm, even though his pulse had picked up. "You saw something nobody else saw."

"Because they were watching the show," she said. "That suit fight was deliberate, wasn't it? A distraction."

"My money says they've used that routine before," Hank replied. "Heidi and Marcus throw a fit, everyone looks, Einstein plays surgeon in the corner."

Her mouth tightened. "So what do you do now? Tell someone? Get the officials to look?"

His instincts yelled yes, but another part of him ran the odds. The Dragons had money, sponsors, and history. He had suspicion and the word of a woman the paddock barely knew.

And that wasn't what scared him most.

"You realize," he said slowly, "if I march over there and accuse them, the first thing they'll ask is how I know. Who saw what? How somebody got close enough to spot a hidden bottle in a frame channel."

Color drained from her face. "You think they'd come after me."

He saw again how alone she'd looked in that pit. Not in a crowd of fans; surrounded by their people. Their crew. Their security.

"The kind of people who cheat like that and build a whole circus to hide it aren't big on leaving loose ends," he said. "You saw what they didn't want anyone to see. That puts a target on your back, whether we say something or not."

"I didn't do anything wrong," she protested, but there was a tremor under the words.

"I know that." He stepped closer, needing her to feel the certainty in him. "You didn't; you did exactly the right thing. You saw something off, you got out, and you came straight to me. That's textbook."

Her eyebrows flicked. "Textbook what?"

"Textbook field work," he said. "You stumble into something dirty, you don't confront the guy kneeling over the bomb; you back out, you tell your team, you let the people with the right gear handle it."

Her eyes searched his. "You're scared."

"Yeah," he said, because there wasn't any point lying. "I am."

The admission cost him, but not as much as the thought of her walking through that pit again with Einstein's eyes on her.

"You're good at reading people, Bree," he said. "Did he see you watching him?"

She thought for a moment. "I don't think so. He glanced over once when the argument got louder, but I was standing near the edge. He rolled his eyes at Heidi, not at me. He never stopped working."

"Okay," Hank said. "That buys us time."

"Time for what?"

He exhaled, long and slow. "Time for me to put some things in motion and for you to stay somewhere they can't reach you."

Her spine straightened. "I'm not a package you can store in a locker, Hank."

"I know you're not." He met her gaze head-on. "You're the only reason I know what they've done. You're sharp and observant, and you walked into a dangerous place, and you walked back out with intel. That doesn't make you a liability. It makes you an asset."

Something flickered in her eyes, something like pride fighting with fear.

"But assets have to be protected," he went on quietly. "If they realize you saw what you did, you're vulnerable. You don't know this paddock like I do. You don't know who's on whose payroll. I can't go out there and do my job if I'm picturing you walking around while the Dragons are looking for a leak."

Her throat worked. "So what are you asking me to do?"

He could've softened it. Could've dressed it up as a suggestion. Instead, he gave her the respect of honesty.

"I'm asking you to stay inside tomorrow," he said. "Race day, I want you in the hotel, door locked. No boardwalk, no pits, no balcony. Not until the Cup race is over and the bikes are back in the tech barn. After that, we can reassess."

Her eyes widened. "All day."

"All day," he confirmed. "I'll make sure you've got whatever you need. Food, sketching supplies, and a live feed of the race on your TV. Brian and Colby will know you're off-limits. If you need anything, you call me or one of them; you don't open the door to anyone else, not even if they say they know me."

Her fingers tightened on the sketchbook. "I came here to paint. To see the race. To watch you do the thing you love. And now I'm supposed to sit in a room like a kid in time-out."

He hated that it sounded like that. Hated it more because he understood.

"I wish like hell I wasn't asking this," Hank said. "But this isn't just about a dirty bottle and a crooked mechanic. The Dragons play rough. Marcus plays rough. If they think you're a threat, they'll push back. I've seen what that looks like off-track."

She watched his face, really watched it, and he knew she saw more there than he usually let anyone see. Old dust, old heat. The kind that clung to your lungs no matter how many years passed.

"How bad," she asked softly.

"Bad enough," he said. "In the desert, it was explosives on the side of a road or a kid with a phone and a detonator. Here, it's a bike that mysteriously malfunctioned or a woman who tripped on a set of stairs when no one was watching. Different stage, same play."

Her breath hitched. "You really think they'd go that far?"

"I think people who cheat at a level that can kill someone are already comfortable crossing lines," he said. "And I think you're important to me. That's not a variable I'm willing to risk."

The last words slipped out before he could filter them.

Her eyes went dark and soft all at once.

"Important to you," she repeated quietly.

"Yeah." His voice came out rough; he didn't try to clean it up. "You are. I've had maybe three months where my head shut up and the noise dropped to something livable; one of them was here, with you. I can't walk into turn one tomorrow wondering if the Dragons have decided to send a message to the woman who caught them with their hand in the cookie jar."

A quiet beat stretched between them, full of engine rumble and shouted orders from the far side of the trailers and the pulse of his own heart.

Bree's chin lifted a fraction. "So this is about your focus."

"It's about your safety," he said. "And yeah, it's about my focus, because my focus is one of the things that keeps me alive on a bike. I'm better on track if I know you're behind a locked door than if I think you're out here trying to get perfect reference photos in a war zone."

Her mouth twisted. "When you put it like that, you make Copper Moon sound very un-touristy."

He almost smiled. "Tourists don't normally stumble into performance-enhancing sabotage."

She looked down at the sketchbook, then back up at him. Conflict flickered across her face; the artist who'd come for light and motion, the woman who'd just seen the underbelly.

"I hate feeling useless," she admitted. "Like my job is to stay out of the way while the grown-ups handle it."

"You're not useless," he said. "You've already done more than you know. You're giving me a way to protect my team and level the field. But sometimes the bravest thing you can do is sit tight and let the people with muscle and experience take the hit."

"And you're the muscle," she said.

"Among others," he replied. "I'll loop Brian and Colby in. I've got a buddy working tech in the regional series; I'll see who's around on this crew that still gives a damn about clean racing. We'll be smart."

Her gaze searched his, looking for cracks. "And what if they find another way to cheat?"

"Then we'll keep watching," he said. "But we can't be everywhere. We start with what we know."

She exhaled, long and slow. "You're asking a lot."

"I know."

Silence fell again, thicker this time. She stood close enough that he could see the fine spray of freckles on her nose, the tiny smudge of graphite near her thumb where she'd apparently rubbed at something without thinking.

He realized he had braced his hand against the trailer beside her head at some point and leaned in, angling his body toward hers as if gravity had shifted.

Her eyes flicked to his mouth, just for a second, then back up.

The fear in her gaze hadn't disappeared, but something else lived there too; a warmth that had been growing in stolen mornings and late-night texts and quiet walks in the dunes.

"You're serious about this," she said. "You're not just being a caveman."

"I've been accused of worse," he said, half a breath from her now. "But yeah, I'm serious."

"If I promise to stay in my room tomorrow," she asked slowly, "do you promise to be careful out there? No extra risks, no proving-a-point bullshit. Just you and the bike and whatever clean race you can get."

He almost laughed at the way she mirrored his terms. Almost.

"I'll do everything I can to bring her home in one piece," he said. "And me with her. That's already the plan."

Her throat worked. "Okay."

"Okay, you'll stay inside," he pressed, needing to hear it.

"Okay." She nodded once. "I'll stay inside. Hotel room, door locked. No balcony, no boardwalk. I'll draw from memory and the TV feed. I'll text you when I'm in and when I'm tempted to break the rules, so you can tell me not to."

Relief hit him so hard he had to close his eyes for a second. He hadn't realized how tightly he'd been wound until that knot loosened.

"Thank you," he said quietly.

When he opened his eyes, she was watching him with a softness that punched through his ribs.

"Don't thank me like I did you a favor," she said. "I'm doing it because you're right. And because I don't really want to find out what happens when cheaters feel cornered."

He lifted his hand from the trailer, hesitated only a heartbeat, then cupped her cheek.

Her skin was warm from the sun, softer than he'd imagined the first time he'd watched her on that balcony. She leaned into his touch without seeming to realize it, her eyes fluttering closed for a second.

He didn't plan the kiss.

One second, he was looking at her, at the worry in the set of her mouth and the stubborn tilt of her chin; the next, he was leaning in, driven by an impulse as old and simple as breathing.

Their mouths met in a collision of pent-up fear and something sweeter. Her hand shot out, fingers catching his T-shirt at the shoulder, holding on.

He kept it slow at first, letting her feel his intent, not just his adrenaline. The brush of his lips over hers, the taste of coffee and salt, and the faint citrus of whatever soap the hotel stocked. She made a small sound in the back of her throat that went straight through his chest and settled somewhere beneath his sternum.

Her lips parted on a breath. He deepened the kiss, angling his head, letting his hand slide back into her hair. It was still damp from her shower, curls catching against his fingers. His other hand found her hip, thumb stroking the curve there through soft denim.

She came up on her toes without breaking contact, closing the last inches between them. The sketchbook pressed into his chest between them, edges digging in. He didn't care. Her fingers tightened in his shirt, anchoring herself.

The noise of the pits faded to a dull roar. For a heartbeat, there was only the two of them, the scrape of his stubble against her skin, the tiny hitch in her breathing when he licked gently into her mouth, the way she answered with her own tentative stroke that had his knees threatening to buckle.

He pulled back slowly before he forgot where they were entirely. Her eyes opened, pupils wide, cheeks flushed with something that had nothing to do with the sun.

"Wow," she whispered.

"Yeah," he said, equally shaken. "That about covers it."

She let out a breath that might've been a laugh if it hadn't sounded so unsteady. "You picked one hell of a moment."

"I've been trying to pick a good one for a while," he admitted. "Turns out there isn't a good time to kiss the woman who makes your heartbeat jump when there's a race and a cheating scandal hanging over your head."

Her mouth curved. "You could've led with that, you know. 'Hey Bree, I'm terrified the Red Dragons might kill you, also I really want to kiss you.'"

"Yeah, I'm not putting that on a greeting card."

She leaned her forehead briefly against his chest, drawing in his scent like she was memorizing it. When she straightened, some of the panic had settled into something more solid.

"I meant what I said," she told him. "I'll stay in tomorrow. I'll lock the door, keep my head down, pretend the outside world doesn't exist until you knock."

His gut tightened in a different way at that image. "Careful. You keep talking about me coming to your room like that, and I'm not going to be able to think about apexes."

A slow, shy smile touched her mouth. "Maybe you can think about it as a reward for not dying."

"High stakes," he said, and it came out more intimate than he'd intended.

She sobered. "You'll be careful."

"I will," he promised. "And if anything feels off, if you hear or see anything weird from your window, you call me. Or Brian. Or Colby. In that order."

She rolled her eyes lightly. "Yes, Sergeant."

Somewhere beyond the trailer, Brian shouted his name. A bike revved, the note familiar; Julie clearing her throat.

Duty called.

Hank brushed his thumb over Bree's lower lip once, unable to help himself. "I've got to get back."

"I know." She angled her face into his hand for one more second. "Go do your thing. Break physics in a legal way."

He huffed a quiet laugh. "I'll try."

He stepped back reluctantly, already feeling the absence of her warmth. "Text me when you're in your room tonight. I'll sleep better."

"You sleep," she said. "I'll be the one chewing my nails."

"I'll text you too," he amended. "We can chew together."

She smiled, small and real. "Deal."

He watched her walk away toward the hotel entrance until she disappeared past the line of trailers. Only then did he turn back toward his pit.

Brian was waiting with a torque wrench in hand, eyebrows raised.

"Everything okay?" Brian asked. "You were MIA for a minute."

Hank glanced once toward the gap where he'd last seen Bree, then back at his crew chief, his friend.

"Not yet," he said, taking the wrench. "But we're working on it. I need to talk to you and Colby tonight; we've got a problem with the Dragons."

Brian's grin faded, his expression sharpening. "How bad."

"Bad enough," Hank said. He looked out across the pits toward the gleam of red and black. "But we've got eyes on it. And we've got something worth fighting for."

He thought of Bree, hands shaking around her sketchbook, still walking into the lion's den because her friend had asked.

He thought of the way she'd kissed him back.

Yeah. Worth fighting for.

He dropped into a crouch beside Julie, mind already shifting gears as he reached for the next bolt.

CHAPTER

TWELVE

Bree woke before the alarm, heart racing like it had heard a starter's pistol in her sleep.

For a few seconds, she lay very still, listening. The room was dim and cool, the air conditioner humming in the corner. Beneath it, muffled by glass and curtains, came the low, restless growl of engines starting up.

Race morning.

She shut her eyes again, and Hank's mouth was right there; the press of his lips on hers; the way his hand had settled at her hip like he had always known it belonged there; the rough scrape of his jaw when she had leaned in without thinking. Her chest tightened with the memory; warmth and fear braided together.

Then another image shoved in beside it; Einstein's gloved fingers cradling a dull silver cylinder; the tiny gauge that had jumped when he pressed the horn; the way everyone else had watched Heidi and Marcus while he hid a secret inside the frame.

She opened her eyes and swung her legs out of bed.

The hotel carpet was soft under her bare feet. The

bedside clock glowed just after seven. Light seeped around the edges of the curtains; pale and tentative, as if the sun was still deciding whether it wanted any part of this day.

Her phone sat on the nightstand where she had left it.

She picked it up and thumbed the screen awake.

Two messages from Hank waited.

You awake, honey? The first one read. *Techs are doing spot checks before the main rounds. Brian and I had a word with a couple of them. You did good.*

The second: *Remember your promise. Door locked, no balcony, no boardwalk. I need to know where you are.*

Her throat went tight. She glanced at the door; the deadbolt was turned; the security bar engaged. She had done that last night without thinking, his words still in her ears.

She typed back, *I'm awake. Door's locked. I'm being very boring.*

He answered fast; he always did with her.

Boring is underrated, he wrote. *Boring keeps you breathing. TV should have coverage on the local sports channel; you'll see more from up there than I can from the queue.*

Despite the knot in her chest, she smiled.

Bossy, she replied. *How are you?*

There was a longer pause. She pictured him in the pits with his phone in one hand, helmets and bikes and people all pulling at his attention, and still making space for this.

Head's on straight, he sent. *Julie passed initial checks; no surprises. Dragons are up soon. I'll keep you posted as much as I can.*

She stared at the words for a beat.

Thank you for believing me, she wrote.

Always, he answered. *Now turn the TV on and pretend I am very calm and very professional down here.*

Liar, she sent, the letters a little wobbly under her thumb.

She set the phone down and crossed to the TV. The remote lay on the dresser; she grabbed it and clicked through channels until Copper Moon's logo appeared in the corner of the screen, a little stylized crescent tucked beside the network name.

The feed showed highlights from yesterday: bikes flicking through the long curve by the dunes; slow-motion shots of sand spraying; riders' bodies low and fluid. A pair of commentators sat in a booth with the ocean behind them; bright polos; teeth a little too white; voices a little too cheerful.

She muted them for a moment and went to the balcony door.

Habit tugged at her, as strong as the tide. That balcony had become her studio; her favorite place in Copper Moon; all that space and motion framed in glass.

Her hand closed around the handle.

She could feel the cool metal against her palm; the subtle give when she pulled, just enough to crack the door; the rush of air that would follow; the roar of engines coming in clean instead of muffled.

Hank's voice threaded through the temptation.

Hotel room, door locked. No balcony, no boardwalk.

She let the handle go.

Her fingers left little crescents on the wood where she had squeezed too hard. She stepped back and tugged the curtains closer together until the view outside was just a faint glow.

"Fine," she said under her breath. "You win."

She grabbed her sketchbook and pencils from the side table and curled up on the end of the bed. When she unmuted the TV, the commentators had shifted to live shots; the camera perched somewhere high above the pits, looking down on the grid of trailers, awnings, and taped-off rectangles.

From up here, the world she had walked through yesterday looked like a toy set; tiny people moving between splashes of color; the bikes slim as matchsticks on their stands.

She let her pencil start moving. Broad strokes first; blocking in the shapes; the canyon of haulers; the spine of the main lane. Her lines steadied her; always had. When the rest of her felt shaky, her hands usually remembered what to do with graphite and paper.

Her phone buzzed again.

Bree?

She smiled.

Yeah, she replied.

Love that you want to help, his next text read. *Remember, the best thing you can do for me today is stay safe. Let me handle the ugly.*

Heat prickled behind her eyes; not tears exactly; something heavier.

You handle the ugly, she wrote. *I'll handle the pretty.*

Deal, he sent.

On screen, one of the cameras zoomed in on the tech inspection area. The announcers' tone brightened; words like "pre-race checks" and "safety protocols" floated over the image.

She watched the officials move from bike to bike, checking levers, looking at screens, bending to peer into frame gaps. They looked oddly gentle with the machines, like doctors with patients.

A line of text ran along the bottom of the screen: identifiers; team names; numbers. She saw Hank's name flick past: Hank James, number twenty-four; Copper Moon Performance.

Her chest gave that little lurch when she saw his name in print.

The camera shifted again, panning toward a section of pits she recognized even from this distance.

Red and black dominated the frame. The Red Dragons' hauler gleamed; their pit taped off neatly. Heidi stood with one hand on her hip, sunglasses on, hair perfect, posture loose in a way that did not match the tension in her jaw.

Marcus and Stoke were both in shot; Stoke pacing; Marcus talking to one of the judges; Einstein behind them near Marcus's bike.

Bree's hand tightened on her pencil.

Her phone buzzed.

They're with Julie now, Hank wrote. *Clean check. Dragons are next.*

She looked back at the TV.

The camera zoomed; the commentators started the kind of upbeat chatter they used when something might be interesting. They talked about "a closer look," "rumors of stricter enforcement," and "whispers in the paddock," careful and vague.

One of the tech officials pointed toward Marcus's bike. Another rolled a cart closer. Einstein looked stiff even at this distance; shoulders too high; hands a little too still.

"Hands off the bikes for a moment," one of the officials said; his voice picked up by a boom mic somewhere.

The pit microphones did not always catch every word, but they caught enough. Heidi's complaint about timing, Stoke's exaggerated sigh, Marcus's smooth reassurance that his team had nothing to hide.

The horn, Bree thought.

Her heart started to climb.

Her phone vibrated in her lap.

Eyes on Dragons, Hank wrote. *Mac's pushing for deeper checks. Breathe for me.*

She realized she had not done that in a while.

She inhaled through her nose, held it, let it out slowly. She counted like her therapist had taught her after Bryn died: four in, four hold, six out. Her shoulders dropped a fraction.

On the screen, one of the techs crouched by Marcus's bike, following a line of wiring. Another loosened something on the frame.

Bree's stomach twisted so sharply she had to press a hand there.

"Please find it," she whispered. "Please find it; please find it."

A change rippled through the body language on screen. One inspector straightened and looked at Mac, whoever he was, the older one with gray hair at his temples. There was a brief exchange she could not hear clearly, a hand gesture toward the lower frame.

Then the camera zoomed in tight.

The view turned grainy, blown up, but she could still see enough.

The panel she had seen Einstein open yesterday sat on the concrete now, leaning against a stand. A gloved hand reached into the frame channel and eased something free.

A small cylinder; dull silver; hose attached; tiny gauge.

Her pencil slid out of her hand and rolled across the duvet.

"There," she said, voice cracking. "There it is."

The commentators went quiet for a beat; then they

started talking again. Their tone had changed: less breezy, more measured. They used words like "non-standard equipment," "alleged performance enhancement," and "further investigation required."

They did not say nitrous. Lawyers somewhere were probably allergic to the word.

Her phone buzzed.

Tech found the nitrous, Hank texted. *You were right.*

She slapped a hand over her mouth, not sure if she wanted to laugh or throw up.

I was right, she typed. *I hate that I was right.*

Me too, he replied. *But I'd rather be mad than plan a funeral.*

On screen, everything got louder.

The microphones picked up Heidi's furious voice, calling it a misunderstanding, and accusing the tech inspectors of targeting them. Stoke stepped closer to one of the officials, his body language all sharp angles and clenched fists.

The camera angle changed again, widening to catch more of the pit lane.

Bree watched Stoke shove the nearest inspector; saw tools scatter as the man stumbled into a cart. Security moved fast; two men in black polos closed in, hands catching Stoke's arms. He fought them with jerky movements, his mouth moving in words that blurred into static through the speakers.

Her nails dug into her palms.

Someone in a darker uniform arrived, a woman with sergeant stripes on her sleeve, hand resting near her belt; her posture was calm in a way that made everyone around her look more frantic.

The commentators scrambled to keep up, explaining

that local law enforcement had a presence at the track and that any altercation with officials would be taken seriously.

Bree's phone buzzed again.

Stoke just shoved a tech, Hank wrote. *Cops involved now. Nobody's hurt. Stay where you are.*

She realized she had half risen without noticing, weight on the balls of her feet; muscles ready to run.

She sat back down.

Is it safe for you? she wrote. *Are they going to blame you for this?*

No one said your name, he answered. *Brian was careful; so was I. To the Dragons, this looks like Mac doing his job. I'm just another rider watching the show.*

She did not like the word show, not with that much anger in the frame, but she understood what he meant.

On TV, security and police steered Stoke out of the center of the pit; the sergeant talking to him with the kind of firm patience Bree had seen cops use with drunk patrons outside bars. One of the techs kept taking photos of the exposed frame; another wrote on a clipboard; glance sharp and focused.

You saved them, she thought. *You saved them from their own bad choices.*

Her phone screen lit again.

How are you, pretty girl? Hank wrote. *Not just watching. You.*

The endearment hit her like a warm hand between her shoulder blades.

Shaky, she answered. *I'm glad they found it. I kind of want to vomit. And I hate that they're yelling at the inspectors instead of apologizing.*

Same, he replied. *They'll spin it; they always do. But the bottle is out in the open. That's not going back in the frame quietly.*

On the broadcast, the commentators started talking about possible penalties, how an impounded bike complicated the lineup, and what sponsors might say. They kept their voices neutral, stretched thin over the tension like a fresh coat of paint.

Bree got up and walked to the curtains again.

She let herself open them just enough to see the edge of the track far below, a thin gray ribbon between blocks of color. She did not touch the balcony door; she was not even tempted to slide it open now. She just looked at the sliver of world she could see and tried to picture Hank in it: tall and solid and unflinching.

Her reflection hovered faintly in the glass; hair messy, eyes wide, T-shirt twisted.

This is what you wanted, she thought. You wanted to matter.

She had not wanted Bryn to die. She had not wanted to sit in a hospital waiting room after Bryn's diagnosis and feel completely powerless. That helplessness had sunk claws into her and never fully let go.

Seeing the hidden cylinder, connecting the details, getting out, telling Hank, that had been the opposite of helpless. It had been focused; clear. It had mattered.

It just did not feel heroic from this side.

She went back to the bed, picked up her pencil again with fingers that trembled a little less.

On a fresh page, she sketched the rectangle of the Red Dragons' pit; the open frame; the small cylinder in a gloved hand. She drew Einstein as a shadow at the edge, his face half-turned away. Then she added a tiny figure at the far margin; herself, sketchbook clutched to her chest; nothing more than an outline.

Underneath, in small letters, she wrote: Caught.

Her phone buzzed again.

Mac just thanked whoever tipped him, Hank texted. *I told him I'd pass it along. So consider yourself officially appreciated by the safety gods.*

A laugh bubbled out of her, surprised and wet.

Safety gods, she wrote. *That sounds like a terrifying pantheon.*

They're cranky but fair, he answered.

The commentators announced that qualifying would be pushed back to account for "ongoing discussions with team representatives." The graphic at the bottom of the screen was updated with a new start time and a little note about schedule adjustments.

So you're still racing, she typed. *After all that.*

Yes, he sent. *Tech did their job. Bad variable is out of the equation. Honestly, the safest place for me is on a bike I trust, doing the thing I know how to do. Knowing you're upstairs and not walking past Einstein helps.*

His honesty wrapped around her like a blanket.

Okay, she wrote. *I'm here. TV on; sketchbook out; chewing my nails as we planned. Bring Julie home in one piece, James. I'd like another chance to kiss her rider.*

A beat, then, *Planning on it,* he replied. *On both counts.*

Heat bloomed low in her belly; her gaze unfocused for a second as she remembered the angle of his mouth, the way he had tasted, the quiet, stunned "wow" she had breathlessly offered when they finally broke apart.

She flipped to a new page without even thinking, and her pencil started tracing lines: the curve of his jaw; the slope of his nose; the little dent in his left eyebrow where some old scar had broken the skin. It felt like a prayer in graphite.

There was a knock at a neighboring door; someone laughing loudly in the hallway; a child's voice squealing about race bikes. Life went on around her; hotel noises, the clatter of people who had no idea they had come within inches of watching a disaster later that day.

She paused, listening to it all, and then went back to her drawing.

Her phone buzzed again, shorter this time.

They're impounding Marcus's bike, Hank wrote. *There'll be hearings and sponsors and a lot of yelling somewhere with air conditioning, but from a tech standpoint, they're off the table for now.*

So you're safer? he sent.

We're all safer, he answered. *You, me, every rider out there. That's on you as much as anyone.*

Tears pushed at the back of her eyes again. She blinked them away; she didn't need them spilling onto the paper.

All I did was watch, she wrote.

Sometimes watching is the part that saves people, he replied.

She set the phone on her knee and stared at those words until they went a little blurry.

Outside, a distant announcer's voice floated up through the glass when she muted the TV for a moment, amplified by speakers on the boardwalk. Inside, the air conditioner hummed; the curtains shifted a fraction in the barely-there draft.

She took a deep breath.

"Okay," she said quietly. "I can do this."

She texted, *When does qualifying start now?*

In about forty minutes, he answered. *I need to put the*

phone away for a bit and dial in. I'll text you again after. You still good?

I'm good, she wrote. *Nervous, but good. Go do your thing, Hank. Break physics, but in a legal way.*

A little checkered-flag emoji popped up beside his next words.

Yes, ma'am, he sent. *Keep a light on for me.*

She felt that line everywhere.

Always, she wrote.

She watched the typing indicator blink, disappear, and reappear.

One more, he sent. *If the cameras catch my interview after, just know I'm actually talking to you.*

She bit back another rush of tears.

Then say something nice, she wrote. *I'll be critiquing your script.*

Pressure's on, he replied.

The typing dots vanished for good this time.

Bree set the phone on the pillow beside her, close enough to touch, and turned back to the TV. The commentators had shifted the conversation to tire choices, weather, and how cooler air off the ocean might change grip levels; things she barely understood but listened to anyway to fill the space in her head where the fear tried to creep back in.

She sketched their faces too, half listening, half sunk in the lines of her own private world.

Every time the camera found Hank's bike on the grid, every time it lingered on his leathers, his helmet, the way he rested one hand on Julie's tank like he was checking her pulse, she felt something steady inside herself.

He was down there, doing the thing he loved, the thing he was built for.

She was up here watching, bearing witness, doing the thing she was built for.

It was not the role she had expected when she came to Copper Moon to paint waves and tourists, but it was the one she had, and for the first time since Bryn's death, she did not feel like the universe had put her on the wrong side of the glass.

She felt necessary.

She lifted her pencil again.

"Bring her home," she whispered toward the screen. "And then bring yourself to me."

CHAPTER

THIRTEEN

Bree told herself she was going to behave.

She sat at the foot of the bed with her sketchbook open and the TV on, the broadcast already cutting between shots of the grid and sweeping views of Copper Moon's shoreline. Her phone lay beside her thigh, screen dark for now, but she knew that if Hank could grab ten seconds between obligations, he would use them to check on her.

She wanted to be able to answer honestly.

You still in your room, honey?

Yes. I'm here.

Door locked. Just like you asked.

She had meant that when she typed it earlier. She still meant it in theory.

Then the network cut away to a pre-race montage: crowd shots, kids with homemade signs, couples in Copper Moon Cup T-shirts. The camera lingered for a few seconds on the north grandstand, packed from end to end, a slow wave of people fanning themselves in the sun.

Something in her chest pulled hard.

She could almost feel the heat coming off that many bodies; hear the rise and fall of real voices instead of the tinny echo through hotel speakers. She imagined the smell of hot asphalt and fried food and salt, the way the engines would vibrate underfoot.

Here, in the room, the air conditioner hummed steadily. The carpet was soft. The curtains, drawn mostly shut, turned the day outside into a pale blur.

Safe, she reminded herself. You promised. This is safe.

Safe felt a lot like trapped.

Her brain flashed an image so sharp she had to close her eyes. Plastic chairs. A narrow waiting room. A TV turned to a channel no one watched. Bryn somewhere beyond a set of double doors, unreachable. Every sound distorted, every minute stretched.

She had waited then, because there had been no other option. She had waited and waited until the waiting ended in the worst possible way.

Now she was supposed to sit and wait again, while someone she loved did something dangerous out of sight.

Her hands went cold.

She set the sketchbook aside and stood, pacing once between bed and dresser.

On the screen, the cameras were on Hank's pit; the sound was off, but she saw him clearly. Helmet dangling from one hand, he listened to Brian, nodded once, then looked up, straight into the closest lens. The director cut to a wider shot, but not before she saw it, the tiny tilt of his head that said he knew she would be watching.

He was down there, sealed in his world of torque settings, tire choices, and brake markers.

She was up here, staring through glass.

Her gaze slid to the hat on the back of the chair. Wide

brim. Neutral color. The sunglasses she had bought on her first day in Copper Moon sat beneath it, folded neatly.

You're not a child, she thought. *You are not helpless. You know how to be careful.*

She walked to the door and checked it again, deadbolt, security bar. Both in place. She picked up the hat and glasses and hesitated, listening.

Somewhere outside, far below, an announcer's voice rolled over the speakers toward the boardwalk. The words were indistinct from here, but the excitement in them was clear. The engines that had been idling during warmups had shifted; more focused now.

"Twenty-four riders on the grid," the commentator said a second later as the broadcast sound rose. "All eyes on local favorite Hank James, starting from pole in his Copper Moon Cup repeat."

Bree's heart knocked into her ribs.

The safest place for him is on a bike, he had told her. The safest place for you is behind a locked door.

Both statements could be true. So could the bone-deep need in her to see him fly with her own eyes.

"I'll stay away from the pits," she said quietly. "I can live with that."

She grabbed her room key and slid it into her pocket with her phone, and tucked her hair under the hat. In the mirror, she looked like one more tourist who had underestimated the sun and overcompensated with accessories.

She paused one last time, palm pressed to the door.

"I am so going to tell you the truth about this," she told the empty room. "Please still want to kiss me after."

Then she opened the door and stepped out.

The hallway felt cooler than the room; the carpet muffled the sounds of her sneakers. A couple in matching team shirts walked past, debating tire compounds like it was a normal conversation, which, here, it probably was. She kept her head down, brim low, and moved toward the service stairwell at the far end.

Yesterday, she had noticed that door on her way back from grabbing ice; a plain gray exit with a laminated sign that said staff access. No one had yelled when she used it then. No one yelled now.

Inside, concrete steps and stark lighting greeted her. The air was warmer, tinged with detergent and grease. She moved quickly, trusting memory to guide her: down two flights; out through a nondescript side door that had opened, last night, onto a small service lane between the hotel and the first vendor tents.

Today, the lane was busier, but still not crowded. Two men pushed a dolly stacked with soda cases toward the concession area, a teenager in a volunteer T-shirt took a drink of water and checked his watch.

"General admission access?" she asked when he saw her, pointing toward a walkway marked with a banner and an arrow. "North stand that way. You'll get a decent view of the back straight and the start."

"Thanks," Bree said, pitching her voice a little lower.

He looked right past her, eyes already moving to the next cluster of people. She took that as a good sign.

She merged into the flow heading toward the stands; families and couples and groups of friends, all in various stages of sunburn. Someone had a radio clipped to a belt; the same broadcast she had left behind in the room crackled from it, a slightly delayed echo of the PA system.

Around her, the air vibrated with engine noise and anticipation.

When she reached the base of the north grandstand, a

woman with a lanyard checked wristbands. Bree held up the bright strip the ticket booth had given her earlier in the weekend when she had come down with Carmen to watch a support race. The woman barely glanced at it before waving her through.

Up in the stands, she chose a place near the end of a row, not too high, not too low. From there, she could see the front straight clearly, the start grid painted bright, and the sweeping turn by the dunes in the distance. The giant screen across from the stands showed what the cameras saw.

Her heart thudded so hard it felt like a drum in her ears.

Down on the grid, Hank swung a leg over Julie's seat. He settled into position like it was the only place in the world he belonged. The sun glinted off his helmet, off the small Copper Moon emblem near the base of his visor. Brian crouched beside the bike, last words lost in the roar of the crowd.

The commentators' voices rose. "Riders are clear. Fifteen laps to decide the Copper Moon Cup."

The light sequence started.

Red. One. Two. Three.

Bree's lungs forgot how to work.

The lights went out.

The bikes launched.

Sound became a living thing, slamming against her chest, echoing through the metal under her feet. Hank held the lead into turn one; his start clean, his line perfect. The pack behind him jostled and shifted, two bikes nearly touching into the second corner before sorting themselves out.

The first lap blurred by in color and noise and flickers of the timing tower.

H. JAMES – P1.

MENDES – P2.

KROLIK – P3.

Bree's fingers bit into the aluminum bench.

"Come on," she whispered. "Do what you do."

She had thought watching the tech inspection from the safety of her room that morning had been nerve-wracking. This was something else. Every time Hank disappeared behind the dunes, her heart stopped; every time he appeared again on the front straight, alive and flowing and in control, her heart restarted with a lurch.

On the third lap, Mendes closed in.

He took a fraction more curb through the fast sweeper; his bike twitching, correcting, the gap shrinking on the screen's little timing graphic. By the end of the back straight, he had tucked into Hank's slipstream, so close Bree could barely see the space between their bikes.

"Don't you dare," she muttered.

Hank did not flinch. At the next braking zone, he held his line with almost stubborn discipline; did not lock up; did not run wide. Mendes tried the inside; he had to back out or risk contact.

People around her jumped to their feet and shouted. A boy a few seats down waved a handmade sign with twenty-four scrawled across it, the ink slightly smudged.

It went on like that, lap after lap. Mendes attacked; Hank responded. Sometimes the gap grew; sometimes it shrank. The commentators filled the spaces with analysis, tire degradation, fuel loads, and the mental game.

Under it all, Bree felt that same low hum of dread she had carried for so long. The knowledge that things could go wrong in an instant, that someone else's recklessness could still undo skill and caution and preparation, or by a bit of bad luck.

Only this time, someone had already removed the worst odds from the table. She had seen to that. The Red Dragons' stolen advantage was sitting in an evidence locker somewhere, not hidden in a frame.

It helped. Not enough to make her calm, enough to keep her from folding in on herself.

Halfway through the race, a gust of wind kicked sand across the far section of the circuit. Several bikes wobbled; one ran wide, through the runoff, then rejoined safely.

Julie stayed planted.

Hank changed his line by inches, not feet; the adjustment so precise it looked almost casual. His body moved with the bike, loose but connected; a rider in harmony, not fighting for survival.

Bree let out a breath she'd been holding.

"Okay," she whispered. "Okay, you've got this."

With four laps to go, Mendes finally made a pass stick. He dived late into the left before the front straight, back tire chattering, the bike on the edge of grip. Hank ceded the corner instead of forcing it, tucked in behind, and waited.

It hurt to watch his number drop to P2 on the board.

It would hurt more if he let pride put him on the ground.

"Smart," she murmured. "Be smart."

He waited two laps.

On the penultimate lap, coming into the complex by the dunes, he made his move. Where Mendes braked in one smooth, late squeeze, Hank feathered the lever just a hair earlier, turned in a fraction deeper, picked the bike up a fraction sooner. It was the kind of difference you would never see on a casual ride down a coastal road. Here, it translated into drive.

Julie shot out of the curve with a cleaner exit and a stronger run. Side by side, then nose ahead. By the time they hit the short chute, Hank was in front again.

The stands exploded.

Bree clapped a hand over her mouth, laughter and something like a sob tangling together.

The last lap felt like it lasted an hour and a heartbeat at the same time. Every corner was a small miracle. Every straight, a test of faith.

When Hank came around the final turn with clear track behind him and pointed Julie at the checkered flag, she did not cheer; her voice would never have made it past the knot in her throat. The crowd did it for her, a wave of sound that crashed across the grandstand.

He crossed the line.

The graphic changed: P1 – H. JAMES.

Bree bowed her head and pressed her fingers hard into her eyes.

"Thank you," she whispered, to no one in particular, to any safety gods who might be listening, to Bryn, to the universe.

On the giant screen, she watched him complete the cool-down lap, sit up, and pat Julie's tank. In parc fermé, Brian and Colby grabbed him, shaking him with delighted violence. Someone shoved a microphone in his face, and he said something, but she could not hear it now over the blood pounding in her ears.

She stayed long enough to see him step onto the top podium spot and take the trophy.

Then she slipped out while everyone else was still watching the stage.

Getting back to the hotel felt like moving through a dream. Her legs were shaky, her chest felt light and heavy at the same time. She kept the hat brim low and the glasses on until she reached the relative quiet of the service lane, then took them off and hugged them to her chest as she ducked back through the side door.

In the stairwell, where the concrete walls deadened the race noise to a distant hum, everything caught up.

She had broken her promise. She had gone out into the crowded world he had asked her to stay away from. Nothing bad had happened, but that did not erase the choice.

She stopped on the landing between floors and leaned her shoulder against the cool cinderblock.

"You always wanted to see the finish line, Bryn," she said softly. "Guess some habits die harder than others."

By the time she reached her room, her heartbeat had settled a little. Her guilt had not.

She let herself in, locked everything again, and tossed the hat and glasses onto the chair.

The TV still played the broadcast on a short delay. She turned the volume down to a murmur and stared at her phone.

No new messages yet.

He would be doing media, debriefs, the endless whirl that came with winning something like this. He did not owe her immediate reassurance. He did not owe her anything but the truth he had already given.

She owed him the same.

The knock came sooner than she expected.

Three quick raps, pause, two more. Her entire nervous system lit up in anticipation.

She crossed the room fast and opened the door.

Hank stood there with his hair still damp from a quick shower, a Copper Moon Performance T-shirt stretched over his chest, jeans hanging low on his hips. He had the trophy in one hand and a paper bag in the other.

The sight of him there, whole and breathing and grinning, nearly brought her to her knees.

"Hey," he said. His voice was rough, like it had been scraped over gravel. "Heard you know a guy who won a race."

"Rumor reached me," she managed. "Congratulations."

He stepped inside; set the trophy on the dresser with a satisfied clunk. The paper bag landed beside it. Before she could say anything else, he was in front of her, big hands settling at her waist.

"Bree," he said.

"Hank," she answered.

He kissed her.

Everything that had been wound tight inside her poured into that contact. She went up on her toes as his mouth claimed hers, arms flying around his neck. He tasted like mint and a faint hint of champagne; his lips firm and sure; his body radiating heat through the thin cotton of his shirt.

He lifted her without effort, hands sliding under her thighs; her legs wrapped around his hips on reflex. She gasped against his mouth; laughed when her shoulders hit the wall; the sound swallowed by another kiss that went deeper, slower.

"God, you feel good," he murmured against her lip. "Kept thinking about this every time I hit that straight. Probably not ideal race prep."

"Whatever you did worked," she said, slightly breathless. "Maybe we should add it to your routine."

"Pre-race visualization, huh," he said. "Might have to keep that one between us."

He eased her back to her feet, though his hands did not leave her for long. He cupped her face, thumbs brushing her cheekbones; eyes searching hers.

"You okay, honey?" he asked. "You look like you have about six extra thoughts bouncing around in there."

She swallowed.

Here it was.

"I'm okay," she said. "And I owe you the truth."

His fingers stilled.

"Okay," he said slowly. "Hit me."

She didn't back away; she didn't look at the floor. She met his gaze and lifted her chin a fraction.

"I watched the race from the north grandstand," she said. "Not on TV."

His jaw flexed. "Start at the beginning."

"I stayed in the room for tech and the whole Red Dragons mess," she said. "I swear I did. I watched the inspection, the fight, and Stoke getting hauled out. I texted you from this bed. But when they put the bikes on the grid for the race, I... I panicked."

"Because of Bryn," he said quietly.

"Because of Bryn," she agreed. "I kept thinking about that hospital room. Sitting there while someone you love is dying. The interminable waiting, holding my breath, trying to be strong, all the while sitting bedside and not moving because the fear of stepping from the room and the unthinkable happening while I was gone was stronger than anything. I couldn't do that again, not exactly like that."

She took a breath.

"So I put on the hat and sunglasses. I went down the service stairs and out the side door I found yesterday. I bought a general ticket, sat in the public stands, stayed away from the pits, and away from the Dragons. The cops and security were all over them, Hank. They were not looking at the crowd. I watched you race, and when you crossed the line, I left before you even hit the podium. Came straight back here."

Silence settled between them, thick and heavy.

He closed his eyes for a second; opened them again. The way he looked at her made her feel like he was looking through skin and bone, directly at the place she tried hardest to keep hidden.

"Thank you for telling me," he said at last.

"You're not yelling," she said.

"Thinking about it," he replied. "Trying not to."

She winced.

"I'm not mad at you," he went on. "I am mad at the picture in my head of you in that crowd while I was riding, like you were behind three layers of hotel security. I made decisions out there based on the idea that I knew exactly where you were. You changed the plan and did not loop me in."

"I know," she said. "And I'm sorry. I picked the least risky way to break the rules, which is a terrible sentence when you say it out loud."

The corner of his mouth twitched, despite everything. "Yeah, it is."

He let out a breath, his shoulders loosening a fraction.

"I get why you did it," he said. "If I had been through what you have, I might have done the same. That doesn't mean I like it."

"I don't like it either," she said. "I hated lying to you, even for a couple of hours. I hated that I felt like I had to choose between being safe and being present."

He brushed his thumbs across her cheeks again, a small, grounding touch.

"Okay," he said. "So next time, we do not put you in that position. If my safety plan involves you, we build it together. No assumptions. No heroics in a floppy hat."

She huffed a weak laugh. "Deal."

"Good," he said softly. "Because I am very attached to the idea of you being around for a long time."

"Yeah," she said. "Me too."

Something eased between them then. Not completely, this was not something one conversation could fix. But a knot she had been carrying in her chest loosened enough for air to move more freely.

He kissed her again, slower, a question instead of an explosion.

She answered yes with the way she pressed closer, with the way her fingers curled into his shirt and then under it, seeking skin.

The rest of the world faded to a low hum.

They made their way to the bed half by accident, half by design. Touches punctuated every step, the slide of his hand along her spine, the curve of her fingers over the back of his neck. When he peeled her T-shirt away, he did it with a care that made her feel cherished, not exposed.

"You're beautiful," he said simply, looking at her like she was the first good thing he had seen in days.

"You're biased," she said, cheeks warm.

"Not even a little," he answered.

His own shirt went next, tossed somewhere toward the chair. The lines of his chest and stomach were familiar enough from earlier glimpses that they did not startle her, but the reality of his bare skin under her hands still made something in her curl tight.

He touched her like he had ridden; focused, attentive, reading feedback and adjusting. When she sucked in a breath or tensed, he slowed; when she arched into him, he followed.

"Tell me if you need anything different," he murmured into the curve of her neck. "Faster, slower, more, less. I'm not on a solo ride here."

She laughed softly; the sound breaking on a sigh when his mouth found the sensitive spot just below her ear.

"I'll tell you," she promised.

She did. When a particular pressure was too much, when she wanted his hand to move, when she needed a second to chase away an old ghost that tried to creep in when his weight settled more fully over hers.

"I'm here," he reminded her each time. "You're here. No one else in the room."

By the time he slid into her, she was ready; not just physically, but in all the ways that mattered. She met him halfway, hips rising, hands framing his face. The stretch hurt a little; then it did not, then it felt so right she could have cried.

He moved with a rhythm that felt almost like the race: steady, sure, pushing and easing at all the right moments. Except here, there were no opponents, no lap times, no flags. Just the two of them, figuring out a new way to fit together.

When release swept over her, it felt nothing like the shattering she had feared and everything like coming back into alignment. She heard herself cry out; heard him answer with a rough sound that was part her name, part relief.

He followed her, his whole body shuddering; forehead dropping to her shoulder.

For a little while afterward, they did not speak; they just lay tangled in the sheets, her leg thrown over his, his hand resting low on her stomach. His heartbeat thumped against her palm, steady and strong.

"You alive?" he asked eventually, voice sleep-rough.

"Very," she said. "Dangerously so."

He laughed, the sound vibrating through her.

"Good," he said. "I like you that way."

They shifted so she could lay half on top of him, her cheek on his chest. He stroked lazy patterns along her spine, fingers following the curve of each vertebra.

"So," she said after a long, contented silence. "You mentioned something earlier about a shop."

He smiled; she felt it under her ear.

"I did," he said. "The mayor cornered me after the podium. Apparently, having a Cup winner stick around and hang a shingle is good for tourism. There's an old warehouse off Bay Street that they want to turn into mixed-use. They figure a performance shop downstairs, and some artsy space upstairs gives them bragging rights."

Her eyebrows lifted.

"Artsy space," she repeated. "That sounds suspiciously like a studio."

"Depends on who we convince to move in," he said. "I hear there is an artist in residence at the Copper Moon hotel who has been making a lot of staff very curious."

She smiled.

"An artist who is thinking about staying," she said quietly. "About painting more than waves and tourists."

His hand stilled against her back.

"Yeah," he said. "Is she now?"

"She might be," Bree answered. "If there was a place where she could put down roots again without feeling like she was betraying someone she lost. If there was a man who made her feel like living was not a selfish act."

"Sounds like she should meet this guy," Hank said. "He sounds pretty smitten already."

"She has," she said. "He kissed her against a hotel wall after winning a race, which is very hard to argue with."

He huffed.

"Is that going in your next painting?" he asked. "Because I'm not sure how I feel about being immortalized as Wall Guy."

"You'll live," she said. "And yes, it probably is."

He went quiet for a moment.

"I don't need an answer right now," he said. "About the shop. About staying. About any of it. I just needed you to know the option is real. It's not just a daydream I trot out when I am tired of hotel rooms."

She shifted so she could look at him, propping herself up on one elbow. He met her gaze without flinching.

"Hank," she said. "I've been operating in survival mode for a long time. Paint, eat, sleep, repeat. I came here to try to feel something that was not grief. I didn't expect to find a possible future."

"But you did," he said softly.

"But I did," she agreed. "I'm ready to imagine what my name would look like on an upstairs mailbox. I am ready to sketch floor plans for a studio instead of escape routes. That feels like a lot."

"It is a lot," he said. "And it is enough."

She leaned down and kissed him, slow and sure.

"Then maybe after you deal with contract offers and sponsor calls and whatever fallout comes from exposing the Red Dragons, we can take a walk down Bay Street," she said. "Look at this warehouse."

"You want the grand tour?" he asked.

"I want to see where you picture yourself when you are not on a bike," she said. "I want to see where I might hang a canvas without feeling like it could all disappear tomorrow."

His eyes softened.

"Then yeah," he said. "We'll do that. We'll look at bad insulation, cracked concrete, and potential. We'll argue about where the coffee pot goes."

"That is an important decision," she said.

"Maybe the most important," he replied. "And Bree. I love you. I want you to know that. I love you."

Her breath hitched, and a knot formed in her throat. Tears filled her eyes, her emotions scattered through her body. Smiling, she stared into his beautiful brown eyes. "I love you too, Hank. It scared me when I first realized it. But I love you too."

His lips met hers, softly, reverently, and sweet.

Outside, the roar of the crowd had faded to a low hum; the late afternoon light slanted through the gap in the curtains, painting a thin stripe across the floor. Somewhere down on the boardwalk, someone laughed, a sound carried on the same breeze that brought the smell of the sea.

Inside, Bree felt like something inside her had just been set carefully back on its feet after years of stumbling.

"You know what the weirdest part is?" she said.

"What?" he asked.

"I actually want to paint this," she said. "You. The race. The warehouse. All of it. Not because it is an assignment or a commission or a distraction. Because it is mine."

He tipped his head up to kiss her again, a quick, soft press.

"Then paint it," he said. "Paint the hell out of it. Copper Moon could use a few more stories on canvas."

She smiled, eyes stinging in the best way.

"I think we've got one," she said. "Maybe more than one."

"Good," Hank said, settling deeper into the pillows and pulling her close. "Because I am not done writing it with you."

For the first time since Bryn's death, Bree believed that might be true.

And that belief, fragile and fierce, felt like its own kind of victory.

H ank sat in a plastic chair that had seen better days, trying not to bounce his knee.

The conference room at race control, which was in the back of a garage near the water, smelled like burnt coffee, dry-erase marker, and the faint lingering tang of race fuel that seemed to seep into everything at Copper Moon. A wall-mounted TV looped slow-motion highlights of the Cup finish on mute; his own number flashed past every few seconds, which was surreal in this setting.

Across the table, Mac, the head tech inspector, flipped through a stack of forms. Beside him sat a woman from series operations with a tablet, a man in a sponsor golf shirt whose smile never quite reached his eyes, and Sergeant Diaz from Copper Moon PD.

On Hank's side of the table, Brian slouched with deceptive ease, arms folded, while Colby sat very straight, hands laced, gaze sharp.

"Let's pick this up," Mac said, tapping the top sheet. "We've documented the equipment found on Marcus

Stoke's primary bike and taken statements from his crew. I'd like to get yours on record now."

Hank nodded. "Sure."

Mac clicked his pen. "Walk us through when you first suspected the Red Dragons might be running something illegal."

Hank thought about Bree, sketchbook clutched to her chest, eyes wide and certain as she described Einstein's hands closing around a dull silver cylinder. His gut tightened.

"I've been around racing my whole life," he said. "You hear things. The Dragons have always pushed the gray areas. Aggressive mapping, borderline fuel mixes. This weekend, some of their speed did not line up with what I was feeling on my own bike or what I was seeing from other top guys. I talked with Brian and Colby, and we decided it was worth asking tech to give them a closer look."

Mac's gaze searched his face. "On what grounds?"

"Pattern of behavior," Hank said. "How they treated access to the bike. The way Einstein worked. It felt like they were guarding something. I couldn't ignore it and still sleep at night."

It wasn't the whole truth, but it wasn't a lie either. It was the version that protected the woman upstairs, who had already risked more than he liked.

Brian chimed in. "We didn't point fingers and walk away. Colby came to you, Mac. Respectfully. All we asked was that you run the book on them, like you ran it on us."

Mac's mouth twitched. "Appreciated. For the record, Copper Moon Performance's bike passed with flying colors."

The sponsor rep cleared his throat. "We're not here to

re-litigate the Stoke situation." His tone was smooth, but it still made Hank's hackles rise. "Our concern is the integrity of the series moving forward. We can't afford a narrative that this is a den of cheaters."

Diaz rested her forearms on the table, expression calm and unbothered. "You can't afford bikes exploding under riders either. Let's keep perspective."

The man's jaw worked, but he shut up.

Diaz turned her attention to Hank. "From what my officers heard in the paddock, there was a previous... altercation between you and Marcus. Any chance this was personal?"

Hank held her gaze. "Marcus tried to run me wide in practice and nearly put me into the wall. He plays dirty on the track. I don't like that. But I didn't ask tech to strip his bike because of a grudge. I did it because I saw enough off-notes to know the song was wrong. And what difference does it make if it's personal? They were trying to cheat. Doesn't make it okay because I don't like Marcus."

Mac grunted. "That hidden bottle wasn't a home game hack. Whoever plumbed it in knew exactly what they were doing. Clean install. Proper routing. Right materials. If I hadn't been looking for it, I might've missed it too."

Brian made a disgusted sound. "So you're saying there's a professional business in the 'make your bike into a rolling grenade' field."

"Wouldn't be the first time," Mac said. "Back when I worked Supercross, we had a guy doing illegal ECU flashes on three continents before we shut him down."

The operations woman swiped on her tablet. "Our preliminary assessment is that the nitrous system was fitted off-site by a specialist, not installed by Einstein alone. He doesn't have the background for that level of work."

Diaz nodded. "We picked him up on charges related to the illegal equipment, but he's already out on bail. His lawyer is claiming he was following marching orders and didn't know the full extent of the risk. Heidi Renner's calling this a smear campaign. Their sponsors are... concerned."

"Of course they are," Colby muttered. "Got caught with their hand in the cookie jar and now they're worried about the crumbs."

Hank's jaw set. "What happens now?"

Mac checked a page. "From the technical side, the Dragons' Cup results are void. They lose all points from this weekend. The bike stays impounded until we finish our analysis. Depending on what else we find, the penalty could extend to the rest of the season and likely a permanent ban from racing."

Diaz added, "From PD's side, we're digging into where that hardware came from. I can tell you this much, James. The machining on that bottle, the gauge integration, the switch routing. That's not something some backyard mechanic cooked up. Someone's supplying pro-grade illegal kits to whoever'll pay."

She let that hang in the air.

Hank felt the old familiar shift in his brain, like someone had flipped a switch from race mode to threat assessment. He'd seen that pattern before, in a different desert, with different hardware. Someone with expertise cuts corners for money; regular people pay the cost.

"Do you think they installed those kits for anyone else here?" he asked.

Mac and Diaz shared a look.

"It's on our radar," Diaz said. "Right now, we have no direct evidence of other bikes running that setup in this paddock. That doesn't mean it's not happening elsewhere."

The sponsor rep cleared his throat again. "We can't go on a witch hunt."

"No one's talking about that," Diaz replied calmly. "We're talking about following leads. Which, Mr. James, brings us back to you."

Hank raised his eyebrows. "To me."

Mac tapped the folder. "You've got credibility with other riders. You talk, they listen. If you hear anything about these kits, about people bragging, about a guy who knows a guy who can find speed for a price. You come to us. Quietly."

It wasn't a request. It was also not unfamiliar. Back in the Corps, he'd been the guy who kept an ear out for the rumor that saved lives.

He nodded once. "You have my word."

Diaz studied him for a moment, then relaxed a fraction. "Good. Because whoever's selling this junk isn't going to be thrilled that their work just got plastered all over the evening news."

Hank thought of the way the Dragons' pit had looked when the cylinder came out of the frame. Shock. Anger. Panic. Somewhere in that mix, he'd seen something that looked a lot like fear.

"I figured as much," he said. "We'll keep our eyes open."

Brian shifted beside him. "We'd appreciate a heads up if the Dragons' people decide to channel their rage in our direction too."

Diaz's mouth tipped up. "Already in motion. Patrol will be heavier around the paddock tonight and tomorrow. We're not letting this turn into a soap opera in the parking lot."

The operations woman looked up from her tablet. "That concludes what we need from you for now. Hank, congratulations again on the win. Please don't let this overshadow what you accomplished."

"I won't," he said. "But I'm glad we didn't look the other way."

As they filed out into the hall, Brian let out a low whistle. "Well. That was a party."

Colby shoved his hands in his pockets. "We poke the bear, now we get invited to the bear's performance review."

Hank's phone buzzed in his pocket. He pulled it out, and his chest eased a notch when he saw the name.

Bree: *How'd the meeting go?*

He smiled.

Hank: *Long. Boring. Good boring. Dragons are officially in trouble.*

Her reply came almost instantly.

Bree: *Good. I just had a text from Carmen. She wants to meet for coffee. She says she needs to talk, and she understands if I tell her to go to hell.*

Hank huffed a breath. "Carmen wants to talk to Bree," he told the guys. "Coffee in the lobby."

Brian arched a brow. "That should be interesting."

"You okay with that?" Colby asked.

He thought about the guilt that had pinched Bree's voice when she admitted how she'd broken the plan. About the loyalty in Carmen's eyes every time Heidi snapped her fingers.

"That's between them," Hank said. "But I'm not letting Bree navigate it completely alone."

He texted back.

Hank: *I've gotta grab something from the pit, then I'll hover somewhere nearby. If you want an extraction, text me the word 'dragonslayer.'*

Bree: *You're ridiculous.*

Bree: *Thank you.*

He slipped the phone away, feeling a warmth settle under his sternum that had nothing to do with the afternoon sun.

"Where are we headed after a beer or two?" Brian asked as they walked toward the stairs.

Hank glanced at his watch. Plenty of daylight left. Enough time to do something that didn't involve legal threats or debrief forms.

"Bay Street," he said. "I promised Bree a field trip."

Colby's eyes lit. "We're going to look at the warehouse."

"Yeah," Hank said. "Time to see if this dream has actual dimensions."

Brian clapped him on the shoulder. "About damn time."

From his spot at the far end of the lobby café, Hank watched Bree approach Carmen's table.

They met halfway between the coffee line and the seating area. Carmen stood when she saw Bree, tension visible even from here; shoulders high; hands wrapped around a paper cup like it might bolt. Bree's chin lifted a fraction, her steps steady.

Good girl, he thought. Walk straight in.

They hugged, awkward at first; then Carmen held on a beat longer. Hank couldn't hear the words over the low murmur of other conversations and the hiss of the espresso machine, but he could read the body language well enough.

Carmen talked fast, hands moving. Apology. Explanation. Some version of I didn't know.

Bree listened, arms folded loosely across her chest; guarded but not closed. When she spoke, Carmen's shoulders sagged with what looked like relief. A minute later, Bree laid a hand over Carmen's and smiled, small and real.

He let himself exhale.

"Looks like that went okay," Brian said, sliding a bottle of beer onto Hank's table and dropping into the opposite chair. "Nobody threw a scone."

"Low bar," Hank said. "I'll take it."

Colby set a bowl of popcorn between them. "Carmen is giving up the red and black."

Hank watched as Carmen scrubbed her hands over her face and laughed at something Bree said. "She'll never give up, Heidi," he said. "They're family. But I think she stopped pretending the Dragons are misunderstood underdogs."

"Good," Brian muttered. "I've got enough to worry about without wondering which side the PR team is on."

A few minutes later, Bree and Carmen stood. Carmen hugged her again, more solid this time, then headed toward the elevators. Bree scanned the room, found Hank, and walked over.

"You survived," he said, standing to meet her.

She rolled her eyes. "Barely. She bought me a latte and apologized so many times the barista started looking nervous."

"Did she know about the nitrous?" Brian asked.

"No," Bree said firmly. "Carmen's a lot of things, but she's not okay with cheating. She's furious. At Marcus. At Einstein. At Heidi for trying to spin this as an overzealous tech crew instead of what it was. She wanted me to know she'd never have pulled me down there if she'd had any idea what they were up to."

Hank nodded, filing that away. "And how do you feel about that?"

Bree considered. She said, "Less angry. She's planning

on taking a break from the Dragons after this season. She says she needs to remember who she is when she's not helping Heidi be Heidi."

Colby whistled. "That's an identity crisis waiting to happen."

"Yeah," Bree said softly. "But it's hers. I told her I'd still answer her texts. That's all I can promise right now."

"That's enough," Hank said.

She tipped her head, studying him. "How did your meeting go?"

"We can recap on the walk," he said. "You up for a short field trip?"

Her eyes lit with cautious excitement. "Bay Street."

"Bay Street," he confirmed. "The mayor left a key at the desk."

Brian grabbed his beer and stood. "Let's go look at our future, then."

The warehouse sat two blocks off the water on Bay Street, a hulking rectangle of brick and corrugated metal that had clearly been built when people cared more about function than charm.

Hank loved it at first sight.

"Okay," Bree said, staring up at the faded letters barely visible on the front. "It looks like every serial killer movie I've ever seen."

Brian chuckled. "That's just the lighting. And the peeling paint. And the fact that there's exactly one sad little plant trying to survive by the door."

"That plant is a metaphor," Bree said.

"For what?" Colby asked, fishing the keyring out of his pocket.

"For potential," she said. "And stubbornness."

Hank's chest did something warm. "I'm going to steal that for the sales pitch."

Colby got the lock to turn with a grating protest, then shouldered the heavy door open. The smell of dust and old oil rolled out, along with a faint chill.

Inside, the main floor stretched back farther than Bree had expected. High ceilings with exposed beams, overhead lights that probably hadn't worked in years, a concrete floor scorched with old tire marks. A large roll-up door took up most of the back wall, currently shut, rust streaked down from its hinges.

Sunlight slanted through grimy windows high along the side walls, catching dust motes in the air.

"Oh," Bree breathed.

Hank heard it, that little hitch between surprise and inspiration. He watched her step inside, slow and careful, as if she half expected the floor to give way. When it held, she moved farther in, turning in a slow circle.

Brian whistled low. "We can fit at least four bays along this wall," he said, pacing out imaginary lift positions. "Plenty of clearance. You could put the dyno in the back corner. That roll-up door opens right onto the alley. Perfect for loading."

Colby wandered toward a metal staircase that hugged one wall. "Upstairs office or storage," he called. "Maybe both. We'd need to redo the wiring. This panel looks older than I am."

Beneath their chatter, Hank could hear the quiet start of Bree's attention locking on. She drifted toward the stairs, fingers trailing along the railing, eyes tracking the way light fell from windows near the ceiling.

"What do you think?" he asked, coming up behind her.

"It's ugly," she said. "And dirty. And it smells like

someone stored a year's worth of bad decisions in here and forgot to take them out."

"Tell me how you really feel," he said.

She huffed, then smiled. "And it has bones. Good ones. Those beams." She pointed up. "You could hang track banners between them. Or canvases. The light's terrible right now, but if we clean those windows and add some north-facing ones upstairs..."

"Careful," Hank said. "You sound like you're about to start nesting."

She looked up the stairs. "Can we go up?"

"After you," he said.

The steps creaked under their weight but held. At the top, the space opened into a long, narrow room that ran the length of the building. Dust lay thick on the floor; old file cabinets sagged against one wall. A cracked window at the far end offered a sliver of Bay Street and, beyond it, a glimpse of water.

Bree walked toward that window like it was a magnet.

When she reached it, she wiped a sleeve over the glass, clearing enough grime to see the curve of the shoreline and the line of the boardwalk.

"This could be my studio," she said quietly. "I could put easels here to catch the morning light. Shelves along that wall. A couch over there. People could sit for portraits and listen to the sea."

Hank came up beside her. "You wouldn't hate having the smell of oil drifting up through the floor."

"I grew up with a dad who rebuilt engines in our garage," she said. "I find it comforting."

He slid his hand into hers. "That's a good sign."

Brian appeared in the doorway, dust on his boots. "Found a leak in the roof near the back corner," he reported.

"And some questionable wiring choices. We're going to need a real electrician and probably a new panel."

Colby nodded. "And the city's going to want to talk zoning. Mixed-use means building codes. Fire escapes. ADA access. The fun stuff."

Bree looked from one to the other. "Can we even afford this?"

Hank squeezed her hand gently. "We're not signing anything today. But between prize money, some savings, and the mayor's enthusiasm for having a Cup winner with a storefront, we've got leverage. There are grants available to revitalize this kind of space. We can talk to someone who knows more about paperwork than carburetors."

"Gabe will know," Brian said. "He and Lena jumped through a bunch of hoops for The Breakwater. He's got opinions."

"Of course he does," Colby said. "He's Gabe."

Bree laughed, the sound bouncing off the bare walls. "Okay. So we call in experts. We make lists. We take our time."

She turned back to the window, looking out at the hint of water.

"I could paint Copper Moon from here," she said. "Not just the pretty parts the tourists see. The alleys. The race prep. The back doors of the boardwalk bars where the staff sneak out for air."

Hank watched her profile, the way her eyes had gone bright. His chest felt too small for the feeling that rose there.

"This is the first place I've been in a long time that feels like more than a stopover," he said. "I like the idea of putting your name on the door upstairs and mine on the one downstairs."

She looked at him, all the usual doubts and caveats in her gaze, but layered now with something sturdier.

"Then let's keep walking toward it," she said. "One permit, one paint swatch, one busted light fixture at a time."

He grinned. "Deal."

As they headed back down the stairs, he caught movement through the grimy front windows. A dark sedan eased past, too nice for this section of town. The driver didn't slow down, but the passenger glanced toward the warehouse.

Suit. Sunglasses. Expression careful and blank.

Hank tracked it out of instinct. The car continued down the block and turned toward the civic center, where the Dragons' disciplinary hearings were being held.

"Friend of yours," Brian asked quietly, following his gaze.

"Doubt it," Hank said. "Probably a lawyer late for yelling practice."

Colby snorted.

On the sidewalk outside, Sergeant Diaz waited, hands tucked into her jacket pockets. She looked strangely at home against the rough brick.

"Officer," Hank greeted. "You slumming it?"

She raised a brow. "Says the guy shopping for fixer-uppers in the industrial district."

Bree joined them, brushing dust off her jeans. Diaz's gaze sharpened for a moment, as if noting her and filing the information away. Then her posture eased again.

"You kids having fun?" she asked.

"We're making spreadsheets in our heads," Bree said. "That's my idea of a wild afternoon."

Diaz's mouth quirked. "You picked an interesting time to consider putting down roots."

Hank sobered. "What's the latest?"

"We processed Einstein and his statement," she said. "He claims a contact approached the team months ago with 'performance solutions.' Says the guy's name is Vic, no last name, no business card. Meetups in parking lots, cash transactions. You know the type."

Brian's tone flattened. "Real reputable fellow."

"He described the kit, though," Diaz continued. "Materials, install time, price point. It matches rumors I've heard out of other regional series. Same style bottle. Same horn trigger. We're looking at a supplier who's been doing this a while."

"Any idea where he's based?" Hank asked.

"We've got a few leads," Diaz said. "Nothing I can share yet. Just know this. You didn't just catch one dirty team. You stepped into the middle of somebody's income stream. That puts you, and anyone close to you, on their radar."

A cool thread slid down Hank's spine. He glanced at Bree; she stood very still, jaw tight, but her eyes were steady.

"We can handle attention," Hank said. "We have before."

"I figured," Diaz said. "Still. Watch your backs. You see that sedan again, or anybody asking weird questions about tech, you call me. Direct."

She handed him a card. He slid it into his pocket.

"You have a lot of those out there?" he asked.

"More than I like," she said. "It's a small town. I intend to keep it that way instead of letting it become a cautionary tale."

She tipped two fingers in a casual salute, then moved off toward her cruiser.

Bree watched her go. "She's scary," she said. "In a reassuring way."

"That's the best kind," Hank said. "Keeps people honest."

He slid an arm around her shoulders and felt her lean into him, light and warm.

"You still in?" he asked quietly. "Knowing that whoever ran this little black-market speed shop isn't thrilled with us."

"Do they know my name?" she asked.

"Not from me," he said.

"Then I'm in," she said. "Besides, Einsteins of the world don't get to scare me back into a life that's already too small."

That made something fierce and protective rise in him again, but there was pride there, too.

"All right, then," he said. "Let's go eat with people who are happy we're here instead of plotting revenge."

The Breakwater Bar was packed, which was exactly what he'd expected on Cup night.

String lights crisscrossed the ceiling, casting the whole place in a warm, golden glow. The staff rolled up the big garage doors at the front to let in ocean air. Surfboards and old race photos lined the walls; trophies perched on high shelves beside jars of seashells.

Gabe Ortiz manned the bar, big shoulders filling out a faded band T-shirt, dark hair pulled back. He'd swapped a mechanic's creeper for a bar mat a few years back and never quite lost the grease-under-the-nails vibe.

He looked up when Hank, Bree, Brian, and Colby stepped in and grinned.

"Copper Moon's new favorite son," he called. "Get your ass over here, James."

Lena Ortiz appeared at his elbow, curls piled on top of her head, a bar towel thrown over one shoulder. "And bring that pretty painter with you," she added, eyes dancing.

Bree laughed, the tension of the day easing off her shoulders as they wove through the crowd.

"Congratulations," Gabe said when they reached the bar, sticking his hand across to Hank. "Hell of a race."

"Thanks," Hank said, shaking it. "Place looks good."

"Winning does that," Lena said, leaning over to kiss Bree's cheek. "How are you, honey?"

"Tired," Bree said truthfully. "Happy. Mildly terrified about the idea of wiring a warehouse."

Gabe's eyebrows rose. "So the mayor got to you."

"The mayor and this one," Bree said, hooking her thumb at Hank.

Gabe wiped his hands. "We should talk. When we took over this place, the permits nearly killed me. I've got advice and a list of people you should absolutely not hire unless you enjoy watching a man fall off a ladder."

"Noted," Hank said.

They grabbed a corner table that looked out toward the water, drinks in hand. The band slid into a softer set; couples drifted onto the small dance floor. The whole town felt like it was exhaling together after holding its breath for days.

Carmen arrived a little later, sliding into a spare chair with a sigh. She'd changed out of team gear into jeans and a simple top. Without the Dragons' colors, she looked ten pounds lighter.

"You guys good if I crash this?" she asked.

"Only if you don't bring any dragons," Brian said.

"Left my fire-breathing accessories at home," Carmen said dryly. She glanced at Bree; they shared a small, private smile. "Thank you again. For earlier."

"You're welcome," Bree said.

They ordered food: fish tacos, burgers, a mountain of fries that disappeared faster than any of them admitted. Conversation flowed easily: racing stories, town gossip, Gabe's anecdote about the time some guys at a bachelor party tried to body-surf down the boardwalk stairs.

Every so often, someone would clap Hank on the back in passing or raise a glass from another table. He took it in with a mix of pride and discomfort. He was used to being noticed on a track, not in a room.

Bree seemed to sense it. Under the table, her hand found his thigh, thumb rubbing small circles that pulled him back into his body.

"You doing all right?" she asked quietly between bites.

"This is a lot," he admitted. "But a good lot."

She smiled. "Good. Because I like seeing people happy you exist."

Later, when the plates had been cleared and the band shifted into something slow, Gabe nodded toward the floor.

"You two better dance," he said. "Otherwise, the locals will think you're fighting."

Bree's eyes widened. "Is that a rule?"

"It is now," Gabe said.

Hank stood and held out his hand. "May I?"

She rolled her eyes fondly. "You already kissed me against a wall. I think we've skipped past 'May I'."

"Humor me," he said.

She slipped her hand into his. "You may."

He led her onto the small dance floor. The song was something with a lazy beat and lyrics about second chances. He set one hand at the small of her back and took her other hand in his, moving them into the gentle sway.

She fit against him like she had in the bed and in the hallway, like her body already knew the map of his.

"Careful," she murmured, cheek resting against his chest. "This is dangerously close to contentment."

He smiled into her hair. "You say that like it's a bad thing."

"I'm still getting used to it," she said.

He didn't rush her. They just moved, letting the music and the murmur of Copper Moon wrap around them.

From the corner of his eye, he caught Carmen at the bar talking with Lena, hands moving as she described something, probably the blowback from the Dragons' hearing. He had a feeling that story was far from over. Somewhere out there, a man named Vic was watching his market contract and taking notes.

But here, in this moment, his world had narrowed to the woman in his arms and the way she relaxed a little more with each turn.

When the song ended, he pressed a kiss to her temple. "Walk back with me."

She nodded.

Outside, the night air was cooler, carrying the salt tang of the sea and the last faint sounds of the day's festivities. The boardwalk had thinned; most families had taken kids home to bed. A few couples lingered on benches. A street musician picked out a tune on a guitar near the fountain.

Hank and Bree walked side by side, hands clasped. Their steps fell into sync without trying.

"So," he said. "A warehouse?"

She chuckled. "Yeah."

He said. "We still have to look at the warehouse in

daylight. Talk to the mayor. Find a decent electrician. Convince my family I haven't lost my mind."

"Meet my parents," she added quietly. "Tell them I'm not running from my grief anymore, I'm carrying it somewhere new."

He squeezed her hand. "When you're ready, I'll be there."

She stopped walking and looked up at him, eyes reflecting boardwalk lights.

"You know you just promised to meet my entire complicated life, right?" she said. "Not just the painter who likes your bike."

"I've seen enough pieces to know I want the whole picture," he said. "Bryn and all."

Her throat worked. "You say her name like it doesn't scare you."

"It doesn't," he said. "Seems like disrespect not to."

She stepped closer, free hand coming up to rest on his chest. "You're not an easy man, Hank James," she said. "You're stubborn and bossy, and you make terrible puns when you're tired."

"I feel like there should be a compliment coming," he said.

"There is," she said. "You make me feel like the future's not a cliff I'm going to fall off. It feels like a road I can walk, even if I'm not sure where all the turns are yet."

He cupped her face, thumb tracing her cheek. "Good," he said softly. "Because I'm planning on being on that road with you. Warehouse. Studio. Whatever comes after."

She smiled, slow and genuine. "Then I guess we should start packing."

"For the warehouse or for your old place," he asked.

"Both," she said. "Eventually. Not tomorrow. But soon."

He kissed her under the glow of the Copper Moon Cup banner that still fluttered over the boardwalk, the taste of salt and possibility on her lips.

When they finally headed back to the hotel, fingers intertwined, Copper Moon felt less like a stop on his racing calendar and more like the place his life could actually unfold.

The race win had been one line of the story.

This, walking into the future with Bree at his side and trouble brewing quietly at the edges of town, felt like the beginning of everything else.

FIFTEEN

Bree woke to the sound of waves and the feel of steady heat at her back.

For a few seconds, she lay still with her eyes closed, breathing in the mix of hotel soap and motor oil that clung to Hank. The curtains were cracked just enough to let in a sliver of pale light. The Copper Moon Cup banner out on the boardwalk snapped faintly in the breeze; she could hear it if she listened.

His arm lay heavy across her waist, hand splayed low over her stomach. Every time his chest rose, it nudged her a little closer to believing last night had not been some elaborate dream.

The dance. The warehouse. The way he had said our future like it belonged to both of them.

Her phone buzzed on the nightstand.

She winced and reached blindly for it, trying not to jostle him. The screen lit her face in a soft glow.

One new text from Mom. A second from Dad beneath it; shorter, more practical.

Mom: *How are you doing this morning, sweetheart? Call when you can. xx*

Dad: *Weather's decent. We're going to the cemetery this afternoon.*

The words sent a familiar ache through her chest. Cemetery. Bryn. The life that had ended so painfully short.

Hank's voice came low and sleepy behind her. "You okay?"

She jumped a little, then relaxed back into him. "Sorry. I didn't mean to wake you."

"Your breathing changed," he said, sliding his palm in a slow arc over her stomach. "You tense when something hurts."

She swallowed. Of course, he would catalog that. "Text from my parents."

"Bad news?"

"No." She stared at the screen again. "Just normal news that still stings."

He propped himself up on one elbow, looking down at her. His hair stuck up on one side, flattened on the other; the sight made something soft pull in her. Hank James, Copper Moon Cup champion, race helmet traded for bedhead.

"You want to call them now?" he asked. "I can take a walk, find coffee."

She turned onto her back so she could see him properly. "No. Not yet. I need to figure out how to say 'hey, remember how you thought this was a short trip, surprise, I might have accidentally found a life.'"

His mouth curved. "You make it sound like you tripped over it in the hallway."

"Feels a little like that." She brushed her thumb over the

tattoo on his shoulder, tracing the edges of the ink. "How are you doing?"

"Physically?" He did a quick mental inventory; she could see it on his face. "Sore in the usual ways. Brain's still doing after-action reports."

"About the race, or the nitrous situation?"

"Both." His gaze searched hers. "And about a warehouse, I may have already mentally filled with lifts and toolboxes."

She smiled, nervous and excited all at once. "You really meant it. That you want to do this."

"Bree." His tone sharpened gently. "I don't say stuff like that to hear myself talk. We walked into that place yesterday, and for the first time in a long time, my head didn't immediately go to exit routes. It went to possibilities. That feels important. Brian, Colby, and I have talked about doing this for a long time. I started it, planted the seeds, but the more we joked, talked, and planned, the more real it became. The issue was...where? Back home, there wasn't anything like this warehouse that we could afford. The fact that this came up, here and now, along with the mayor offering concessions through tax credits and support, makes me believe it has to be here."

She heard the unspoken part; the Marine who had spent years in places where a building meant cover or a target or both. The fact that he could stand in that ugly old warehouse and think about lifts instead of ambushes said more than any speech.

"Okay," she said quietly. "So let's talk about what possibilities cost."

He huffed a soft laugh. "Spoken like a woman who has actually looked at her bank account in the last six months."

"I'm a working artist," she said. "I check my balance more than I check my email."

He rolled onto his back and hooked one arm under his head. "All right. Practicalities. We've got prize money from the Cup. After taxes, team percentage, and the usual slices, I still come out ahead enough to make a solid down payment on renovations. I've got savings from the last few seasons. I'm not rich, but I'm not living on instant noodles."

"Instant noodles are underrated," she said, then sobered. "I've got some savings. Most of my paintings go to people who pay me in actual money, not exposure. I sold that series in Milwaukee. The one with the industrial waterfront."

He nodded. "The one you hate talking about."

"I don't hate talking about it." She did, a little. It had been the last thing she'd completed before Bryn died. "It just feels like part of a different life."

He waited. He was getting good at that. At letting silence stretch until she filled it with something real.

"There's also..." She stared at her phone again, thumb resting on the screen without unlocking it. "There's the insurance money."

His brows drew together, but he didn't speak.

"When Bryn died," she said, words awkward and thick, "she had a small life insurance policy through work. Not huge. Enough to help with funeral costs and a cushion. She hadn't changed my parents' names as the beneficiary when she and Charlie married. My parents refused to touch it. They insisted it go to me. 'For your future,' my mom said. I offered it to Charlie for the kids, but he said Bryn would love that I have it, and he was fine, financially. The money wouldn't bring her back. I put it in an account and haven't touched a cent."

"Because?" he asked gently.

"Because spending it felt like… stealing from her." She blinked hard. "Like I'd be cashing in on the worst thing that ever happened to us."

He reached for her hand and laced their fingers. "Money doesn't know where it came from," he said. "You do. And you get to decide whether it just sits there like a rock in your pocket, or whether you use it for something that would've made her smile."

Bree swallowed again. "She would've liked the studio idea."

"Then maybe," he said, squeezing her hand, "using some of it to build a studio with her name on the door is not stealing. Maybe it's the exact opposite."

She let that sink in; the idea of a space where Bryn existed in more than framed photos. A place where Bree could paint, and maybe hang one canvas that never went to a gallery; one that stayed because it belonged there.

"I could paint a series about her," she said slowly. "Not just portraits. Pieces of her. Her boots by the door. The coffee mug she stole from that diner we loved. The way she left paint on everything she touched."

"I'd stand in line to buy that," Hank said quietly.

"You're biased."

"Sure," he said. "But I also know what good art feels like. The warehouse upstairs with your work, people climbing those stairs to see pieces of your heart on the walls? That's worth betting on."

She exhaled. "Okay. So, finances. If we pool what you've got, what I've got, and whatever the mayor can conjure up in grants, we could probably manage a modest renovation and a few months of breathing room."

"Throw in some sweat equity," he said, "and favors

from friends like Gabe, and we're in better shape than most."

"Your family," she said quietly. "How are they going to feel about you planting yourself in Copper Moon instead of, I don't know, buying a house back home and racing out of there?"

He smiled. "My mom's initial reaction will be to ask what the healthcare options are in town and whether there's a decent grocery store that sells real vegetables. My brother will want to know if there's space for a lift with his name on it. My sister will remind me she called it, because she always knew I wasn't done with small towns."

"And your dad?" she asked.

His gaze flicked away for a second, just long enough for her to see the shadow. "He'll be fine. He likes a project. He'll probably send unsolicited advice about shop organization just to feel useful."

"You say that like it's a bad thing."

"I say it like I know I'm going to be rearranging wrenches at midnight to avoid arguments." He looked back at her. "What about your parents?"

Bree's stomach did a slow flip. "That's the part I'm still working out. They've already lost one daughter. The idea of the other one living eight hours away instead of two... that's not going to be their favorite news."

"You're not exactly close by now," he pointed out. "And Copper Moon's an actual town with actual people who care whether you make it home at night. That counts for something."

"I know." She chewed the inside of her cheek. "But it's not just distance. It's... permanence. I came here to breathe for a week. Not build a life. In their heads, I'm still going home when the race weekend is over."

"Then maybe," he said, tone gentle but firm, "it's time to tell them that home shifted a little."

She made a face at him. "You make it sound simple."

"It's not," he said. "But you're good with hard things. You stayed when everyone else left the paddock yesterday. You saw something wrong, and you spoke up. You can have a tough conversation."

She looked at his mouth; at the small line that formed when he was absolutely certain of something. Then she looked back at her phone.

"Will you be here when I call?" she asked.

"Do you want me here?"

"Yes," she said. "But maybe not in the room for the whole thing. I don't want them to feel like I'm performing for you."

"I can grab coffee," he said. "Loiter in the hallway like a proper anxious boyfriend."

The word pinged around the room.

Boyfriend.

Her heart did a small, startled dance. "Is that what you are?"

He met her gaze. "Unless you'd like to renegotiate my contract."

She laughed, the sound wobbling. "No. That title's fine."

"Good." He kissed her forehead, then her mouth, slow and reassuring. "I'll shower first, then I'll get out of your hair. We're supposed to meet with the mayor at eleven anyway."

"Right." She pushed herself up on her elbows. "Preliminary lease talk. Contractors. Adult stuff."

"You say that like we didn't already talk in bed about wiring a warehouse," he said.

Her cheeks warmed. "That was different adult stuff."

He grinned. "Both important."

He slid out of bed and headed to the bathroom, pausing in the doorway to look back at her. "Call them, Bree. You don't have to have every answer. Just tell them the truth."

She nodded, fingers tight around her phone. "Yeah. Okay."

The shower started; water hit the tile in a steady rush.

Bree opened her mom's text and hit the call icon.

Her parents picked up on the second ring. That alone told her they had been waiting.

"Hi, honey," her mom said. "How are you feeling? We watched the race on TV. Your dad kept yelling at the announcer."

Her dad's voice came faintly in the background. "He kept calling the corners by the wrong names."

Bree smiled despite the nerves. "Hi, Mom. Hi, Dad. I'm okay. Hank's okay. It was a big day."

"So we saw," her dad said, taking the phone from her mom by the sound of it. "That pass on the last lap. Damn, Bree. That was something."

"I didn't do anything except clutch my sketchbook and forget how to breathe," she said. "Hank did the hard part."

"You were there," he said. "Counts for something."

Her mom reclaimed the phone. "We heard there was some kind of cheating scandal," she whispered. "Are you safe? Are you staying away from those people?"

"Yes," Bree said quickly. "I'm safe. Copper Moon PD is on top of it. Sergeant Diaz could probably take down an entire biker gang with a look."

Her mom made a doubtful sound. "I don't like that you needed to find out."

"None of us liked it," Bree said. "But Hank did the right

thing. He spoke up. They found the illegal equipment. Nobody got hurt."

Not physically, anyway. She could still see the panic in Einstein's face.

Her mom sighed. "All right. So long as you're being careful."

"I am."

A beat of silence settled. Bree could hear the hum of the fridge at her parents' house, the distant tick of the hallway clock that had been there since she was six.

"So," her mom said. "When are you heading back?"

There it was.

Bree swallowed. "That's kind of what I wanted to talk about."

"Okay," her dad said. His tone shifted; sturdy, prepared. "What's up?"

She walked to the window and pushed the curtain aside. The boardwalk stretched below; the Cup banner still fluttered. Down near the fountain, a kid chased a bubble that had drifted free from a street vendor's wand.

"I think I want to stay," she said. "In Copper Moon. For a while. Longer than we talked about."

Silence.

Her mom recovered first. "Stay how long?"

"I don't have an exact date," Bree said. "But Hank's looking at opening a performance shop here. And there's space above it that would make a perfect studio. I stood in it yesterday, and for the first time since Bryn died, I could actually picture myself working somewhere that wasn't temporary."

Her dad cleared his throat. "This is about the racer?"

"It's about the town," she said quietly. "And the racer. And me. I came here to hide and figure out if I could still paint. Instead, I found a place that feels like I can grow something. With him, yes. But also for myself. We're together. Seeing if it works."

Her mom's voice was soft and worried. "You're not coming home."

"I'm not saying never," Bree said. "You two are still my home. But I think... I think I need a home that doesn't feel like a memorial service all the time. Every corner of the house has a ghost. Every street reminds me of driving behind the hearse. I've been living there like I'm waiting for someone to hand me a script for how to move on, and it turns out the pages might be in a different town."

She waited, heart pounding.

Her dad exhaled slowly. "You know we only kept it that way because we thought it helped you," he said. "We were afraid changing anything would erase her."

"I know," Bree said. "And I love you for that. But she's not in the throw blanket on the couch or in the shoes by the door. She's in us. And she's in what we do with the fact that we're still here."

Her mom made a small, strangled sound.

"Mom?" Bree asked.

"I'm all right," her mom said after a second. "Your father is patting my shoulder like I'm about to collapse, and I'm not. I'm just... hearing you."

"I'm not running away from Bryn," Bree said. "I'm trying to carry her somewhere new. I want to use some of the insurance money for the studio. For a series about her. I want people who never knew her to see pieces of her in my work."

Her dad cleared his throat again, rougher this time. "She'd like that," he said. "She hated that you hadn't painted her yet."

Bree laughed through the tightness in her throat. "She kept saying she wanted to sit for me when she 'felt less like a raccoon.' Her words."

"She always stayed up too late," her mom said, voice thick. "You really think you can be happy there?"

"I think I can try," Bree said. "And if it turns out I was wrong, I'll figure it out. But right now, when I picture the future, it's not a cliff anymore. It's a road. And Hank's on it. And so are you, just... at a different mile marker."

More silence. Not empty this time; full of things they were both turning over.

"Will we get to meet this Hank properly?" her mom asked at last.

"If you want to," Bree said. "He'd like that."

"Good," her dad said. "If he's keeping our girl in one piece, I want to shake his hand."

Bree's eyes burned. "He's trying. So am I."

"We know," her mom said. "We just worry. It's our hobby."

Bree smiled, breath catching. "I'll come back for a visit soon. Maybe after we know more about the lease and the timing. We're meeting with the mayor this morning to go over details. I can show you pictures of the warehouse."

"Send some today," her dad said. "I want to see this place where my daughter suddenly discovered gravity."

"That's not how gravity works," Bree said reflexively.

"Art people," he muttered to her mom. "Always nitpicking the metaphors."

Her mom laughed, shaky but real. "We love you, Bree."

"I love you too," Bree said. "Tell Bryn hi for me at the cemetery. I know that's not how it works, but... just do it."

"We always do," her mom said. "Call after your meeting with the mayor, okay? We want to hear."

"I will. And I'd love for you to come here and see the place. Do you remember all the things Bryn used to say about Copper Moon?" She swallowed the knot in her throat. "She was right. It's all she said and more."

Her father's voice was gruff when he responded. "That's a good idea. That's probably why you feel you need to be there..." He took a deep breath. "She loved it so much, you can feel her there."

"I absolutely can. At every turn, I remember something she said about the area. I see and feel her everywhere here."

Her mom sobbed quietly, but she could still hear her. Her dad scoffed, "That's good. Yeah, good."

They disconnected. Bree stood there for a moment, phone pressed to her chest, letting the relief and the ache wrestle it out.

The bathroom door opened; Hank stepped out with a towel around his hips, hair damp, another towel slung over his shoulder. She appreciated, briefly and thoroughly, the way his muscles moved under his skin when he scrubbed at his hair.

"How'd it go?" he asked.

She sat on the edge of the bed. "They didn't have a heart attack, so that's a win. They're worried, but they're listening. My dad wants pictures. My mom wants to meet you."

He smiled. "I like them already."

"He also wants to make sure you're not a flighty jerk."

"Reasonable concern."

"He didn't use those exact words, but it was implied."

Hank crossed the room and tipped her chin up with one finger. "You okay?" he asked.

She nodded. "Scared. Relieved. Some weird combination of both."

"That's usually where the good changes start," he said. "You were brave. I'm proud of you."

The word proud slid under her ribs and settled there. "Don't you dare make me cry. I have a meeting with the mayor, and I don't want to go in with puffy eyes."

He brushed his thumb under one eye anyway. "I like your eyes," he said. "Puffy or not."

She rolled hers. "You're impossible."

"Accurate." He paused. "We've got about forty minutes before we need to head out. You want breakfast, or you want me to distract your brain for a while?"

Her gaze dropped briefly to the strip of skin between his towel and his hip.

"Why not both?" she said.

His laugh was low and pleased. "Yes, ma'am."

An hour later, showered, dressed, and only slightly late, they walked hand in hand toward the civic building where the mayor's office lived. Hank carried a folder with notes he'd scribbled on hotel stationery; Bree carried her sketchbook because she felt naked without it.

The morning sun had burned through most of the haze, leaving Copper Moon sharp and bright. Workers swept up confetti and paper cups from the previous night's celebrations. The Cup banner hung a little crooked now; someone would fix it later.

"Okay," Bree said as they climbed the steps. "Game plan."

"Listen more than we talk," Hank said. "Ask about terms, timeline, and what improvements the city will cover for code compliance. We keep options open. We sign nothing without reading every page twice."

"Look at you," she said. "Responsible adult."

"Don't spread it around," he said. "I've got a reputation to maintain."

Inside, the building smelled of old paper and lemon cleaner. The receptionist greeted them by name and pointed them toward a conference room.

Mayor Rochelle Meyers stood at the window when they walked in, looking out over the harbor. She was small and wiry, with silver-streaked hair pulled into a low knot and a blazer that had seen a few campaign cycles. Beside her stood a broad-shouldered man in his forties with a rolled-up set of blueprints under one arm and a pencil tucked behind his ear.

"Hank, Bree," the mayor said, turning with a smile. "Thank you for coming. And congratulations again on the win. Copper Moon's very proud of you."

"Thank you, Mayor Meyers," Hank said, shaking her hand. "You remember Bree."

"Of course." The mayor shook Bree's hand warmly.

"So." The mayor gestured to the man beside her. "This is Jason Keene. He's one of our preferred contractors on city projects. He oversaw the renovation of The Breakwater and the boardwalk restrooms. He has opinions about wiring and roofing."

Jason nodded. "I like buildings that don't fall down when it rains."

"High bar," Hank said. "Appreciated."

They all took seats around the table. A slim folder lay in front of Hank and Bree; the mayor tapped it with one finger.

"This is a preliminary sale proposal," she said. "It's not binding. Think of it as a starting point. The city owns the Bay Street warehouse outright. It's been a storage headache for years. We'd like to turn that into a revenue stream and a revitalized block. Having a Cup champion's performance shop and a local artist's studio in that space fits nicely with what we're trying to do."

Hank flipped open the folder. The first page outlined the purchase price, far lower than he'd expected, especially for a building that size.

"That number real?" he asked.

"Yes," the mayor said. "It's an introductory rate; in exchange, you commit to specific improvements that bring the building up to code and create street-facing activity. After two years, the taxes step up to a level closer to the market average, with caps on annual increases. We're not looking to gouge you. We're looking to keep you."

"What improvements would be on us?" Bree asked.

"Interior build-out," Jason said. "Electrical upgrades. Plumbing for whatever bathroom and utility setup you need. Cosmetic stuff like paint. The city will handle structural work, roof repairs, and exterior masonry. We've already budgeted for window replacements as part of a safety initiative in that district."

Hank tracked the numbers in his head; what he had, what he could reasonably expect from next season, what he could not count on from sponsors.

"It's doable," he said slowly. "If nothing catastrophic happens."

"Catastrophic like nitrous kits blowing up our reputation," the mayor said dryly.

Bree stiffened. "About that..."

The mayor lifted a hand. "You did us a favor," she said. "You and your crew. I don't like the press using the words 'cheating scandal' and 'Copper Moon' in the same sentence, but I'll take one ugly news cycle over a fatality. Sergeant Diaz concurs."

"Speaking of Diaz," Jason said, "she mentioned you

might be interested in security measures. Cameras, reinforced doors. That kind of thing."

Hank nodded. "She told us we might've stepped on somebody's business plan. I'd like to make sure my shop isn't an easy target."

Bree felt tension slide under her skin. "I don't want to live in a fortress," she said before she could swallow it.

Three pairs of eyes swung to her.

"I mean," she said, forcing herself to stay steady, "I spent the last year feeling like my life was made of caution tape. If we turn the studio into a bunker, I'm going to feel like I never left."

"I'm not talking about sandbags and razor wire," Hank said, tone calm. "I'm talking about smart locks, camera coverage on entry points, solid glass instead of the 'a stiff breeze could punch through it' that's in there now."

"The glass upstairs is the only reason the light's decent," she said. "If we start slapping bars over it, I might as well paint in a closet."

Jason leaned forward. "There are options between closet and fortress," he said. "Tempered glass with security film. Roll-down shutters you only deploy at night. Discreet cameras. From the street, it looks like any other cool mixed-use space. From a would-be thief's perspective, it's more trouble than it's worth."

Bree considered that. "You're sure it doesn't have to look like a prison?"

"Promise," Jason said. "My wife would divorce me if I started turning half the town into bunkers. She runs the bookstore; she has opinions."

The mayor smiled. "She also sits on the arts council, which would be thrilled to have a working studio downtown."

Hank looked at Bree. "I'm not trying to cage you," he said quietly. "I just don't like leaving doors open for people who mean us harm. That's all."

She heard the echo of Diaz's words yesterday. You stepped into somebody's income stream. That puts you, and anyone close to you, on their radar.

"I know," she said. "I just spent a year being scared of everything. Of crossing the street, of getting in the car, of answering the phone. I don't want this to become another thing fear takes from me."

He reached across the table and rested his hand over hers. The mayor and Jason politely examined their notes.

"What if," he said, "we design the space so your studio is light and open and very Bree, and the security sits underneath that. Like a frame. You won't see it day to day, but it'll be there if we need it."

She exhaled slowly. "So long as we're not talking about metal detectors at the door."

"Only for Brian," he said. "He sets off alarms just on principle."

Her mouth twitched. "Okay. I can live with that."

Jason nodded. "I can draw up some options," he said. "We'll prioritize natural light upstairs. Downstairs, we can keep it more utilitarian without making it look like a chop shop."

"I don't own any neon underbody kits," Hank said.

"Let's keep it that way," the mayor replied.

They moved through more details. Fire code. Parking allocation. Loading access. The mayor mentioned potential small-business grants. Jason offered to walk the building with them that afternoon and flag immediate concerns.

At the end, the mayor folded her hands. "No pressure," she said. "You take this with you. Talk to your team. Talk to your families. If you decide it's too much, I'd rather lose you now than halfway through construction."

Hank glanced at Bree. "We plan on doing both," he said. "Talking and staying."

Bree lifted her chin. "We're not signing on the dotted line today," she said. "But we are serious. This isn't just a post-win sugar high."

"Good," the mayor said, satisfaction flickering. "Copper Moon could use a few more people who stick. Lord knows we've had enough passersby."

She stood and offered her hand again. "Whatever you decide, you've already made this weekend one for the books. Thank you."

They shook, thanked Jason, and stepped back into the hallway.

As they walked toward the front doors, Hank's phone buzzed. He checked it, thumb skimming the screen.

"Diaz," he said. "She wants us to know they picked up chatter about a guy asking questions at one of the smaller regional races. Same description as Einstein's contact. She's sharing data with other departments. Her exact words are 'stay aware, not paranoid.'"

Bree snorted. "That should be on a T-shirt."

He pocketed the phone. "You okay?"

She thought about Vic. About mysterious parking-lot meetups and illegal bottles and cash in duffel bags. About the way Diaz's eyes had sharpened when she looked at Bree outside the warehouse.

"I don't enjoy being on anybody's radar," she said. "But I like the idea of pretending nothing's wrong even less."

"Then we stay aware," Hank said. "We put cameras where they should've been years ago. We keep in touch with Diaz. We don't let fear drive the bus."

She frowned. "That's a terrible metaphor."

He grinned. "You knew what I meant."

She chuckled. "I did."

They stepped out into the sunlight. The harbor glittered; gulls wheeled and complained overhead. Across the street, a dark SUV idled at the curb before pulling away. Hank watched it for a beat, attention narrowing, then relaxed when it turned toward the highway instead of the industrial district.

"Problem?" she asked.

"No," he said. "Habit."

He looked down at the folder in his hand, then back at her. "So. You still in?"

Bree thought about her parents' voices on the phone. The relief under the worry. The way her mom had said, "We always tell her, you said hi."

She pictured the warehouse, dust motes in the air, the view of the water through the cracked upstairs window. Hank's hand in hers as she'd imagined easels and canvases and people climbing the stairs to see what she made.

"I told my parents I was," she said. "I'm not walking that back."

He smiled slowly, warmth softening his features. "Good. Because I just promised a mayor and a contractor that James Performance is going to be more than a temporary sticker on the door."

She laughed. "We're really doing this."

"Yeah," he said. "We are."

He lifted the folder slightly, like a toast, then leaned down and kissed her right there on the civic center steps. It was not the desperate, I might never get to do this again kind of kiss. It was steady and sure, the kind that tasted like commitment and morning coffee.

Across the street, someone honked and whooped. A kid's voice shouted, "That's the Cup guy!"

Bree smiled against Hank's mouth.

"Fame is exhausting," she murmured.

"It has perks," he said.

They broke apart reluctantly.

"Come on," he said. "Let's go show Brian and Colby the numbers so they can tell me all the reasons my timeline is too aggressive."

"And I'll tell you all the reasons it's not aggressive enough," she said.

He chuckled. "I look forward to the arguments."

They walked down the steps side by side, their footsteps finding an easy rhythm as they headed toward the future they had just nudged a little closer into focus.

Hank walked Bree down the steps of the civic center, their hands still linked, the folder with the city's proposal tucked under his arm. The harbor glittered like someone had scattered broken glass across the water. A gull screamed overhead, offended about something only gulls understood.

Bree's smile kept flickering in and out, like she was testing whether it fit.

"We really just told a mayor we were serious," she said.

"Yep."

"And I told my parents we're together."

He squeezed her hand. "Also true."

Her cheeks went a little pink, but she did not pull away. "Where are Brian and Colby?"

"Dockside," he said. "Brian texted while we were in there. He found pastries the size of his face and decided it was a sign."

She laughed; the sound loosened something tight in his chest. "Okay. Let's go tell them we're about to become small business owners, and we're possibly insane."

They crossed the street, stepping around confetti and the occasional flattened paper cup with the Cup logo on it. Someone in a souvenir T-shirt gave Hank a double take, then nudged his friend and pointed. Hank lifted a hand in a casual half-wave and kept moving.

"You're getting recognized," Bree murmured.

"It's the hair," he said. "Stands out."

"It was the pass on the last lap, and you know it."

He did know it. His muscles still remembered the lean of the bike, the split second when the gap had opened, and he'd taken it. The adrenaline from that would probably still be working its way out of his system when they were signing mortgage papers.

Dockside smelled like coffee, bacon, and the ocean. The bell over the door chimed as they stepped in. The same mechanic crowd from earlier weekends mixed with tourists wearing brand-new Copper Moon Cup caps.

Brian already occupied a corner booth, a plate of pastries in front of him, and a coffee mug in his hand. Colby sat opposite, his tablet propped against the sugar caddy; he looked up as soon as Hank slid into the booth.

"Well?" Brian asked. "Did the mayor offer you the keys to the city or just the cool abandoned building?"

"Preliminary sale proposal," Hank said, dropping the folder on the table between them. "Price is better than we hoped. City handles major structural, roof, masonry, and new windows. We cover interior build-out, electrical, plumbing, and finishes."

Colby's brows went up. "What's 'better than we hoped' mean, in actual numbers, boss?"

"Look for yourself," Hank said.

He opened the folder and turned it so they could read. Bree slid in beside him, close enough that her thigh pressed against his; her presence grounded him more than the coffee in his hand.

Brian whistled. "Damn. They know they're sitting on a problem."

"They know they're sitting on an opportunity," Bree said. "They want more people to stick around instead of treating this place like a long weekend."

Colby scanned the second page, lips moving as he did mental math. "Taxes stay low for the first two years. Step up after that, but capped increases. That's not bad."

"We'd be buying the building outright," Hank said. Saying it out loud made the idea more solid. "No lease; no landlord deciding they want to sell out from under us."

"Three units on paper," Colby murmured. "Ground floor shop, back bay that could be separate if we ever needed it, and upstairs." His gaze flicked to Bree. "You still good with making that studio yours?"

She nodded. "Yeah. I am."

Hank watched the way her hand tightened around her sketchbook. She looked scared and determined at the same time. He'd seen that expression on Marines going into a raid; he'd never expected to see it on a painter heading toward a mortgage.

"So this is the part where we talk percentages," Brian said. "Who owns what."

"I figured we'd split the shop three ways," Hank said. "Equal partners. The studio upstairs is Bree's. We can figure out how that works on paper so the city stays happy, but I don't want her space getting tangled up in arguments about dyno schedules."

Colby leaned back, considering him. "You're coming in with the biggest cash chunk," he said. "Prize money plus savings. You okay with an equal split?"

"I didn't get here alone," Hank said. "You two kept me upright and fast. I won the Cup because my bike ran like it was supposed to and because there was someone in my ear keeping me from doing anything too stupid. I'm not interested in being the guy who owns everything and barks orders."

Brian grinned. "That's sweet. You're still going to bark orders."

"Probably," Hank said. "But I'd rather do it to partners than employees."

Brian tore off a piece of pastry and popped it in his mouth. "All right. I'm in. I've been half living in this town for three seasons anyway. Might as well get a proper address."

Colby nodded slowly. "I want to walk the building again with Jason," he said. "Get a better sense of what his 'that's an easy fix' face means. But yeah. I'm in. We're going to need an excellent accountant and a lawyer who doesn't scare easily."

"The mayor had a list of people who've handled business sales in town," Hank said. "We can talk to a couple, see who feels like the least painful option."

"Least painful is a high bar," Brian said. "You're trusting lawyers with your future."

"Careful," Bree said. "Their future involves my paintings. I need contracts that don't make me want to light them on fire."

Hank nudged her knee under the table. "We'll let you vet the language."

She smiled, but her thumb still stroked the edge of her sketchbook. He knew her head was half at this table and half in Milwaukee, in the house where her parents had just hung up the phone.

"Did you tell your folks about this idea?" Brian asked Bree.

Bree glanced at Hank; he tipped his head, giving her the choice. She took a breath.

"They were... okay," she said. "Sad. Worried. But they listened. I told them about the building and the studio. And about using some of Bryn's insurance money for the build-out."

Brian's calm expression sobered. "Was that a hard sell?"

"It was a hard start," she said. "But my dad said she'd like it. That she hated I hadn't painted her yet." Her mouth quirked. "He also wants pictures of the warehouse and said something about gravity, which made little sense, but it was sweet."

"Parents rarely make sense," Colby said. "It's part of their charm."

Hank watched Bree's shoulders; they were relaxed in a way he hadn't seen since the first night. She'd just taken one of the hardest conversations of her life and walked out of it standing.

"You were brave," he said quietly.

A flush climbed her neck. "You already said that."

"I'm going to keep saying it until it sinks in," he replied.

His phone buzzed against the table. The screen flashed Diaz's name.

He swiped to answer. "Sergeant."

"James," Diaz said. In the background, he could hear the low murmur of a station. "You got a minute?"

"Yeah." He glanced at the others. "We're at Dockside. What's up?"

"Short version, we've got confirming chatter that Eisen's supplier is not happy their product got yanked off the track," Diaz said. "One of our neighboring departments picked up talk at a regional race about 'the guy who ratted.' No names, but the description's close enough to you that I'm not calling it a coincidence."

Hank's hand tightened around his mug. "Is he in this region?"

"Probably not yet," she said. "But he has friends who are. I'm not telling you this to freak you out; I'm telling you so you keep your head on a swivel. Awareness, not paranoia. You understand the difference."

"Yes, ma'am."

"I'm talking with the mayor about fast-tracking security cameras around the Bay Street block," Diaz went on. "If you move forward with that warehouse, I want your exterior covered. I'll connect you with a guy I trust. No junk equipment."

Bree watched his face, worry flickering in her eyes. Hank reached for her hand under the table and squeezed once.

"We were already talking security with Jason and the mayor," he said. "We'll loop your guy in."

"Good." Paper rustled. "If you see anyone hanging around that doesn't fit, get me a plate if you can. Don't play hero at the warehouse, James. You already did that once."

"I hear you."

She exhaled. "I'll pass along anything else that crosses my desk. For now, finish your coffee. Enjoy your victory. Let us do our jobs."

"Yes, ma'am."

He ended the call.

"Well?" Brian asked.

Hank relayed the gist. Brian's easy grin vanished; Colby went still.

"So we're officially on somebody's list," Brian said.

"We were already on it," Hank said. "This just means Diaz knows the list exists."

Bree's fingers tightened on his. "Does this change anything?" she asked.

"Yeah," he said. "It changes how fast I want to get cams on that building. It changes how often I want you walking alone."

Her jaw set. "I don't want to live like a target."

"You're not a target," he said. "You're a witness who helped stop something lethal. That's going to irritate people who think they're untouchable. I'm not saying we board up the windows. I'm saying we make it harder for them to cause trouble without consequences."

She looked down at their joined hands, thumb rubbing along his knuckles. "You're falling into *Marine brain*," she said softly.

"Probably," he admitted. "Hard to shake. But *Marine brain* kept a lot of people alive. I'd like to put it to work here."

Colby cleared his throat. "I'm with him on this," he said. "We can design the shop so it feels open and still leaves us control of the entry points. Cameras, alarms, smart locks. None of that has to be ugly."

"Jason said the same," Bree said. "If my studio looks like a prison cell, I'm out. But if we can hide the security in the bones, I can live with that."

"We can," Colby said. "I'll talk to Jason about wiring and camera placements when we walk the place."

"Speaking of," Brian said, checking his watch, "you're meeting him when?"

"Half an hour," Hank said. "He's finishing a walk-through at one of the boardwalk places."

Brian slid out of the booth. "Then we'd better get moving. I want to see my future lift bay."

They paid, said quick goodbyes to the staff who recognized Hank, and walked back toward Bay Street. The farther they got from the waterfront crowds, the quieter the streets became. The warehouse loomed at the end of the block, brick stained and windows clouded with years of salt and dust.

Jason Keene already stood out front, blueprints under one arm, a hard hat dangling from his hand. He wore the same pencil behind his ear and the same practical boots he'd had on in the mayor's office.

"You came back," he said. "Always a good sign."

"We brought reinforcements," Hank said. "Jason, this is Brian Knight and Colby Landon. The other two-thirds of the brain cell."

Jason shook their hands. "Good to meet you. Let's go see what we're dealing with."

Inside, the warehouse smelled like old wood, motor oil, and the faint tang of salt driven in on sea wind. Dust motes spun in shafts of light. The ground floor stretched long and deep, the concrete cracked but solid.

Jason walked them through the space, pointing out support columns, water lines, and electrical panels that needed to be replaced yesterday. He spoke in practical phrases, the way Hank remembered engineers talking in briefing rooms.

"We replace this panel," Jason said, tapping a metal box that had seen better decades, "run new lines along here, reroute for whatever heavy equipment you want. Where are you thinking lifts and dyno?"

"Lifts along that wall," Hank said, pointing. "Dyno at

the back, with exhaust ventilation tied into that existing duct if we can salvage it."

Jason measured with his eyes. "We can. We'll have to reinforce that wall if you want to anchor anything serious. But it's workable."

Bree drifted toward the steel staircase leading upstairs, her steps soft on the treads. Hank watched her go.

"She okay?" Jason asked quietly.

"She's thinking," Hank said. "That's good for all of us."

Jason nodded. "Upstairs is in better shape structurally," he said. "Less water intrusion. More natural light. It's going to clean up nice."

They climbed after her. The second floor opened out into a wide expanse with tall windows facing the harbor. The glass was cracked in places, but the light poured in.

Bree stood near one of the windows, palm flat against the dusty sill, eyes half closed. Her sketchbook dangled from her other hand.

Hank came up beside her. "What do you see?"

"Walls knocked back," she said. "White paint, but not too clean. A big work table there. Easels along that side. A couch in the corner for when I forget how to sit like a normal person. And that entire wall..." She pointed opposite the windows. "Gallery space. Rotating work. Maybe a couple of pieces that never move."

"Security film on the glass," Jason said. "New frames. We can keep the size. The light's kind of the whole point."

Bree chewed her lower lip. "No bars," she said.

"No bars," Jason agreed. "We'll put shutters on the outside that roll down at night; from the street, they'll look like part of the building. Cameras at the stairwell and entrance. That way, anyone who comes up here is either invited or recorded."

Hank saw the tension in Bree's shoulders, saw it ease a fraction at the word recorded. "You okay with that?" he asked.

She nodded slowly. "I can live with shutters if they're up when I'm working," she said. "And if the cameras aren't giant, blinking red eyes."

"I leave the blinking to smoke alarms," Jason said. "We'll keep them discreet."

They walked farther into the space. Brian and Colby peeled off, talking excitedly about mezzanines and storage. Jason stopped near a section of floor where the boards creaked.

"We'll need to reinforce this area," he said. "Especially if you plan on holding openings with more than a handful of people."

"Openings," Bree echoed, soft and almost to herself.

"You're going to have them," Hank said. "Might as well plan for it."

She looked at him, eyes bright in the filtered light. "You really think people are going to climb those stairs to look at my work?"

"I think people are going to climb those stairs to feel something they didn't expect to," he said. "Your work does that. I've seen it."

Her throat moved as she swallowed. "You keep saying things that make it harder to be rational."

"Rational's overrated," he said. "Calculated risk, that's the sweet spot."

Jason cleared his throat politely. "Before this turns into a Hallmark moment and I have to pretend I'm not here," he said, "let me talk timelines. If we get permits moving next week, they can complete the structural and roof work in three months. Windows, wiring, and plumbing will layer in as we go. You're probably looking at six months before you're ready to open the doors to customers."

"Next season," Colby said from across the room. "We could be running under our own sign by the time the Cup roll-out returns here."

"That's the idea," Hank said.

"Money?" Brian asked. "Just so we know whether we're eating instant noodles all winter."

Jason gave them ballpark figures. They weren't small, but they weren't impossible. Hank felt the numbers click into the mental spreadsheet he'd been carrying since the mayor's office.

Prize money. Savings. A percentage of past seasons he'd never touched. The studio build-out was from Bree's account. Possible small-business grants, the mayor had mentioned.

"Assuming nothing catastrophic hits your budget, you're okay," Jason concluded. "I'll give you a detailed quote once my engineer runs the structural calcs."

"Thank you," Hank said. "We appreciate you being straight with us."

"Straight's the only way I know how to be," Jason said. "I'll email the preliminary breakdown tonight. You three talk it over. If you decide to move forward, we'll get the paperwork started."

He headed back toward the stairs with Brian and Colby. Their voices drifted down as they started arguing about whether the shop's logo should feature flames, a piston, or both.

Hank stayed where he was, next to Bree, letting the quiet settle.

"How's it hitting you?" he asked.

She turned in a slow circle, taking in the space. "Like

standing on the edge of a canvas that's too big," she said. "My brain's trying to fill it all at once, and I know that's not how it works."

"You start with one line," he said. "Then another."

She smiled faintly. "You say that like you've done it."

"I've built a couple of things," he said. "Teams. Bikes. A life or two."

Her hand brushed his chest lightly, right over his heart. "You sure you want to build this one here?" she asked.

He didn't hesitate. "Yeah," he said. "I am."

She looked up at him, eyes dark and serious. "Then we have to make it hard for anyone to knock it down."

"That's the plan," he said. "We'll layer the security in like primer. You'll notice it when it's going up; after that, it just becomes part of the walls."

She nodded, but he could see the lingering shadow. Losing her sister had taught her that bad things did not bother with fair warning; they just happened and left holes.

"Hey," he said softly. "We're not helpless bystanders here. We have a capable police chief, a mayor who wants this to succeed, and a contractor who is honest. Plus three stubborn idiots who don't know how to quit."

"And one painter with questionable life choices," she said.

He smiled. "Those are my favorite kind."

Her gaze softened. "You keep being like this," she said, "and I'm never going to find my rationality again."

He leaned down and kissed her gently in the dusty sunlight, a promise rather than a diversion.

"They called this quiet aftermath," he murmured against her mouth. "Feels more like the starting line to me."

Bree stood at the upstairs window and watched Jason's truck pull away from the curb. Brian and Colby lingered on the sidewalk, still talking, their gestures big and animated. Hank leaned against the warehouse's brick wall, arms folded, listening.

From this height, with the harbor spread out beyond them, they looked like pieces in a sketch she hadn't finished.

Her phone buzzed in her pocket.

Mom.

She hesitated only a second before answering. "Hey."

"Hi, sweetheart," her mom said. "We just left the cemetery. Your father insisted on telling your sister you're talking about moving. As if she doesn't already know."

Bree's throat tightened. "Thank you," she said. "For telling her. I know…"

"I know it's not how it works," her mom finished. "We say it anyway."

Bree leaned her shoulder against the window frame.

The light was warm on her face, smelling faintly of dust and salt. "How are you?" she asked.

"Tired," her mom said. "The good kind, where you've cried it out, and your husband made you sit on a bench and eat half his granola bar. Your father wishes me to inform you that the grounds crew needs to mow the north slope more often."

Bree smiled. "Of course he does."

"How are you?" her mom asked. "And don't say 'fine.'"

"I'm... hopeful," Bree said slowly. "Scared. But hopeful."

"Tell me about this place," her mom said. "The building. I've been picturing some kind of haunted shack by the docks."

"It's not haunted," Bree said. "It's old. Brick warehouse on Bay Street, two blocks from the harbor. Ground floor's going to be the performance shop. High ceilings, concrete floor, lots of space for lifts and whatever mechanical wizardry Hank and the guys need. Upstairs..." She turned, letting her gaze travel over the room. "Upstairs is big. Wood floors, tall windows facing the water. It's rough right now, but you can see what it wants to be."

"Which is?" her mom asked softly.

"A studio," Bree said. "And a small gallery. I can see easels, canvases, and a big table in the middle for messy work. A corner where I can just sit and stare at things when I forget how to be a person." Her throat got tight. "And a wall dedicated to Bryn."

There was a quiet sound on the other end of the line; she knew that inhale, that small intake that meant her mom was holding back tears.

"She'd like that," her mom said. "What kind of wall?"

"Not portraits," Bree said. "Not just her face. Pieces of her. Her Doc Martens under a bench. The coffee mug she stole from that diner. The paint on her knuckles. The way she'd leave smudges on doorframes like little fingerprints of color everywhere she went."

"She did make a mess," her mom said, a watery laugh threading through the words.

"A beautiful one," Bree said. "I want people who never knew her to stand here and feel like they're meeting her anyway."

"I can't decide if that makes me want to cry or clap," her mom said. "Maybe both."

"Same," Bree admitted.

"Do you have to decide about the money now?" her mom asked quietly. "The insurance."

"No," Bree said. "But I want to. I've been letting it sit like a stone in my pocket for a year. It feels heavier every day I don't use it. Hank said something this morning that stuck, about money not knowing where it came from, only what we use it for. I think I want to turn some of it into walls and light and paintings instead of letting it gather dust in a bank account."

Her mom was silent for a moment. When she spoke again, her voice had steadied. "Then that's what you should do," she said. "We gave it to you for your future, not for guilt."

"I know," Bree said. "I just had to catch up to the idea."

"Is it safe?" her mom asked suddenly. "This warehouse. This town. You said there was cheating at the race. People being shady."

"There was," Bree said. She glanced out the window at the street. Hank stood with his back to the wall, his gaze sweeping the block, automatic and practiced.

"And?" her mom prompted.

"And we spoke up," Bree said. "Hank turned in the

illegal kit. The police are on it. There's some fallout there; Sergeant Diaz said the people who were profiting from it aren't thrilled. But the mayor's on our side. The cop in charge knows what she's doing. They're putting cameras in the area. We're not walking into this blind."

Her mom let out a low sound. "I don't like the idea of you being anywhere near people who make money by hurting others."

"Nobody does," Bree said. "But pretending they don't exist doesn't make them go away. At least here we're surrounded by people who give a damn. Hank's not going to ignore it. Neither is Diaz."

"And you," her mom said.

"And me," Bree agreed.

She noticed movement across the street; a silver sedan had eased to the curb, idling. A man in a ball cap sat behind the wheel, his posture just a little too stiff for someone taking a phone call. He looked toward the warehouse, then down the block.

"Bree?" her mom asked. "You still there?"

"Yeah," Bree said. Her artist's brain cataloged the angle of the man's head, the way his hand tightened on the steering wheel. "Just... looking at the view. The harbor's so close it feels like you could fall into it."

"You always did like getting close to the edge of things," her mom said. "You sure about this? Staying there. Building a life that isn't two hours down the road."

Bree watched Hank push off the wall and glance up, checking windows automatically. His gaze found her; he tipped his chin in question. She lifted a hand and gave a small wave, pointing subtly toward the street.

He turned, casual, like he was only stretching. His eyes tracked to the sedan. After a beat, the car pulled away, merging into light traffic and disappearing around the corner.

"I'm sure I need to try," Bree said, pulling her focus back to the phone. "If I come back now, before I've given this a real shot, I think I'll always wonder what would've happened if I'd stayed."

"And if it doesn't work?" her mom asked.

"Then I'll figure something else out," Bree said. "But right now, when I picture the future, it's not just me in an apartment full of half-packed boxes and memories. It's this building. The shop downstairs. The studio up here. Hank. People climbing stairs to see what I made of all this grief."

"You always did make things out of what hurt," her mom said softly.

Bree swallowed. "I learned from the best."

Her mom made another small sound.

"Can you and Dad come down when we get closer?" Bree asked. "I'd like you to see it before it's finished. Help me decide where the Bryn wall goes."

"We'd like that," her mom said. "Your father's nodding. He says he'll bring a level."

Bree laughed. "Of course he will."

"I know you're going to be okay," her mom said. "I just need a little time to catch up to it."

"Take all the time you need," Bree said. "I'm not going anywhere for a while."

"We love you," her mom said.

"I love you too," Bree replied.

They hung up. Bree stood there a moment, phone slipping back into her pocket, listening to the building breathe.

Boot steps creaked on the stairs. Hank appeared in the doorway, the light behind him haloing his shoulders.

"You okay?" he asked.

"Yeah," she said. "They're... adjusting. My mom's picturing you and trying really hard not to ask if you have tattoos or a criminal record."

He smiled. "Do you want to tell her the answer to one of those is yes?"

"Not yet," she said. "I'll let you scandalize her in person."

He crossed the room and leaned his hip against the windowsill beside her. "Guy in the sedan," he said quietly. "Anything feel off about him to you?"

"My stomach didn't love it," she admitted. "But that might've just been all the feelings."

He nodded. "Could be nothing. Could be somebody curious about why four people are standing outside an old warehouse with blueprints. Either way, I got the plate. I'll send it to Diaz."

"Awareness, not paranoia," she said.

"Exactly."

She looked at his profile, the way his jaw worked when he was thinking. "Do you ever get tired of feeling responsible for everything within a fifty-yard radius?"

"Constantly," he said. "Doesn't stop me."

"I know," she said. "I'm not asking you to change. Just... remember that I can also notice weird sedans."

"I saw you clock him," he said. "You went still without freezing. There's a difference. I'm not trying to turn you into a porcelain doll I have to carry around."

"Good," she said. "Because I'd be terrible at that."

His gaze dropped to her mouth; warmth flickered there, layered over the concern. "You'd be terrible at sitting still," he agreed. "You did good with your parents."

She let her head tip against his shoulder. "You did good

with the mayor," she said. "Very grown-up. There were terms and everything."

He huffed a laugh. "Wait until you hear me talk depreciation schedules."

"Sounds sexy," she murmured.

He tilted her chin up with one knuckle. "Careful," he said. "You keep saying things like that, I'm going to forget we're standing in a room with broken boards and no curtains."

She kissed him before she could talk herself out of it, slow and deliberate. Dust and light wrapped around them; the harbor scent drifted through the cracked glass.

"We should probably not christen the studio while your friends are downstairs," she said against his mouth.

"Probably not," he agreed. "But later..."

"Later," she said.

They grabbed a late lunch at a little place on Main, then parted ways. Brian and Colby went back to the paddock to tie up loose ends with the team hauler. Hank and Bree returned to the hotel, the quiet of the hallway a strange contrast to the noise in her head.

Inside the room, Bree set her sketchbook on the small table by the window. Blank pages waited, daring her.

Hank tossed the folder onto the desk and sat heavily on the edge of the bed, scrubbing his hands over his face.

"You look like someone just made you run stairs," she said.

"I've had easier briefings," he replied. "Fewer zeroes."

"Are you freaking out?" she asked.

"A little," he admitted. "Feels a lot like planning an op. Only this time, the worst possible outcome isn't on the battlefield; it's a foreclosure notice."

She sat beside him and laced their fingers. "Hey. We went over the numbers three times with Jason. We'll go over them again with the accountant. We're not leaping blind."

He glanced at her. "You're not scared?"

"I'm terrified," she said. "I'm just... more scared of going back to my tiny apartment and pretending I don't know what this feels like. The building. The studio. You. So I'm choosing the fear that comes with possibility instead of the one that comes with being stuck."

He stared at her for a long beat, something raw and grateful flickering in his eyes. "You keep doing that," he said, "choosing hard things on purpose."

"Trick I picked up," she said lightly. "Grief had a lot of practice making choices for me. I'm trying to return the favor."

He lifted their joined hands and kissed her knuckles. "Have I mentioned that I'm proud of you?"

"Once or twice," she said. "Keep it up. It's starting to sink in."

His mouth curved. "We've got a few hours before we have to show our faces at the team thing tonight," he said. "Dinner at the tent, sponsor pictures, all that fun stuff. Any plans for the immediate future?"

She glanced at the sketchbook. Then at him. "Yeah," she drawled. "I was thinking about starting the first piece for the Bryn series. While the building is still a skeleton in my head, I want to catch how it feels right now. And then later... I kind of want to lie in bed with my boyfriend and talk about absurd things like what color we're painting the bathroom."

He smiled. "I'm available for both those tasks."

"I thought you might be."

She stood and opened the sketchbook, flipping to a

fresh page. The pencil felt familiar between her fingers. Her heart kicked, not with the sharp panic that had become her normal companion, but with something steadier.

"Do you want me out of your hair while you draw?" he asked.

"I want you right there," she said, nodding at the bed. "You can pretend to look at budget spreadsheets while I pretend not to be staring at your forearms every five minutes."

"That's a fair trade," he said.

He picked up the folder and stretched out on the bed, back against the headboard, ankles crossed. The sight of him there, utterly at home, tightened something sweet in her chest.

She sat at the table and began to sketch.

The first lines were hesitant. The outline of a boot. A chipped mug. A section of wood floor with sunlight pouring over it. Not exact replicas of Bryn's things, but echoes. Memories translated into shapes.

Hank's low voice drifted over as he muttered to himself about square footage and estimated labor costs. It was oddly soothing, like the distant hum of a motor.

After a while, he set the papers aside. "You're frowning," he said.

"I'm thinking," she replied without looking up.

"About?"

"How to make people feel like they know her," she said. "Without ever seeing her face."

"You already know how," he said. "That's what you did with those industrial waterfront pieces."

She glanced back at him. "You saw those for all of ten minutes on my phone."

"Long enough," he said. "They made me feel things I

didn't want to admit to in public. This is going to do the same."

Her chest squeezed. "You keep having more faith in me than I have in myself."

"Occupational hazard," he said. "I spent a lot of years betting on people's potential. I'm not about to stop with you."

She let the pencil still. "Come here," she said.

He obeyed without question, setting the papers aside and crossing to her. She stood, tipped her head back, and kissed him.

Whatever patience they'd shown at the studio, they dropped it now.

He slid his hands to her hips, pulling her in; the contact sent a rush of heat through her. She opened to him, tasting coffee and something purely Hank.

"We should pace ourselves," he murmured against her mouth.

"Why?" she asked. "I like this pace."

He laughed softly, resigned and pleased. "Fair point."

They moved together without spoken coordination, hands finding buttons and hems. The bed caught them when they toppled back; there was a lot of laughing and getting tangled in the comforter before it shifted into something slower.

Hank took his time; he always did. As if he were memorizing, mapping her with his hands, his mouth. He checked in with small touches and the way he watched her face, looking for every flicker of pleasure, every shadow of doubt.

She let herself be seen. That was the true leap, not the warehouse, not the business plan, but this. The way she let him touch the parts of her grief that still felt raw and jagged, even as he worshipped everything else.

When she came apart around him, it wasn't fireworks and fanfare. It was a slow, deep wave that rolled through her, leaving her boneless and full. He followed with a quiet curse, burying his face in her neck, his body shuddering.

For a long time afterward, they lay in a tangle of limbs and sheets, breathing hard. The late afternoon light slanted across the floor, edging toward evening.

"If this is what post-race weekends look like now," he said eventually, voice rough, "I'm never retiring."

She laughed, stroking a hand down his back. "Pretty sure you can't keep racing forever," she said. "Your knees will mutiny."

"Traitors," he muttered. "Fine. I'll run the shop and be your studio's in-house mechanic. Hire a couple junior riders to do the dangerous stuff while I yell at them from the pit wall."

"That sounds terrifying," she said. "For them. Slightly hot for me."

He lifted his head, eyebrow arched. "Slightly?"

"Moderately," she amended. "Possibly extremely."

He kissed her again, quick and affectionate this time, then rolled onto his back, dragging a hand over his face.

"Timeline-wise," he said, "we're looking at permits next week, contracts after that. If all goes well, we're in construction within a month."

"I'll need to go back to Milwaukee," she said. "Pack up my apartment. Figure out what to put in storage and what to bring here. Maybe help my parents shift some of Bryn's things from altars to actual life. That's not going to be easy."

"I'll go with you," he said.

She turned her head to look at him. "You don't have to."

"I know," he said. "I want to. If I'm buying a building

with you and using my power tools in your future studio, I'd like to see where you've been living. Meet your parents. Pay my respects to Bryn."

Emotion punched through her chest, sharp and fierce. "You already did," she said, voice thick. "When you pulled me out of that hotel room the first night and made me walk on the beach. She'd have liked you for that alone."

"Then I want to go stand where she's buried and tell her I'm going to keep trying," he breathed. "If that's okay with you."

She pressed her face into his shoulder for a moment, hiding the sudden sting in her eyes. "Yeah," she said. "That's okay."

He wrapped an arm around her, holding her close. "We'll figure the schedule out after Diaz gives us the all clear on your mystery sedan."

"Awareness, not paranoia," she reminded him.

He huffed. "You're going to throw that back at me forever, aren't you?"

"Forever's a big word," she said. "But it's getting less scary."

He kissed the top of her head. "Good."

"We should also talk to a realtor and find a house."

He chuckled. "I've been thinking that too. I want to live with you. I want you to live with me."

She smiled softly as she stared at their joined hands. "I want that too."

Outside, the sounds of Copper Moon drifted up from the street. A distant motorcycle engine. Laughter from the boardwalk. The faint echo of someone calling out about fresh fish at a stall.

Inside, the room smelled like them: soap, sweat, hotel sheets, and something new that felt a lot like home.

Bree closed her eyes and let herself imagine it. Not just this room, temporary and anonymous, but the upstairs of the warehouse with their life layered into it. Paint-stained floors. The thump of tools downstairs. Hank's laughter slipping under the studio door. Her parents sitting on a mismatched couch at an opening, pointing out details in the Bryn paintings to anyone who would listen.

The future wasn't a cliff anymore.

It was a long, winding road, full of potholes and unexpected turns; she knew that. Some people out there didn't like what they had done with Marcus and the nitrous kit. There were conversations ahead that would hurt.

But she wasn't standing at the edge of nothing.

She was already walking.

"Hey," Hank murmured. "You zoning out on me?"

"Just plotting," she said.

"Anything I need to be worried about?"

"Only if you hate the idea of the studio bathroom being teal," she said.

He groaned. "You're going to turn my shop into an art installation."

"Don't worry," she said. "We'll keep the flames on your logo."

He laughed, the sound low and easy. "I look forward to the arguments."

She smiled into his skin. "Me too."

They lay there a little longer, letting the light change and the day shift around them. In a few hours, they'd pull on clean clothes and go be public faces again, shaking hands and taking pictures and pretending to be slightly more put together than they actually were.

For now, it was just the two of them, the echo of the future humming quietly between their heartbeats.

CHAPTER

EIGHTEEN

Hank leaned his shoulder into the tent pole and let the noise of the celebration wash over him for a minute.

The team dinner had turned into more of a loose, wandering gathering; half the paddock seemed to be crammed under the big hospitality tent, plates balanced on laps, beer bottles sweating on folding tables. Someone had dragged a speaker over; classic rock threaded through the hum of voices and the occasional burst of laughter.

Brian stood near the buffet, telling a story with his hands as much as his mouth. Colby was perched on a cooler with his tablet on his knees, alternating between taking notes and swatting at Brian when he got too close.

Across the way, Bree stood with Carmen, the two of them forming a small island in the chaos. Bree's head was tipped back in laughter; the sight hit him as hard as any adrenaline spike he'd had all weekend.

He felt Diaz before he saw her; a shift in the air, a different kind of alertness.

"James," she said at his elbow.

He straightened. "Sergeant."

She wore plain clothes tonight, dark jeans and a Copper Moon Cup staff T-shirt, her badge clipped to her belt instead of riding her chest. It did nothing to make her look less like she could take down half the tent with a raised eyebrow.

"Relax," she said, reading his stance. "I'm off duty in about thirty minutes. Right now, I'm just a woman who wants a paper plate of pulled pork before Brian eats it all."

"He will," Hank said. "You should probably cut in line."

She smiled briefly, then nodded toward Bree. "How's she doing?"

"Better than I expected," he said honestly. "She told her parents she's staying. Told the mayor we're serious about the warehouse. Started a sketch for a new series."

Diaz's gaze followed his. "Good," she said. "We need more people who stick."

He heard the unspoken because. Because people who stick are more likely to fight for a place.

"You said you'd call if there was more chatter," he said.

"I did," she said. "I'm still sorting through what's useful and what's background noise. Your plate-check from earlier goes to a rental, paid in cash by a shell company that has one purpose: buying cars and moving them between states. I've seen it tied to two other investigations, neither local."

"So not a tourist," he said.

"Probably not," she agreed. "But I can't prove intent yet. He didn't loiter long, he didn't approach you, he didn't do anything except look too interested, and then drove away. Suspicious, yes; actionable, no."

"Do we need to be doing anything different tonight?" he asked.

"Tonight you eat, you smile for the cameras, you go

back to your room and lock the deadbolt," Diaz said. "Tomorrow, you keep an eye out. I've already asked patrol to do a few extra passes near your hotel and the Bay Street block. We're putting a marked car in sight as often as we can; deterrence is worth something."

"Thanks," he said.

She gave him a long look. "I'm telling you this because I know you get it," she said quietly. "Not so you can run your own op. You see something off, you call it in. You do not follow anyone into dark corners."

The words hit memories he didn't dwell on; sand under his boots, radio crackle, a door that opened on something none of them had wanted to see.

"I hear you," he said. "I won't go cowboy."

"Good," she said. "I don't feel like writing that report."

Across the tent, someone called Diaz's name. She lifted two fingers in acknowledgment.

"Your guy Colby," she said, nodding toward the cooler. "He asked me earlier if there's a way he can see any public bulletins about illegal parts circulating. I told him no; then I told him where to look anyway. He's got a brain for patterns."

"Yeah," Hank said. "He does."

"You keep him pointed at the legitimate side of that line," Diaz said. "People who can see systems are valuable; they're also tempting targets for the wrong kind of work."

"I will," Hank said.

She clapped his shoulder once, surprisingly warm. "Enjoy your night, James."

He watched her head for the food line, then took a breath and went to find his own center of gravity.

Bree looked up as he approached. Her face lit; that still felt like a miracle.

"There you are," she said. "I was telling Carmen about your *Marine brain* and how you tried to turn the studio into Fort Knox."

"I did not," he said. "Jason and I merely suggested that glass that shatters if you breathe on it is not optimal."

Carmen smiled. "I like him," she said to Bree. "He sounds like my insurance agent."

Hank laughed. "Not the look I'm going for, but I'll take competent over cool."

Carmen shifted her weight, her Dragon-branded jacket suddenly looking out of place in a tent full of mixed fans and teams. She caught his eye, something like an apology crossing her face.

"Can we grab a few minutes later?" she asked. "You and Bree both. Somewhere quieter."

"Sure," he said. "You okay?"

"Yeah," she said quickly. "Just... time for some overdue conversations."

He filed the phrasing away. Overdue conversations rarely meant anything simple.

"Come find us," Bree said. "We're hard to miss."

Carmen's phone buzzed; she glanced at it and groaned. "That's Mom," she said. "She's worried about the issues here."

Bree slipped her hand into Hank's. "You good?" she asked.

"Diaz gave me a status update," he said. "Rental car, shell company, nothing she can move on yet. They're watching, they're making themselves visible around our places. She reminded me not to chase anyone into alleys."

Bree's mouth twitched. "You needed that reminder?"

"Apparently," he said. "I have a history."

Her gaze softened. "You're not on a deployment anymore."

"I know," he said. "Sometimes my muscle memory forgets."

She squeezed his fingers. "I'll remind you. Awareness, not paranoia."

"Exactly," he said.

A staffer from the Cup organization appeared with a camera and a harried expression. "Hank James? Can I steal you for a second? We're grabbing a few shots for the recap reel."

"Sure," he said. He kissed Bree's temple. "Back in a minute."

He posed for a handful of photos; the practiced half-smile came easy now. He signed a program for a kid whose hands shook with excitement. His real calculations remained tucked away, as he answered some innocuous questions.

When he made it back to the edge of the tent, Bree and Carmen were gone.

His chest tightened until he spotted them near the paddock exit, stepping into the cooler dark beyond the lights. Carmen caught his eye and lifted a hand; the invitation was clear.

He followed.

The night outside smelled like damp asphalt and salt. The rumble of voices faded as soon as the tent flap fell back into place behind him. Overhead, the sky was a deep navy bruise, streaked with faint clouds.

Carmen stood near the temporary fence, arms folded, Dragon jacket zipped to her throat. Bree leaned against a concrete barrier, her expression curious and open.

"Sorry to drag you away from your adoring public," Carmen said. "I just... wanted to talk without an audience."

"Sounds serious," Hank said.

"It is," she said.

Bree tilted her head. "What's going on?"

Carmen drew in a breath. "I quit," she said. "The Dragons. I told Heidi I'm done after this weekend."

Bree's brows climbed. "Wow. That's... big."

"Yeah." Carmen gave a short, humorless laugh. "I'm only along to help Heidi, but as the evidence stacks up against the Red Dragons, I want no part of any of that. I love my sister, but if they're cheating, and it looks as though they are, I don't need that reflecting on me."

Hank nodded slowly. "Are you sure they're cheating?"

"I heard talk in the trailer afterward about 'finding a source that is a little more discreet next time'." Her jaw tightened. "Because when I told them if they ever pulled that kind of stunt again I'd turn them in myself, one of the guys laughed and told me I'd never do it. Like I'm some kind of decoration they can ignore."

Anger sparked low in Hank's gut. "You told Diaz any of that?" he asked.

"Yes," she said. "I went by the station after the driver's meeting this afternoon. Gave her my notes, names, dates, everything I had. She asked if I'd be willing to testify if it comes to that; I told her yes."

"That's brave," Bree said, her voice soft.

Carmen shrugged one shoulder. "Feels more like overdue," she said. "I don't really care much for the personality of the team. It's exciting to be part of the race and all the prep that goes into it. I got caught up in that. I let the excitement for racing take over, and I've questioned myself over and over on my attention to detail. Maybe I would have seen something myself if I'd paid attention. But it never occurred to me that they'd cheat. I thought they were just obnoxious and cocky.”

Silence sat for a beat, heavy with things all three of them knew in different ways.

“Marcus will land on his feet,” Carmen went on. “He's good at spinning. He'll pitch it like they cut me loose for not being a team player; I don't really care. I've got enough contacts to pick up freelance PR work somewhere else.”

“Where are you thinking?” Hank asked.

She hesitated, then looked at Bree. “I've been talking to the Cup operations folks,” she said. “Off the record. They need someone to coordinate community engagement stuff in the smaller markets. Charity events, school visits, all the things that keep locals from hating the noise and the traffic. Copper Moon's on that list.”

Bree's eyes widened. “You'd be based here?”

“Probably in a weird hybrid way,” Carmen said. “Some travel, some home base. I haven't said yes yet; I wanted to be sure I was really not going back to the Dragons before I jumped. But after this weekend…” She shook her head. “I can't be the person smiling in the background while they cheat. And it could only be a matter of time before they actually hurt someone.”

“You're not,” Hank said quietly. “You stopped being that the second you walked into Diaz's office.”

“Yeah, well.” Carmen looked away, blinking fast. “Doesn't erase the years I stayed because it was convenient.”

“That's not all you did,” Bree said. “You supported the riders who weren't assholes. You kept Heidi out of the worst of it. You watched for things that didn't feel right, and you spoke up. That counts.”

Carmen gave a small, crooked smile. "You're too generous," she said.

"Maybe," Bree said. "Or maybe I know what it feels like to stay somewhere because the alternative is a big, terrifying unknown."

Carmen closed her eyes briefly. "Yeah," she said. "I guess you do."

"This is a clean break," Hank said. "That matters."

"It also means some people who already don't like you are going to like you even less," Bree said gently. "Are you safe?"

Carmen's mouth twisted. "I'm not stupid," she said. "I'll be careful. Diaz made me promise I'd call if anyone from the Dragons started getting too friendly outside official events. Most of them will just be pissed in a loud, macho way for a while and then move on to the next thing. The ones who worry me are the guys who were benefiting from the shady deals you exposed."

"Einstein's supplier," Hank said.

"And his friends," Carmen said. "I heard one of them on the phone this afternoon, hissing about 'making examples'."

Cold went down his spine. "You heard a name?" he asked.

She shook her head. "No. Just a voice. Brooklyn accent, smoker's rasp. Diaz said that matches some of what she's hearing from the state. I'm not useful beyond that."

"You're more useful than half the people who think they are," Hank said.

Carmen huffed out a breath. "Point is, I'm out. I wanted you to hear it from me, not through paddock gossip. You put your neck on the line to call out the nitrous; I'm putting mine on the line to back that call."

"Thank you," he said simply.

She nodded, then turned to Bree. "And I wanted to say... I'm sorry."

Bree blinked. "For what?"

"For bringing you into the mix in the first place," Carmen said.

Bree's expression flickered; hurt, then understanding. "You were in a complicated spot," she said. "Doesn't mean you get a lifetime pass, but it does mean I get it."

"Can we call it even if I buy you coffee next time I'm in town?" Carmen asked. "Assuming I'm allowed in your new fancy studio without an appointment."

Bree smiled, the ache in it obvious. "You're always allowed," she said. "We'll paint over the Dragon logo on your jacket if it makes you feel better."

Carmen laughed, startled and real. "Deal."

People began spilling out of the tent, the temperature shifting as bodies moved through the night.

Carmen hesitated, then stepped forward and hugged Bree, quick and fierce. When she pulled back, her eyes were bright.

"Take care of her," she said to Hank.

"Planning on it," he said.

"And let her take care of you, Marine," Carmen added. "You've got that 'I can handle everything' look. It's bullshit."

He smiled. "Noted."

She nodded once, squared her shoulders, and walked back toward the tent; the Dragon logo on her back caught the light, then disappeared into the crowd.

Bree watched her go, her hand finding Hank's.

"That felt like a goodbye," she said softly.

"It was," he said. "But not the permanent kind."

"You think she'll take the Cup job?" Bree asked.

"I think she already has," he said. "She just hasn't said the words yet."

Bree exhaled. "I'm glad she's stepping away," she said. "Even if it hurts."

"Step one," he said. "People who were quiet before are starting to talk. That matters."

"Are you going to be able to sleep tonight?" she asked.

He thought of the shell company rental and the Brooklyn rasp Carmen had described.

"Eventually," he said. "After I watch the hallway for an hour and rearrange the chair under the door handle twice."

She bumped his shoulder with hers. "Good thing you've got a girlfriend who's good with hard things," she said. "Including talking you down when your *Marine brain* plans ambush drills in the stairwell."

He pulled her in, pressing his lips to her hairline. "Yeah," he said. "That is a good thing."

Behind them, fireworks popped over the harbor, painting the sky in brief, bright flashes. The crowd roared in appreciation.

Hank watched the reflection in Bree's eyes; for the first time in a long time, the explosions did not make his muscles tense. They were just light and sound and a town celebrating being alive.

Tomorrow, they would go back to numbers and security plans and shell companies.

Tonight, he wrapped an arm around the woman who had somehow become home and let himself just stand in the warm dark, the threat still out there but held at bay for a few precious hours.

NINETEEN

By late morning, the paddock had emptied out enough that Copper Moon started to feel like itself again.

Trucks rolled slowly toward the exit, haulers groaning under the weight of bikes and gear. Crew members in half-zipped jackets carried toolboxes and coils of hose, the frenetic energy of race day replaced by a tired, satisfied shuffle.

Bree stood near the entrance to Bay Street with her sketchbook tucked under her arm, the breeze from the harbor tugging at the ends of her hair. The warehouse sat at her back, a solid, waiting presence.

Carmen had texted an hour ago.

Coffee? One last civilized beverage before I hit the highway.

Bree had replied with the name of a little place off Main that did decent lattes and had mismatched armchairs that encouraged lingering. She'd walked to the warehouse first anyway; she needed to touch it, to remind herself why everything felt so very in-between.

She let her palm rest against the rough brick for a second, then headed toward town.

Main Street was in that post-event state where everything looked slightly disheveled; banners drooped, trash cans bulged, shop owners stood in doorways with brooms, sweeping confetti and sand back into rough order. People still wore Cup T-shirts, but the edge of excitement had softened into the sleepy satisfaction of having witnessed something big.

The café bell jingled when she pushed the door open. Inside, the air smelled like espresso, cinnamon, and the faint tang of something citrus. A ceiling fan turned lazily overhead.

Carmen already occupied an armchair in the back corner, a to-go cup on the low table in front of her, her jacket folded neatly over the back of the chair. Without the Dragon logo blazing across her shoulders, she looked younger, or maybe just lighter.

"You're early," Bree said, dropping into the opposite chair.

"I wanted to make sure they didn't run out of the good muffins," Carmen said. "They didn't. I got you one." She nudged a napkin-wrapped bundle toward her.

Bree peeled it back: blueberry, with a crumble top. "You know my weaknesses."

"I pay attention," Carmen said. "Eventually."

They sat in companionable silence for a few sips. Outside, a couple wandered past, arguing good-naturedly about whether to stop at the bookstore or the fudge shop first.

"So," Carmen said at last. "How's it feel? Waking up and knowing you're not going home in two days."

"Terrifying," Bree said. "And... right."

Carmen smiled, a corner of her mouth quirking. "Good terrifying, or the 'I made a terrible mistake' kind?"

"Good," Bree said. She picked at the edge of her muffin. "I talked to my parents again this morning. They'd gone back to the cemetery to tidy up, like they always do after a visitation day. My mom was worried about the safety stuff; my dad wanted to know if the warehouse has decent parking."

"He would get along with my father," Carmen said. "Dads and parking stuff! They seemed okay?"

"They're… catching up," Bree said. "It's like I hit fast-forward on my life and they're trying to watch a replay in slow motion. They'll get there."

"And Hank?" Carmen asked. "Is he holding up under all this responsible-adult pressure?"

"He's pretending he's fine," Bree said. "Which means he's quietly freaking out and making lists in his head. He's meeting with Colby and Brian right now to go over Jason's preliminary numbers. He promised to text me if he needs someone to talk him down from ordering a lifetime supply of security cameras."

Carmen snorted. "I might contribute to that fund."

They sipped again.

"I meant what I said last night," Carmen said eventually. "I'm glad you're staying. Copper Moon's better with you in it."

Bree's chest pinched. "You sure you're not just saying that because you think I'll let you use my studio bathroom when you're in town?"

"That too," Carmen said. "I'm going to need a place to change shoes between events when I'm not hauling Dragons' swag anymore."

"You're really taking the Cup job?" Bree asked.

Carmen nodded. "I said yes this morning," she said. "They're putting the contract together. It's part-time to start; I'll coordinate community activities for Copper Moon and two of the other smaller tracks. It's not glamorous, but it feels... clean."

Bree let out a breath. "I'm happy for you," she said. "And selfishly, I'm relieved. Knowing you'll be nearby sometimes makes this whole staying thing feel less like jumping into the void."

"You've got a whole net down there," Carmen said. "Hank, Colby, Brian, the mayor, and Diaz. Me. You're not jumping alone."

"I know," Bree said. "It's just... a lot of new all at once."

"That's kind of your thing, though," Carmen said. "Big moves. Big feelings."

"Please don't tell my therapist that," Bree said. "She'll get ideas."

They both laughed.

A shadow fell over the table. Bree looked up; Colby stood there, tablet tucked under one arm, hair pushed back like he'd run a hand through it one too many times.

"Hey," he said. "Sorry to interrupt. Hank said you were here; he's on his way. I had something I wanted to float past both of you."

"You want coffee first?" Carmen asked. "I'm buying; I heard you're about to be a homeowner."

He shook his head. "I'm operating on espresso fumes already," he said. He glanced at Bree. "You got a minute for nerd talk?"

"Always," she said. "Pull up a chair."

He dragged over a spare and sat, setting the tablet on the table. The screen showed a spreadsheet; lots of numbers, dotted with red and yellow highlights.

"So Diaz showed me how to access some of the public technical bulletins the series circulates to teams and sanctioning bodies," he said. "Stuff about suspected counterfeit parts, flagged vendors, that kind of thing. I cross-referenced those with purchase records for Einstein's team over the past two seasons."

Carmen's brows rose. "That sounds like a fun Saturday night."

"I know how to party," Colby said dryly. "Point is, there's a pattern. Every time a certain vendor in the Southeast region pops up in the bulletins, there's a corresponding bump in spending from at least three teams, including the Dragons. Bigger than would make sense for just replacement parts."

Bree frowned. "You think they're buying black-market performance kits under the table."

"I think they're paying for something that doesn't show up on the books," Colby said. "The shell company Diaz traced that rental car to? It's linked to a warehouse address in that vendor's town. My guess is the parts come in there, get distributed through 'consultants' who show up at tracks, and disappear again."

"Can Diaz use that?" Carmen asked.

"Maybe," Colby said. "It's not enough by itself; she needs something more solid. But it gives her a place to look. And it gives us a sense of the scope. This isn't just one desperate rider with a hot bottle; it's a whole network."

Bree's stomach tightened. "Are we poking a bigger bear than we realized?" she asked.

"Probably," Colby said. "But somebody was going to, sooner or later. We just made sure it happened before someone died on live TV."

She swallowed. "Great. That makes me feel so much better."

He winced. "Sorry," he said. "That sounded less comforting out loud."

"I get what you meant," she said. "I just... don't love knowing there's a network."

"Diaz said the same," Colby said. "Then she told me to keep my nose in the legitimate side and bring her anything I find. She's looping in state and maybe federal if it looks interstate enough."

"Which it does," Carmen said. "Those guys brag about how many tracks they're working."

Bree folded her hands around her cup; they felt cold, even though the coffee was still warm.

"What do you need from me?" Bree asked.

"I actually wanted to talk out loud to someone with a good head on her shoulders to see if it makes sense."

Bree smiled. "It makes sense."

The bell over the café door chimed. Hank walked in, scanning the room automatically. His gaze found their table; his shoulders relaxed a notch as he threaded his way between chairs.

"Sorry," he said, dropping a hand to Bree's shoulder as he sat beside her. "Jason called while I was paying the bill for breakfast; he wanted to double-check a couple of measurements. I think he sleeps with that tape measure."

"How bad is it?" Bree asked.

"Better than it could be," Hank said. "Worse than my optimistic brain wanted. We're not broke, we're not rich. We're in that fun middle ground called 'tight but doable'."

"Story of my life," Carmen said.

Hank nodded toward Colby's tablet. "You show them your conspiracy board?" he asked.

"Cliff notes version," Colby said.

"Good," Hank said. He glanced at Carmen. "You still heading out today?"

"Yeah," she said. "Heidi and I are caravanning back, she's got to be at work in the morning, and Mom will panic if she thinks we stayed in town just to get murdered by your shadow man."

"Reasonable fear," Bree said.

Carmen finished her coffee and set the empty cup on the table with a soft thud. "All right," she said. "I hate good-byes, so we're going to make this quick."

She stood; Bree and Hank followed.

Carmen hugged Bree first, longer this time, her hand pressing warm between Bree's shoulder blades. "You call me if you need help packing," she murmured. "I can be bribed with coffee and the promise of local gossip."

"Deal," Bree said thickly.

Carmen stepped back and looked at Hank. "You too," she said. "You ever need someone to run interference with a sponsor or tell a pushy fan to back off, you call me. I have a scary voice."

"I've heard it," he said. "I'm grateful it's never been directed at me."

"Keep it that way," she said.

She offered her hand; he took it. Instead of shaking, she squeezed hard for a second, warrior to warrior, then let go.

"See you around, James," she said.

"Count on it," he replied.

Carmen nodded at Colby, pulled her jacket back on, the Dragon logo bright for one last time. As she walked away, Bree imagined painting over it in white, then in a color that belonged to Carmen alone.

"You okay?" Hank asked quietly.

Bree watched the door swing shut behind Carmen. "I will be," she said. "Right now I feel... heavy and light."

"Sounds about right," he said.

Colby closed his tablet. "I'm going to head back to the warehouse and measure that upstairs wall again before Jason puts anything in stone," he said. "If we're dedicating it to Bryn, I want the proportions right."

Emotion pinched her throat. "Thank you," she said.

He shrugged, almost shy. "Feels important," he said, then slipped out with a wave.

That left her and Hank in the corner, the café's quiet chatter filling the spaces their friends had left.

He slid back into his chair, turning it slightly so his knees brushed hers. "I've got meetings with the Cup accountants this afternoon," he said. "They want to go over prize distribution, taxes, all that fun stuff. After that, I'm free. You got any plans that don't involve tracking illegal vendors?"

She smiled. "Actually, I had this idea about you taking me on a real date," she said. "No warehouses, no mayors, no cops. Just you, me, something Copper Moon-y."

His mouth curved slowly. "I think I can arrange that," he said. "You like boats?"

"As long as they stay on top of the water," she said.

"There's a rental place down by the south pier," he said. "Small day boats, nothing fancy. We could take one out, poke around the shoreline, pretend we're the kind of people who know how to relax."

She tilted her head. "You sure you remember how?"

"I've got a vague recollection," he said. "You willing to help me remember?"

She reached across the table and wrapped her fingers around his. "Always," she said.

He squeezed back. "All right then," he said. "You've got a date with the harbor."

H ank stood at the edge of the south pier and tried not to think about all the ways a boat could go wrong.

The rental outfit was a low, weathered shack with peeling blue paint and a hand-lettered sign that said HARBOR HOPPERS. A row of small day boats bobbed at the dock, their hulls knocking gently against rubber bumpers. A teenager in a faded life jacket sat on a stool out front, scrolling on his phone.

"You the guy who called about the afternoon slot?" the teenager asked without looking up.

"That's me," Hank said.

"Boat's fueled and ready," the kid said, jerking his chin toward a twenty-foot center console with a small outboard. "Keys are in it. There's a chart and a radio; if you get into trouble, call Harbor Patrol on sixteen. Bring it back with the prop still attached, and my boss will love you forever."

"Solid motivation," Hank said.

He signed the waiver on the clipboard, trying not to dwell on the words assumption of risk. The Marine in him cataloged wind speed, wave height, and the placement of nearby buoys; the part of him that had grown up spending summers at the lake remembered the feel of a boat under his hands and relaxed a notch.

Footsteps approached on the wooden planks. He turned; Bree walked toward him, hair pulled back in a low knot, sunglasses perched on her nose, a light sweater over her T-shirt. She carried a small canvas bag and her sketchbook.

"You look like a brochure," he said.

She snorted. "If this ends with me falling in, I'm demanding a refund," she said. "And I'm not paying extra for trauma."

"I've got you," he said.

"I know," she replied.

He helped her into the boat, steadying her with his hands on her waist. The brief press of her body against his, the trust in the way she stepped down without looking, made something warm expand in his chest.

He untied the lines, pushed them off from the dock, and eased the throttle forward. The little boat responded smoothly, carving a path through the gentle chop.

They passed the harbor entrance slowly, idling near the breakwater while he got a feel for the engine. Gulls wheeled overhead; a larger fishing boat chugged by, its wake rolling under them.

"Okay?" he asked.

Bree sat on the padded bench beside him, one hand resting on the rail, the other shading her eyes. "More than okay," she said. "This is... beautiful."

Copper Moon spread out around them in a curve of shoreline; the boardwalk, the old lighthouse, the distant sparkle of the Cup banner still hanging near the civic center. From the water, the town looked both smaller and more solid, like a model someone had built with unusual care.

"Where to?" he asked.

"You're the local now," she said. "Show me your favorite view."

He thought for a moment, then angled the bow south, toward a quieter stretch of coast. After a few minutes, the boardwalk noise faded; low cliffs took over, dotted with scrub pine and patches of wild grass. A narrow strip of sand appeared, tucked between two rocky outcrops.

He cut the engine and let them drift.

"This is where I come when the track noise gets too loud in my head, and there are too many people on the beach."

She looked around, taking in the curve of the cove, the way the light hit the water. "You come out here alone?" she asked.

"Most of the time," he said. "Sometimes Brian tags along and complains about the lack of burgers."

She smiled. "I can see why you like it," she said. "It feels... tucked away."

"Protected," he said.

He dropped the small anchor; the rope pulled taut, the boat settling into a gentle sway.

Bree took off her sunglasses and set them beside her. Her eyes were very green in the reflected light. "So," she said. "What do people do on normal dates again? I feel like I skipped a chapter."

"We sit," he said. "We talk. Maybe we kiss, if the mood strikes. We do not have to make any decisions about mortgages or security systems for at least an hour."

She let out a breath that sounded like relief. "That sounds perfect," she said.

He leaned back, draping one arm along the back of the seat. "Tell me something you've never told anyone," he said. "No pressure."

She laughed softly. "That's low pressure to you?"

"Fine," he said. "Tell me something you usually leave out when you tell your story."

She looked down at the water for a long moment, watching the ripples.

"When Bryn died," she said slowly, "everyone kept telling me to take my time, to not rush into anything. 'Grief has no timeline,' they said. So I did what they told me; I froze. I stopped everything. I took the safe jobs, the small pieces, the commissions that did not require me to feel anything. I kept my apartment like a shrine of Bryn's things because I thought moving on meant leaving her behind. We didn't live together, obviously, but I kept all the little things we'd picked up at festivals, art shows, and sister days." She swallowed. "Little secret? Part of me was angry. At her. For dying and leaving me there to deal with life without her."

He stayed quiet; it was the only thing to do.

"I never said that out loud," she said. "I painted around it. I walked it. I wrote it in sketch margins and then scribbled over it. But I didn't say the words. It felt like betrayal."

"It's not," he said.

"I know that now," she said. "But back then, it felt like wanting anything meant I was choosing something over her. So I chose nothing. For a long time."

He traced a slow circle on the back of her hand with his thumb. "And now?" he asked.

"Now I'm trying to choose," she said. "Even when it's terrifying. The warehouse. You. Telling my parents I'm staying. Using the insurance money for something important and for my future. It feels like shouting into the universe that I want a future. That I believe I might have one. I called Charlie and told him I was staying, and he sounded excited for me. He said Bryn would be proud of me. That means everything to me."

He exhaled. "I wonder if he even knows how much you needed to hear that," he said. "That's survival."

"What about you?" she asked, turning the question back on him. "What do you usually leave out?"

He looked out at the horizon, where the water met the sky in a hazy line. "People like the neat version," he said. "Guy goes over there, sees bad things, comes home, rides fast to keep the ghosts quiet. Wins races, gets the girl. They don't want to hear about the nights I drank too much just to sleep, or the time I stood in my parents' garage and thought about turning on the car and closing the door."

Her breath hitched; her fingers tightened around his.

"I didn't," he whispered. "Obviously. Colby walked in, looking for a torque wrench, and saw my face. He dragged me out by the shirt and sat me on the driveway and talked sports statistics at me for an hour until whatever had me by the throat loosened. Then he made me promise I'd tell him if the dark ever got that loud again."

"Did you?" she asked.

"Not every time," he said. "But enough. Every time I thought about not bothering anyone with my crap, I saw his face in that moment, the way it went white, and I made myself say something."

She blinked hard. "Thank you," she said. "For staying."

He smiled, small and a little crooked. "Kind of glad I did," he said. "Otherwise, I'd have missed out on you calling me responsible in public."

"High praise," she said.

The boat rocked gently; a gull cried somewhere overhead. The air tasted like salt and possibility.

"Can I tell you something selfish?" she asked.

"Always," he said.

"I like this," she said. "Not just the boat. You. The way you talk about the dark without pretending it never touches you. It makes me feel less broken."

"You're not broken," he said. "You're... rebuilt. So am I."

Her smile trembled. "Rebuilt," she repeated. "I can live with that."

He leaned in, slow enough for her to see him coming, and kissed her.

It started soft; a question, not a demand. She answered it with the way her hand slid up his chest, fingers curling at the back of his neck. He deepened it gradually, letting the world drop away until there was nothing but the gentle sway of the boat and the press of her mouth against his.

She shifted closer, one knee pressing against his thigh. He set his free hand on her hip, anchoring her. The kiss turned hotter, the kind of slow burn that had his pulse pounding and his brain shorting out in the best possible way.

She broke away on a breath, eyes dark. "This counts as a normal date, right?" she asked, voice a little rough.

"Pretty sure," he said. "We have a boat, a view, and the possibility of getting sunburned in awkward places."

She laughed; the sound slid right into his bloodstream. "Then I'd say it's going well."

"Want to make it better?" he asked.

Her gaze flicked to the small cuddy cabin under the console, then back to him. "Are we about to become those people?" she asked. "The ones who tell stories about that one time on the boat?"

"We don't have to," he said. "We can just sit here and make out like teenagers."

She considered that for a moment, then shook her head slowly. "Seems a shame to waste the scenery," she said.

He kissed her again, harder this time, his hand sliding under the hem of her sweater to find warm skin. She shivered, but not from cold.

They moved together in the confined space of the bench; bodies twisting, hands fumbling with buttons and zippers, the boat rocking gently under them. Every brush of skin, every small gasp from her, ratcheted his desire higher, but he forced himself to stay present, to watch her face, to listen.

"You okay?" he asked when he had her stretched out along the seat, her sweater bunched near her ribs, his hand splayed over her stomach.

"More than okay," she said, breathlessly. "Keep going."

He did, mapping her with his mouth and hands, tasting the salt of her skin, the faint hint of sunscreen. She arched into him, fingers digging into his shoulders, as if she needed something solid to hold on to while the rest of her came loose.

By the time he slid into her, both of them were already half undone. He moved slowly at first, letting them find a rhythm that matched the sway of the boat. She met him, every roll of her hips saying yes, this, more. The world narrowed to the heat between them, the sound of their breath, the quiet slap of water against the hull.

When she came, it was with his name on her lips, her body tightening around him in a way that dragged him over the edge with her. He buried his face in her neck and let go, shuddering, the release as much emotional as physical.

They lay there for a long moment afterward, tangled and flushed, the boat rocking them in a slow, absent-minded cradle.

"This might ruin all future dates," she said eventually, voice muffled against his shoulder. "The bar is very high now."

He laughed, feeling loose and wrecked in the best way. "I'll try to keep up," he said.

"You usually do," she replied.

He kissed her forehead, then reluctantly disentangled enough to help her sit up and straighten her clothes. They made some attempt at tidying themselves, laughing quietly whenever the boat shifted at the wrong moment and threw them against each other again.

Once they were mostly presentable, she leaned back against the rail, closed her eyes, and tilted her face to the sun.

"This feels like cheating," she said.

"On who?" he asked.

"On our past selves," she said. "The ones who couldn't imagine this. Sun, boat, sex, plans that extend beyond next week. Feels a little unfair to them."

"They got us here," he said. "They deserve to be retired somewhere nice."

She opened one eye and smiled. "You going to put them in a home by the sea?"

"Maybe," he said. "Visit them on holidays."

His phone buzzed in his pocket, disrupting the lazy contentment. He considered ignoring it, then thought of Diaz and shell companies and sighed.

"Sorry," he said, pulling it out.

A text from Diaz flashed on the screen.

Got that plate back from the state. Your sedan friend is connected to an active case in three states. You and your girl stay visible when you can; avoid isolated parking lots for a bit. Coffee at Harbor Station tomorrow a.m.? I want to loop you in on what we can share.

He showed it to Bree.

Her mouth tightened, but she didn't flinch. "Well," she said. "That's one way to bring us back to reality."

"You okay?" he asked.

She took a breath, letting it out slowly. "Honestly? Yeah," she said. "I mean, I'm not thrilled there's a multi-state case attached to our shadow, but I'd rather know than pretend."

"Awareness, not paranoia," he said.

"Exactly," she said.

He typed a quick reply.

We'll be there. And we'll stick to well-lit, populated places.

He slid the phone back into his pocket and looked at her. "We can head in if you want," he said. "I don't want you to feel exposed out here."

She glanced around; the cove was still as quiet as it had been, the only other boat a distant speck near the horizon.

"I feel safer here with you than I did in my own apartment a month ago," she said. "Let's steal a little more time before we go back in. Diaz has us; we're not alone in this."

He nodded, some of the tension easing. "Deal," he said.

They sat there together, watching the light play on the water, talking about small things: paint colors, tool brands, whether Brian would survive if they banned neon in the shop. They argued, cheerfully, about the merits of teal in a bathroom; he lost, mostly willingly.

On the ride back in, Bree sat at the bow, hair whipping

in the wind, one hand curved around the rail. She looked back at him over her shoulder, joy clear on her face; the sight lodged in his chest like a promise.

At the dock, he helped her out of the boat and returned the keys. The teenager barely looked up, mumbling "have a nice day" as he shoved the clipboard into a plastic bin.

They walked along the harbor path toward town, hands brushing, then twining. The sounds of Copper Moon grew louder with each step; kids shouting near the fountain, someone busking with a guitar, the clink of dishes from café patios.

"Tomorrow," Bree said, "we talk to Diaz and hear how big this thing really is."

"Yeah," he said.

"After that," she went on, "we go back to the warehouse and argue about whether the shop bathroom can be teal."

He smiled. "I thought we settled that."

"We settled that I'm right," she said. "You'll come around."

He laughed. "Probably."

"And somewhere in there," she said, "we call the realtor Diaz's assistant recommended and start looking at houses."

He looked at her, at the way she said houses like a thing she believed in now. "You sure you want to tie yourself to a mortgage with a guy whose idea of a good time is running spreadsheets on part shipments?" he asked.

"I just had sex with you on a boat," she said matter-of-factly. "I think I'm pretty in."

He felt the grin spread across his face, unstoppable. "Fair," he said.

They reached an intersection; the light changed. Across the street, a dark sedan paused at the stop sign, then turned the other way, disappearing into the flow of traffic. Hank's muscles tightened for a second, then eased when he saw the local dealership plate frame.

Bree noticed; her fingers tightened briefly in his. He squeezed back.

"Awareness," she murmured.

"Not paranoia," he finished.

They crossed together, stepping into the bright patch of afternoon that lay over Main Street. Copper Moon bustled around them: imperfect, messy, alive.

The threat was out there; they both knew it. A network of people who would rather stay in the shadows. A supplier with a grudge. A sedan with a plate that pinged in three states.

But they were not alone.

They had Diaz and her sharp eyes, the mayor and her stubborn pride, Jason and his honest tape measure, Colby and his spreadsheets, and Brian with his unshakeable loyalty. They had a warehouse that was about to become a shop and a studio, a future painted in light and grease and color.

And they had each other.

Hank squeezed Bree's hand and felt her squeeze back, their steps falling into an easy rhythm as they walked toward whatever came next, side by side.

TWENTY-ONE

Bree traced the rim of her coffee cup, watching the steam curl and vanish in the bright light of Harbor Station.

Morning rush had tapered off; a few tables were still occupied by fishermen in faded ball caps and a pair of tourists poring over a paper map like it was a treasure. The big front windows framed the harbor, boats bobbing gently. Behind the counter, the barista worked the espresso machine like an instrument she knew by heart.

Diaz sat across from Bree and Hank, sleeves pushed up, badge clipped to her belt, a notebook open beside her untouched muffin.

"So," Diaz said, tapping her pen against the margin. "We got confirmation from the state last night. Your sedan friend's shell company is on their list. They're running it under organized crime, interstate trafficking, all the fun labels."

Bree's fingers tightened around the cup. "Trafficking in what exactly?" she asked.

"Parts, money, people," Diaz said. "These guys don't

specialize. The plate that pinged here matched sightings near two other tracks. The pattern's strong enough that the feds are sniffing around. Which means they'll move slower, but they'll move big when they do."

Hank's jaw flexed. "What does that change for us?"

"On paper?" Diaz said. "Nothing. You still go to work, you still buy your building, you still take your girl out on dates instead of camping in stairwells. Practically? You keep doing what you're doing. You're careful. You notice things. You call me when something tastes off."

Bree swallowed. "Are we targets?" she asked. "I mean, specifically."

Diaz held her gaze for a long beat. "You're visible," she said. "You embarrassed someone who doesn't like being embarrassed. That makes you interesting. But you're also useful. The more you see, the more you can feed us. And you're not alone out there. That's important."

Useful. The word settled oddly in Bree's chest; not heavy, exactly, but solid.

"What about the locals?" Hank asked. "People around the track, the businesses on Bay Street. Should we be warning anybody?"

"I'm working with the mayor on that," Diaz said. "We're drafting a bulletin that doesn't cause a full-scale panic. 'Hey, watch out for guys selling miracle horsepower out of the back of vans' kind of thing. We'll roll it out through the Chamber, the track, social media."

Bree nodded slowly. "Is it ridiculous that I'm more nervous about meeting with the mayor this afternoon than I am about your federal friends?" she asked.

"Zoning boards have crushed more dreams than the FBI," Diaz said dryly. "Your priorities are fine."

Hank huffed out a laugh. "We should get going soon,"

he said. "Jason's meeting us at the warehouse to go over the latest quote before the mayor brings her binder of rules."

Diaz slid something across the table: a business card with her name, the station number, and a handwritten cell number on the back. "You already have this, but I'm giving it to you again," she said. "Repetition helps."

Bree tucked it into her sketchbook. "Thanks," she said. "For everything. I know we're not your only problem."

"You're the ones trying to fix something instead of breaking it," Diaz said. "That puts you on my priority list." She pushed her notebook aside. "Okay, enough doom. Tell me your good news. Last time we spoke, you'd just told the mayor you were serious about the warehouse."

Hank's mouth curved. "We signed the purchase agreement yesterday," he said. "Bank's processing the loan. Assuming today's meeting doesn't turn into a bonfire, it's happening."

Diaz's smile was brief but real. "Congratulations," she said. "Copper Moon could use a few more people crazy enough to plant roots."

Bree felt a little flutter at that; at the way Diaz said plant roots as if it were a commendation.

"We'll keep you posted," Hank said, standing. "And we'll be here tomorrow. Same time. You'll want a refill on that muffin intel."

Diaz raised her coffee in a half-toast. "Count on it," she said.

The warehouse didn't care about shell companies or federal cases.

It sat at the end of Bay Street, its brick face catching the midmorning sun, windows like tired eyes. The big bay door was rolled up, the inside cool and shadowed. Jason's truck was already parked out front; so was the mayor's hybrid, the chirp of its lock sounding as Bree and Hank walked up.

"Let's hope this isn't a portent," Bree muttered.

Hank's hand brushed her lower back. "We've handled worse than a meeting," he said. "If they tell us the place is secretly full of asbestos, I'll just add hazmat suits to the budget."

"That's not funny," she said.

"Little bit," he replied.

Inside, Jason stood near the center of the open floor, a roll of blueprints in one hand, and a tape measure hooked to his belt. Mayor Liz Harper leaned against a scaffolding plank, tablet in hand, reading glasses perched on her nose.

"There they are," Liz said. "Our new neighborhood investors."

Bree tried to read her tone. It sounded mostly warm, with a hint of mayoral briskness.

"Hey," Jason said. "You two ready for the fun part? Numbers and forms."

"More ready than you know," Hank said.

They gathered near the makeshift table Jason had fashioned from two sawhorses and a sheet of plywood. Jason spread the blueprints out. The lines and measurements looked like a language Bree was only beginning to understand.

"So here's where we're at," Jason said. "Structurally, she's sound. We need to reinforce a couple of beams if we're going to hang the lift you want, Hank, and if you're serious about that mezzanine for Bree's office, we're talking some steel work. Electrical's going to need a full upgrade if you want both the shop and the studio pulling power without tripping every breaker on Bay."

"We knew that," Bree said, her mind leaping ahead to

the Bryn wall, to the way light would fall across it after they opened the second set of windows.

"Right," Jason said. "So the issue isn't the renovation itself. It's what we're allowed to do under current zoning."

Liz tapped the tablet. "This block is zoned light industrial with restricted commercial overlay," she said. "Which is a fancy way of saying you can fix things here, you can ship things, you can sell wholesale. But retail and public assembly uses are limited. Your machine shop? Perfect fit. Your art studio with classes and gallery openings?" She winced. "Not so much."

Bree's stomach swooped. "Wait," she said. "We talked about community events at the council meeting. Nobody said anything about... limits."

"At that point, you were hypothetical," Liz said. "It's easier for a lot of people to nod along when something's hypothetical. When the forms hit their desks, they start reading the fine print."

"So what does that mean?" Hank asked. "In plain English."

"It means," Liz said, "if you do nothing, you can operate the shop as planned, and Bree can have a private studio. She can sell online, ship from here, and do commissioned work by appointment. But you won't be able to host regular public events or have walk-in gallery hours without a special use permit."

Bree's chest tightened. "The whole point was to have a space people could come into," she said. "Workshops. First Fridays. Kids' art days. Bryn's wall isn't just for us."

"I know," Liz said gently. "I remember."

"So we apply for the permit," Hank said. "What's the problem?"

"The problem," Liz said, "is that special use permits for

mixed commercial on this block have been... contentious. We tried it five years ago with a microbrewery. The neighboring property owners fought it hard. Noise, parking, drunk tourists. The board denied it on a three-two vote. Two of those three are still on the board."

Silence dropped like a weight.

Bree looked around the empty space, seeing it for a second the way a stranger might: old brick, oil stains, echoing roofline. A warehouse, nothing more. Her throat burned.

"So they can just say no," she said. "And that's it?"

"They can," Liz said. "But it's my job to make sure they don't do it quietly."

Jason glanced at Bree, then Hank. "Financially, losing that public-facing piece changes the equation," he mumbled. "Your projections assume workshop income and gallery sales. If the board drags this out or denies it, you're looking at a longer road to break even."

There it was. The snag. Not a dramatic collapse, but a tightening of margins, a slow bleed.

For a moment, Bree felt an old reflex twitch. Walk away before it hurts more. Pack up, go back to what you know. Safe jobs, safe spaces, safe grief.

She looked at Hank instead.

He studied the blueprints, jaw set, thumb rubbing idly over the edge of the table. When he lifted his gaze to hers, she saw her own fear reflected there, but also something steadier underneath.

"We knew it wouldn't be simple," he said. "Simple's not our brand."

Her laugh came out shaky. "You sure you're not just addicted to forms?" she asked.

"Absolutely not," he said. "I hate forms. I'm just more scared of living the rest of my life sitting on the sidelines."

That hit her right in the sternum.

Liz cleared her throat. "I'm not neutral here," she said. "I want this. I want you here. Mixed-use like this is exactly what we need if we want this block to be more than just storage units and empty lots. So here's what I propose. We file the special use application this week. I'll get it on the agenda as soon as the board will let me. Between now and then, we build a coalition."

Bree blinked. "A coalition?"

"Letters of support from neighboring businesses," Liz said. "Petition from residents. Testimonials from people who think it's a good idea to have a memorial wall instead of another warehouse full of old boat parts. We show up to that meeting with more than pretty renderings."

A name flashed in Bree's mind. Charlie.

She swallowed. "Could we include Bryn's husband?" she asked. "He's not from here, but this would... matter to him."

Liz's expression softened. "If he's willing to write something or Zoom in, yes," she said. "It would carry weight."

Bree nodded slowly. The lump in her throat grew, but it wasn't all panic now. Some of it was something fiercer.

"I'll call him," she said. "Today."

Jason tapped the blueprint. "From my end, I'll make sure all the plans emphasize safety and noise mitigation," he said. "We show them this isn't some fly-by-night rave spot. We're talking family workshops and engine rebuilds, not all-night EDM."

"Thank you," Bree said.

"We're not walking away, Bree," Hank whispered. "Not

unless every door slams so hard we're bleeding. And even then, we'll probably look for a window."

She looked at him, at this man who'd once threatened to build barricades around her studio because the glass looked flimsy. The terror hadn't vanished. But it sat alongside something else now. Resolve.

"Okay," she said. "Then let's fight for it."

She called Charlie from the sidewalk around the corner, where the noise of Bay Street thinned, and the gulls seemed louder.

Her thumb hovered over his name for a second. Old muscle memory whispered that she should text first, ease into it. She hit call anyway.

He answered on the second ring. "Hey, stranger," he said. "You missed family night. We're very offended."

Guilt pricked; she'd bailed on their standing video chat last week, everything in Copper Moon tilting under her feet.

"I owe you wine and cheese," she said. "How are you all?"

"Good," he said. "Bobby just got accepted into the doctoral program he wanted. Gracie has a boyfriend. Your favorite brother-in-law has mixed emotions about that."

Warmth slid under her ribs at the image. "Oh, I'm so proud of Bobby. He's going to be a fantastic doctor," Bree said. "Sorry about Gracie. But she's bright, beautiful, and full of life. She will always attract boyfriends."

He laughed. "How's Copper Moon? Have you decided what you'll do? You sound... I don't know. Like you're standing on the edge of something."

"I am," she said. "We are."

She told him about the warehouse again, this time in more detail. The Bryn wall. The shop, the studio, the zoning snag. The way the board could say no with three votes and a shrug.

Charlie listened without interrupting, the way he always had.

"So what you're telling me," he said when she finished, "is that you and Hank finally found a way to combine engines and art, and now some retired dudes on a committee are trying to ruin it."

"Pretty much," she said.

"That sounds on-brand for the universe," he said. "What do you need?"

The question hit her harder than she expected. She leaned against the brick, letting it hold her up.

"Liz, the mayor, thinks letters of support could help," she said. "From people who can show this is more than just a business plan. She thought maybe... if you were comfortable with it...you might write something. About Bryn. About why this wall and this space would matter."

Silence hummed for a moment. She almost rushed to backtrack. Tell him it was okay if he couldn't, that she understood.

"Yeah," he said, voice a little rougher. "Yeah, I can do that."

Relief flooded her eyes before it hit her chest. She swiped under her lashes.

"You're sure?" she asked.

"Bree," he said. "My wife died far too young. If there's a chance some good comes out of that, that someone walks into a building ten years from now and sees her name and remembers her for the person she was... I'd crawl across glass to help."

Her breath hitched. "Thank you," she whispered.

"Besides," he went on, lighter now, "if those board guys

say no after reading my heartfelt prose, they'll have to live with the crushing weight of my disappointment. And my mother's. You know how she gets."

Bree laughed, a wet, hiccupy sound. "Terrifying," she said.

"Exactly," he chuckled, "Send me whatever details you want included. I'll write it tonight. And Bree?"

"Yeah?" she said.

"I'm proud of you," he said. "Bryn would be too. Staying, fighting for this...it's big."

She pressed her forehead against the cool brick. "I'm scared," she admitted.

"Of course you are," he said. "Big things are scary. Do it anyway. You've got people in your corner. One of them apparently drives very fast for a living. You're not alone there, even if it feels like it sometimes."

The words Diaz had used earlier stirred in her chest; not alone. Useful. Planted.

"I love you," she said.

"Love you too," he replied. "Now go buy a building. I have to call Gracie and tell her I'm sorry I balked at her having a boyfriend."

That night, back in her hotel room, she curled against Hank on the bed, paperwork spread across the comforter like a second quilt.

"We sign the special use application tomorrow," he said, tapping the page. "Jason's already filled in most of it. Liz added some notes in mayor-ese."

She traced the line where their names appeared together: applicants Hank James, Aubree Spencer.

"You sure you're up for this?" she asked quietly. "If the board drags it out, we could be bleeding money for months."

"We'll adjust," he said. "Scale back some of the initial studio stuff, ramp up the shop work. I can take more rebuild contracts, and Colby can pick up consulting. Brian's already talking about merchandising."

"Brian's always talking about merchandising," she said.

"True," he said. "Point is, we'll flex. I meant what I said today. I'm more scared of not trying."

She studied his face, the faint grooves near his eyes, the steady line of his mouth. He'd carried weight before. Different, heavier. This was a different kind of load. Chosen.

"You make it sound easy," she said.

"It's not," he said. "It's worth it."

He set the papers aside and tugged her closer, rolling so she sprawled partly on top of him. Heat slid between them, familiar and new all at once.

"You know what else is worth it?" he asked.

She smiled, slowly. "I have a guess."

Their mouths met, the connection immediate; the paper rustled beneath her elbow as she braced herself, laughter bubbling up even as desire curled low in her belly.

"Careful," she said against his lips. "If we crumple the application, the board will definitely deny us."

"We'll just tell them we stress-tested it," he murmured.

They didn't go as far as they had on the boat; clothes stayed mostly on, bodies aligned in a slow, rocking rhythm that left both of them flushed and breathing harder, the kind of release that felt like letting go of breath they'd been holding all day.

Afterward, they lay tangled in the dim lamplight, the muffled sounds of the harbor drifting through the slightly open window.

"Tomorrow," he said into her hair, "we'll deal with all of this."

"Tonight," she said, tracing circles on his chest, "we rest. Because apparently being brave is exhausting."

His chest rose and fell under her hand, steady. "Good thing we're in training," he said.

She smiled against his skin, eyes slipping closed. Scared and hopeful, tired and wired. On the edge of something.

And for the first time in a long time, she didn't look for a way off the ledge.

Jason stood on a ladder near the front windows, drill driver in hand, securing a new bracket to the brick. A soft morning light slanted through the dusty glass, catching motes in the air. Someone had propped the bay door open; the harbor breeze cut the lingering scent of oil.

"You're early," Hank said, rubbing a hand over his jaw.

Jason glanced down. "Are you still staying in the hotel?"

"For now. We're beginning the search for a house today. Bree and I are sharing her room, Brian and Colby have the other. We're all tired of hotel living."

They wanted somewhere real. Somewhere theirs.

"Where's your partner in crime?" Jason asked, climbing down. "She usually beats you here."

"Bree had a call with her accountant," Hank said. "They're going over what happens if the board plays hardball. She'll be by after. We sign the special use application at City Hall in an hour."

Jason grimaced. "I'd rather pull all this wiring through twice than sit through a zoning board meeting," he said.

"Same," Hank said. "But apparently grown-ups attend public hearings. It's in the manual."

Jason snorted. "Colby texted," he said. "He's meeting with the bank rep this morning to go over your revised projections. Wants to make sure they see the 'community benefit' section."

"That guy and his spreadsheets," Hank said, a fondness threading through the words. "He probably didn't sleep at all last night."

Jason said. "He was here at six, measuring the front wall again. Muttering about sightlines and light angles for Bryn's wall."

Hank's chest tightened in a way that wasn't all anxiety. "He's putting his heart into it," he said quietly.

"You all are," Jason said.

The drill whirred again from somewhere behind them. Brian emerged from the back hallway, a paint roller balanced on his shoulder like a ridiculous spear, flecks of white on his forearms.

"Good, you're up," Brian said.

Hank gestured at the roller. "Are you starting without us?"

"Prepping the back room," Brian said. "Figured if the board says yes, we'll need a clean space for the office."

He tried to make it sound like a joke. Hank heard the strain underneath.

"You don't have to be here, you know," Hank said. "You could be on a beach somewhere waiting for your Cup bonus wire to hit."

Brian shrugged. "Meh," he said. "I like this beach. And if you two are jumping off a cliff, I'm not gonna stand at the top and wave. Somebody's got to help build the landing pad. And I like it here. I'm house shopping myself since we're all moving here, and between us, Colby snores."

Hank laughed out loud. "You snore too!"

Brian shook his head. "Not like Colby."

Hank looked at Brian, at Jason, at the half-gutted warehouse. The sense of standing in someone else's life crept up on him again; a life where people showed up with rollers and drills instead of rifles.

"Thank you," he said.

"Don't get sappy," Brian said. "You'll ruin my reputation."

Before Hank could retort, his phone buzzed. He checked the screen: Diaz.

Need a favor. You heading out to the warehouse today?

He thumbed a reply. *I'm here now.*

Her response came fast.

We picked up chatter about a "demo day" at the bike shop just out of town on County Road A. Vendor's supposedly showing off new "tuning tech" to some local riders. I'd rather not let our friends recruit on my turf. I've got plainclothes in the area, but you know the scene better than most of my guys.

His throat tightened.

You want me to run interference?

No. I want you to exist as a very visible reminder that fast doesn't mean illegal. Talk to the kids who look interested. If someone you don't know offers you "free samples," remember what I said about alleys. I'll handle the rest.

He slipped the phone back into his pocket.

"Diaz?" Brian asked.

"Yeah," Hank said. "She thinks our friends might be trying to recruit some locals at the bike shop just out of town. Wants us to be another set of eyes."

Brian's mouth tightened. "I hate those guys," he said. "Like parasites."

"Parasites get removed," Jason said. "Eventually."

Hank glanced at the clock on the exposed pillar. "We should move," he said. "If we're late for the application, Liz'll put our heads on pikes outside city hall."

"Free publicity," Brian said.

City hall smelled like floor polish and old paper.

Bree met him at the front steps, hair twisted up, a folder tucked under her arm. The sight of her, even in the mundane setting, still did something quiet and seismic inside him.

"How bad was it?" he asked, nodding at the folder.

"Bad-ish," she said. "My accountant says if the board says no and we operate as just the shop and private studio, we're tight but not doomed. If they say yes, the workshop income gives us breathing room faster. Either way, there's less cushion than we hoped for the first year."

"You still in?" he asked.

She held his gaze. "I called Charlie," she said. "He's sending a letter to the board. He offered to help financially if we needed it, but I told him no. Bryn's insurance already got me this far. I can't..." She trailed off, eyes bright. "I want this to stand because we built it. Not because the universe felt sorry for us."

Pride swelled under his ribs. "Then we build it," he said.

They filed the application with Liz's assistant, a woman with a perpetually frazzled bun and a stack of color-coded folders. Papers were stamped, signatures collected. A date was set for the hearing. Two weeks. Not long, but not immediate either. Enough time for worry to find footholds.

As they stepped back out into the sunlight, Liz caught up with them, breath puffing a little.

"I talked to a couple of the board members this morning," she said. "Unofficially. One's worried about parking, the other's worried about noise. If you can get written support from the café, the marina, and the antique shop, it'll help. They're the ones who usually complain."

"I'll go by this afternoon," Bree said.

"I'll go with you," Hank added.

Liz smiled. "That's the spirit," she said. "And Hank? Diaz mentioned the situation at the bike shop. You going out there?"

He blinked. "Word travels fast."

"In a town this size?" Liz said. "It's practically a sport. Be careful. I'd rather not hold a memorial next to a zoning hearing."

"I plan on avoiding both," he said.

The beach felt different without the Cup banners.

Quieter, for one. The grandstands had been removed, and people walked with their toes in the sand. The air held the familiar overlay of fuel and rubber, but the buzz of big-race tension was gone, replaced by the more relaxed energy.

At the bike shop, local riders wheeled bikes out of pickups and battered trailers; some wore full pro gear, others mismatched leathers. A handwritten sign at the entrance read TEST DAY – SIGN WAIVER INSIDE.

Hank and Brian signed in with an attendant who looked vaguely starstruck but managed to keep the squeaking to a minimum. Hank kept his helmet in his hand, resisting the urge to turn the day into a full-on practice session. They were here to watch, not set lap records.

"There," Brian murmured.

Near the far end of the lot, a small knot of riders had gathered around a van with out-of-state plates. The van's back doors stood open, revealing shelves of neatly lined boxes. A man in a branded jacket leaned against the bumper, talking animatedly, hands moving like punctuation.

Hank's pulse ticked up.

"See the logo?" Brian asked under his breath. "Different from Einstein's guys, but same vibe."

"Yeah," Hank said. "And look at the plates."

Diaz had texted him a partial plate to watch for. The state matched. So did the first three characters.

He felt eyes on him before he saw Diaz.

She stood near the concession stand, plainclothes, hair pulled back. Sunglasses hid her eyes, but the tilt of her head told him she'd clocked the van too. Another man leaned casually beside her, pretending to be absorbed in his phone. Backup.

"You want to ride or work?" Brian asked.

"Work," Hank said.

They walked toward the cluster like they had every right to be there. Because they did.

The man in the jacket noticed them at once; his smile brightened, shark-quick.

"Well, well," he said. "Celebrity drop-in. Hank James, right? Hell of a race last weekend."

Hank gave him a polite nod. "Appreciate it," he said.

"Come to see what the grassroots scene is doing?" the guy asked. His accent had a hint of Northeast, flattened by time. "We're helping some of these kids find a little extra power on a budget."

"On a budget," Brian repeated, tone mild.

"Factory support's expensive," the man said. "We offer alternatives." He flipped open one of the boxes for the riders' benefit. Inside sat a series of glossy brochures and a small metal canister with a generic label.

Nitrous kits didn't look like much when they were disguised. He knew that too well.

"Alternatives that show up on the series bulletins?" Hank asked, gaze steady. "The ones warning about counterfeit parts and 'unapproved chemical enhancements'?"

A couple of the younger riders shifted, glancing between them.

The man's smile didn't falter. "Bulletins are for scared people," he said. "Guys who like their rules neat. Racing's always been about pushing limits."

"Limits," Hank said. "Not safety. That's where you lose me."

Behind the man, one of the riders spoke up. "Hey, my cousin said his buddy got black-flagged for using one of those kits," he said. "His engine nearly blew."

"That's operator error," the vendor said smoothly. "You follow our specs, you're golden."

Hank took a small step closer, enough that the riders had to shift to keep him in their peripheral vision. "You know what happens when your engine goes south at a hundred and fifty?" he asked. "You don't get to blame the guy who sold you the 'budget boost.' You're the one sliding across the asphalt. Or into the wall. Or not getting up at all."

A hush fell over the small group. The vendor's jaw ticked once.

"Look, man," he said. "We're just showing options. Nobody's forcing anybody."

Diaz's voice cut in, cool and conversational. "That's the nice thing about options," she said, approaching. "They go both ways."

The vendor's gaze flicked to her badge, visible for a

heartbeat as she shifted her jacket. Something hard passed behind his eyes.

"Sergeant," he said. "Afternoon."

"Afternoon," she replied. "I'm sure you already checked in with management and provided full documentation on all your products for liability purposes."

He spread his hands. "We're just handing out brochures," he said. "Free country."

Diaz studied the small canister in the open box. "You're right," she said. "It is. It's also my county. And in my county, traveling salesmen of miracle performance solutions need permits. Which I don't see."

"Didn't realize we needed a hall pass for talking," he said.

"You don't," she said. "But you do for commerce. Why don't we go chat about that in my office while these nice folks enjoy their track time?"

The man hesitated. For a second, Hank's muscles coiled, waiting for the wrong choice.

Then the vendor shrugged, all easy charm again. "Sure," he said. "Can't say no to an invitation from law enforcement."

As he moved away with Diaz and her partner, he glanced back once. The look he sent Hank was pure calculation.

Message received. You're in this.

One of the younger riders cleared his throat. "So, uh," he said. "Those things really that bad?"

Hank considered his answer. He could scare them. Lecture them. Or he could tell the truth in a way that might stick.

"I've seen what happens when they go wrong," he said quietly. "I've held helmets that were still warm. There's no podium worth that. You want to get faster? I'll walk your line with you. I'll look at your setup. Hell, I'll introduce you to Colby and Brian. They'll find you a tenth in your suspension before you ever need a bottle."

Brian nodded. "We'll look at your bikes," he said. "Free. No strings. You show up with those kits on your machines, though, we're out. And I will personally tell Diaz you've got a death wish."

The kids looked at each other. Slowly, a few nodded.

"Yeah," one said. "Okay. I'd rather not die for a trophy."

Hank clapped him on the shoulder. "Good call," he said.

By late afternoon, his head buzzed with numbers, forms, and the echo of engines.

Back at the warehouse, Bree stood in the front bay with a clipboard, talking to the café owner from Main and the antique shop couple, a petite woman and a tall man with a collection of pens in his pocket. The marina manager leaned against the doorframe, arms folded.

"...we'd host open studio nights," Bree was saying. "Live painting, maybe a local musician, nothing wild. We're talking nine o'clock end times, not midnight ragers. And the shop side closes earlier than that. We want this block to feel safe. Alive, but safe."

The café owner, Lila, nodded. "More foot traffic's good for me," she said. "If people are coming down for your events, they'll want coffee and dessert. I'm on board."

The marina manager shrugged. "As long as your events don't block the boat ramps, I don't care," he said. "I'll sign whatever Liz wants."

The antique shop owner's husband adjusted his glasses. "My only concern is parking," he said. "We already get the overflow from the ice cream place on busy nights."

"We've been talking about partnering with the civic

center lot," Bree said. "Most nights after six, it sits half empty. If we can get signage and a shuttle going on event nights, it should ease some of that."

"And I'll put parking management in the application addendum," Hank added, stepping up. "We'll have clear hours, clear capacity limits. You'll have all of that in writing."

The man studied them for a moment, then nodded. "All right," he said. "We'll support you. A little noise's better than another empty storefront."

Relief softened Bree's shoulders.

As they trickled out, promising to email letters to Liz's office, Hank caught her eye.

"How'd it go?" she asked softly. "At the track?"

He told her the condensed version: the van, the vendor, Diaz stepping in.

"Any trouble?" she asked.

"Not today," he said. "But that guy knows we're not just going to look away. So do the kids he was trying to hook."

Bree's expression was steady. "Good," she said. "Let him know Copper Moon isn't an easy mark."

He looked at her, at the smudge of primer on her wrist, the clip holding back her hair, the clipboard full of signatures. She'd spent the day convincing neighbors, calling in favors, and building support. While he'd been on familiar terrain with engines and bad actors, she'd been on a different kind of front line.

"You did good today," he said.

"So did you," she replied.

Later, after Brian left with promises to return in the morning and Jason had locked up his tools, they sat on overturned paint buckets in the middle of the empty floor, pizza box between them.

"This doesn't feel real yet," Bree said, looking around. "Like we're squatting in someone else's dream."

"It's ours," he said. "We just haven't filled it in yet."

She took a bite of pizza, chewed thoughtfully. "Speaking of filling in," she said, "I talked to Diaz's assistant. Her cousin's a realtor. She sent over some listings."

He swallowed a mouthful of crust. "Anything promising?"

"A few," she said. "There's a little bungalow near the marina that's in our budget, but it's tiny. There's a farmhouse on the outskirts with land and a detached garage that keeps winking at me, but it needs work."

"Work we could do," he said.

"Work we'd have to do," she countered. "On top of this."

He thought about it. About walking out of a place that smelled like their coffee, their laundry, their life.

"Can we see the farmhouse?" he asked.

She smiled slowly. "Tomorrow afternoon," she said. "Realtor's meeting us there at three."

He leaned back on his hands, looking up at the rafters. "A house and a shop in the same week," he said. "We don't do anything halfway, do we?"

"Nope," she said.

He looked back at her, at the spark in her eyes that looked a lot like fear and excitement braided together.

"I'm in," he said.

"For the house?" she asked.

"For the life," he replied.

Her breath hitched; she looked away for a second, blinking fast, then back.

"Good," she said. "Because I already started a list of potential paint colors for the kitchen."

He laughed, the sound bouncing off bare brick and old beams. For the first time that day, the knot in his chest loosened for more than a moment.

Tomorrow, they'd walk through other people's rooms and try to imagine their own lives there. The board could still say no. The case Diaz was working on could still get ugly.

But sitting on paint buckets in a half-finished dream with grease on his hands and Bree at his side, Hank felt something he hadn't in a long time.

Steady. Pointed somewhere. Moving.

TWENTY-THREE

The farmhouse sat at the end of a gravel lane, its white paint a little tired, its front porch tilting with the weary charm of something that had held a lot of stories.

Bree climbed out of Hank's truck and stood for a moment, letting the place settle into her bones. A line of old maples bordered the property, their leaves just beginning to hint at gold. Beyond the house, a weathered barn and a long, low outbuilding stretched toward a fringe of trees.

"Okay," she said under her breath. "I see why you liked the pictures."

Hank came around the front of the truck, keys jingling. "Good bones," he said. "Kind of like you, Spencer."

She elbowed him lightly. "Flatterer," she said.

The realtor, Kara, waved from the porch. She was Diaz's assistant's cousin, early thirties, efficient, and tablet in hand.

"Hey!" Kara called. "You must be Bree and Hank. I'm so glad the timing worked. The sellers are already out, so we've got the place to ourselves."

Bree mounted the three creaking steps, hand skimming the rail. The porch boards flexed a little, but held. The front door's paint was chipped around the handle, the kind of wear that came from use, not neglect.

Inside, the air held a faint mix of dust and lemon cleaner. The front room opened into a big, square living space with hardwood floors and tall windows that looked out over the fields.

"It's... bigger than I expected," Bree said.

"The square footage is decent," Kara said. "Three bedrooms, one and a half baths. Kitchen's dated, but functional. The big draw is the land and the outbuildings. And the fact that you're still only fifteen minutes from town."

Hank walked to the nearest window, looking out. "I like the light," he said. "And the fact that you can't see the neighbors."

Bree followed, standing beside him. From here, Copper Moon was a suggestion; a faint line of buildings beyond the fields. Close enough to reach, far enough to breathe.

Her mind flicked briefly to her old apartment; the way the walls had closed in near the end, the way the street noise had felt like an accusation, all those lives moving forward while hers held still.

"This feels..." She searched for the word.

"Open," Hank supplied.

"Yeah," she said.

They moved through the downstairs. The kitchen was as advertised: tired cabinets in an orangey oak, laminate counters, and an ancient stove that looked like it had opinions. But the footprint was good. A window over the sink framed the side yard. There was space for a small table or, if she squinted, a long counter where someone could spread out sketchbooks while another someone chopped vegetables.

She pictured herself here, barefoot, paint on her fingers, Hank behind her with a dish towel slung over his shoulder, Brian dropping by with takeout and unsolicited opinions. The image settled with surprising ease.

Upstairs, the bedrooms were simple; sloped ceilings, more hardwood, and closets that would need organization miracles.

"This one could be your studio," Hank said in the smallest room, where the light hit just right. "If you ever get tired of going into town."

She shook her head. "No," she said. "Studio stays with the warehouse. Bryn's wall belongs there. But this could be a good guest room. Or a library."

"A library," he repeated. "Of course."

"What?" she asked. "You don't want floor-to-ceiling bookshelves and a comfy chair to hide in when my parents come to visit?"

His laugh warmed the dusty room. "Okay, I'm sold," he said. "Library it is."

The primary bedroom overlooked the front field. It was empty now, a blank square of possibility. The faint outline of where a bed had once stood marked the floorboards.

Bree walked to the window, pressing her palm against the glass.

"You okay?" Hank asked behind her.

"I keep waiting for the panic to hit," she said slowly. "For the part of me that likes safe, small spaces to revolt. But it's... quiet."

"Quiet's good," he said.

She turned. His face was open, hopeful, and a little

wary, like he didn't quite dare believe this might be theirs. The same look she imagined she wore.

"Hank," she said, heart thudding. "Do you want this? Not just a house. This."

"Life with you?" he asked. "Yeah. I do."

The words landed like a stone in a pond; ripples spreading.

"Okay then," she said, voice steady. "Let's see the barn."

The barn door protested when Hank slid it aside, wood groaning against old metal. The smell inside hit them in a wave: hay, dust, and old oil. Sunlight filtered through gaps in the boards, striping the packed dirt.

Bree stood just inside the threshold, eyes wide. "This looks like every Pinterest board you've ever denied having," she said.

"I don't have Pinterest," he said.

"Sure," she replied.

The main space was big enough to host a small wedding reception, which she suspected would delight her friend Janice if she ever saw it. Loft space ran along one side, accessible by a narrow staircase. The far end had a raised platform where someone had once stored bales.

"It's solid," Hank said, thumping a support post. "Needs some structural love, but it's not leaning in the wrong directions."

Kara leaned against the doorway, arms folded. "The current owners used it mostly for storage," she said. "There's electricity, but it's old. We can request a recent inspection before you put in an offer."

"What would you do with it?" Bree asked Hank.

He turned slowly, taking it in. "Part of me wants to set up a second lift and turn this into a side shop," he said. "But that's probably my inner workaholic talking." He looked up at the loft. "You could hang pieces from those beams. Install track lighting. Host... whatever art people host."

She tilted her head, imagining. "Mixed shows," she said. "Work from other artists, maybe some music, some community events. Not right away. But someday."

"Workshop weekends," he said. "Moto-art retreats."

"You're terrifying," she said. "And weirdly persuasive."

A breeze moved through, stirring dust motes. The barn groaned, but held.

"What about the outbuilding?" she asked, nodding toward the low structure beyond.

"That's the real prize," Kara said. "Come on."

The outbuilding had a concrete floor and three broad bays, each with its own roll-up door. Inside, old shelves lined the walls; a workbench sagged under the weight of rusted tools.

Hank's eyes lit up. "This," he said. "This is where my heart lives now."

Bree laughed. "The shop at home," she said.

"Exactly," he said. "We could set up bikes here, do small jobs on the side when we're not at the warehouse. Or just keep all the personal projects out of your way."

She walked the length of the space, fingertips trailing over the worn wood of the workbench. The idea of coming out here late at night, mug of tea in hand, while Hank fussed over some stubborn engine part, warmed something deep in her.

"Could I have a corner?" she asked.

"You can have half," he said.

"Corner's fine," she replied. "A little table, some storage. A place to work on messy experiments I don't want near the studio. Sculptures. Large canvases. Things that get... splattery."

He grinned. "You planning on splattering the barn?" he asked.

"Maybe," she said. "You won't know until it's too late."

Kara looked between them, something like fondness on her face. "I like seeing people fall a little bit in love with a place," she said. "You're both doing that thing with your eyes."

"What thing?" Bree asked, startled.

"The one where you're already hanging curtains in your head," Kara said. "And figuring out where the coffee maker goes."

Bree felt a blush creep up her neck. "Rude," she said.

"Accurate," Hank murmured.

They sat at the rickety kitchen table with Kara, running numbers.

"The asking price is here," Kara said, pointing at the tablet. "But based on days on market and the inspections we've seen so far, we might be able to come in a little under. You'll need to factor in immediate repairs; roof work within the next five years, some electrical updates, cosmetic stuff."

Bree thought about her accountant's voice: calm and practical. About the tightened margins on the warehouse if the board dragged their feet. About the way her chest had opened up while walking through the house and barn.

"We can do it," Hank said. "If we're smart. Cut back on some non-essentials this year. Eat more frozen pizza and less restaurant sushi."

"You don't like sushi," she said.

"I was trying to sound sophisticated," he replied.

She studied the line labeled monthly payment. It was a lot. And also... not insurmountable. Not compared to what her old rent had been in the city for a shoebox with mystery stains.

"When do you have to decide?" Kara asked. "The sellers are motivated; they've already relocated upstate. They'd like an offer sooner rather than later, but they're not in full panic mode yet. If you want this, we can put in an offer tonight with a financing contingency and an inspection clause. You'll have outs if the house turns out to be secretly infested with raccoons."

"Is that a thing here?" Hank asked.

"Only on Tuesdays," Kara deadpanned.

Bree met Hank's eyes across the table.

"We're already in deep with the warehouse," she said. "We've got the board hearing in two weeks. We're talking about taking on a mortgage on top of construction loans, permits, insurance..."

"I know," he said. "If it's too much, we walk away. We keep looking."

Her old self, the one who'd frozen after Bryn, would have seized that out like a lifeline. This is too big. Too risky. Stay small.

The one sitting here now thought about waking up in that quiet bedroom with light spilling across the floor. Driving fifteen minutes into town to unlock her studio door and breathe in paint and coffee and engine oil. Walking out to the barn on weekends, Hank's laugh echoing off the rafters.

Fear sat alongside something else. Desire, simple and clear.

"I don't want to walk away," she said softly.

Hank's hand curled around hers on the table, warm and steady.

"Then we don't," he said.

She sucked in a breath. "Let's do it," she said to Kara.

"Make the offer. We can negotiate, but... yeah. We want this."

Kara smiled, tapping quickly on her tablet. "I'll get the paperwork started," she said. "You'll have a dozen things to sign by tonight. Tell your wrists I'm sorry."

They were halfway back to town when Bree's phone buzzed.

She glanced at the screen. A text from Liz.

Just read Charlie's letter. It wrecked me in the best way. Thank you for asking him. Board packet goes out tomorrow. You two ready to charm some bureaucrats?

She swallowed past a lump, typing back.

We'll bring cookies if we have to. Thanks for fighting for us.

Hank's phone buzzed. His brows furrowed, then rose, creating arches above his eyes. He turned his phone to her.

Vendor from test day's on a bus out of Copper Moon for now. We've tied his shell company to three other tracks. You kicked a hornet's nest, but you're not standing there alone. Keep building your life. We'll keep closing the net.

She stared at the words.

"They're making progress. She says we kicked a hornet's nest."

"Feels about right," he said.

"I love that she wants us to keep building our life," Bree said. "And that they'll keep doing their job."

He reached over and squeezed her knee. "Sounds like a good division of labor," he said.

That night, back at the warehouse, they sat cross-legged on the floor of what would eventually be her corner of the shared office, laptops open, contracts glowing on screens.

They e-signed the offer on the farmhouse. Two clicks that felt enormous.

"Too easy," she said.

"Don't jinx it," he muttered.

The warehouse around them hummed with quiet; Jason had left the small heater running in the corner, taking the edge off the chill. From upstairs, where Colby had disappeared to tweak his mural projections, came the faint sound of a pencil scratching.

"What if they say no?" she asked suddenly.

"The sellers?" he asked. "Or the board?"

"Both," she said.

He set his laptop aside and shifted closer, knees bumping hers. "Then we regroup," he said. "If the sellers counter too high, we counter back or walk. There'll be other houses. Maybe not with barns that make you make that face, but something."

"What face?" she demanded.

"The one where your eyes go all soft and you start rearranging walls in your head," he said.

She rolled her eyes. "Fine," she said. "And if the board says no?"

"Then we still have a building," he said. "We make the shop thrive. We build the studio side more slowly. We find other ways to get your work in front of people. Pop-ups, collaborations, traveling shows. Diaz'll introduce us to every cop who wants art for their break room. We'll adapt."

"And the Bryn wall?" she asked, voice small.

He cupped her cheek, thumb stroking her skin. "We build it," he said. "Even if we're the only ones who ever stand in front of it. But I don't think that's how it'll go. This town's showing up for you, Bree. For us. Liz, Diaz, Charlie, the neighbors. They don't always agree on anything. The fact that they're aligning here? That's something."

Tears pricked obnoxiously at the corners of her eyes.

She laughed through them. "Why do you always have to be so reasonable?" she asked.

"It's a curse," he said.

She leaned in, kissing him. It started soft and turned quickly, as it always did, into something deeper; that familiar pull that lived somewhere between fear and want.

When they broke apart, breathing a little harder, she rested her forehead against his.

"Do you ever get scared we're building too fast?" she asked quietly. "Shop, studio, house, this... thing between us."

"Every day," he said. "You?"

"Same," she said. "But I'm more scared of stopping."

He smiled, the slow one that made her stomach flip. "Then we keep going," he said. "One permit, one wall, one room at a time."

She nodded, letting that settle. One thing at a time. Not the whole mountain, just the next foothold.

From upstairs, Colby called down, voice echoing. "Hey! Do you two want to see something?"

Hank groaned. "If it's another spreadsheet, I'm staging a coup," he said.

Bree laughed, wiping her face quickly. "Coming!" she called.

They climbed the stairs together.

In the dim light of the upper level, Colby had rigged a projector against the far wall. A sketch bloomed across the brick; the beginnings of Bryn's wall, not in stark portrait realism, but in lines and shapes that suggested motion, flight, wheels. Around her, abstract swirls hinted at tracks, at waves, at something larger.

Bree's heart punched her ribs.

"I know it's rough," Colby said quickly. "And we'll refine it. But I wanted you to see the scale. The way the light hits."

She stepped closer, fingers hovering just shy of the bricks.

"It's perfect," she whispered.

"Give it time," Colby said. "It'll get there."

Hank stood behind her, hand at her waist. "You're doing good work, man," he said.

"This only works if it works for all of us," Colby said. "She's going to have a lot of company up there. Names, stories. Feels like the least I can do."

Bree imagined that future; people standing here, tracing names with their eyes, seeing Bryn not as a tragedy but as a part of something living.

The warehouse, the house, the barn. The case Diaz was building. The network Colby was helping map. Brian's paint-splattered arms. Liz's dog-eared ordinances.

All of it threaded together, messy and imperfect and real.

Bree reached for Hank's hand, fingers lacing with his.

Whatever the board said. Whatever the sellers countered. Whatever their hornet's nest decided to do next.

They had started. They weren't stopping.

"Okay," she said, voice steady. "Let's build a life."

TWENTY-FOUR

Hank sat in the second row of the council chamber, the wooden chair creaking every time he shifted his weight. The room felt too small for the way his chest kept expanding and tightening, like it was trying to be two sizes at once.

Copper Moon's zoning board looked exactly like every other board he'd ever seen: a long table, nameplates, water pitchers, and stacks of papers. Fluorescent lights hummed overhead. A faded photograph of the harbor hung crooked on the back wall.

Beside him, Bree's knee bounced once, twice, then stilled when he laid his hand over it. Her fingers twitched around the folder in her lap, the edges softened from being gripped all morning.

"You're doing it again," he murmured.

"Breathing?" she whispered back.

He fought a smile. "Looking like you're about to bolt."

Her gaze flicked up to his, brown eyes sharp and scared and stubborn. "I'm not going anywhere," she said. "You're stuck with me."

"Good," he said. "Because I signed a lot of paperwork based on that assumption."

She huffed out a quiet laugh, some of the tension in her shoulders easing.

Across the aisle, Liz Harper stood near the end of the board table, conferring with the clerk. She wore her usual mayoral armor: crisp blazer, sensible heels, the kind of calm that made people think rules were a suggestion she'd already considered and adjusted.

Behind them, the chamber was fuller than he'd expected for a weekday afternoon. Lila from the café sat near the back, hands folded over her purse. The marina manager slouched in a corner, arms crossed. The antique shop couple sat together, the husband already taking notes. Jason lounged against the wall near the door, work boots planted wide, hair still dusty from the job site.

Colby and Brian had squeezed into the row behind Hank and Bree. Brian's knee bumped his chair rhythmically. Colby's gaze tracked the exits, the sprinkler heads, the wall sconces, all the quiet habits Hank had come to recognize from someone who spent his life thinking about worst-case scenarios.

"You know there's a fire extinguisher every twenty feet in here, right?" Hank murmured without turning.

"Yeah," Colby said. "I was just judging them."

"On what scale?" Brian asked under his breath. "One to raging inferno?"

"One to 'I'm going to have a chat with whoever did this layout,'" Colby said. "Those exit signs are a mess."

It should not have been comforting. Somehow, it was.

The chair at the center of the board table scraped back. Elaine Drummond, chair of the zoning board, tapped her microphone.

"All right," she said. "Let's call this meeting to order. First item, continuation of application ZB-24-16, special-use permit for mixed commercial at 412 Bay Street. Applicants, Hank James, Colby Landon, Brian Knight, and Aubree Spencer."

Hank felt Bree's breath hitch.

"That's us," she whispered unnecessarily.

Liz stepped forward. "Madam Chair," she said. "I'll be speaking in support of this application, along with several community members. The applicants are here to answer questions."

Elaine nodded, adjusting her glasses. "We've received the updated packet from your office," she said. "Including letters of support, traffic estimates, and revised floor plans. We'll start with a summary for the record, then move to public comment."

The municipal part blurred a little; Liz was laying out the basics in clear, steady language. Existing zoning, proposed use. Machine shop in the rear, art studio, and memorial wall upstairs. Projected hours, parking plan, noise mitigation.

Bree's hand found Hank's on her knee. He laced their fingers and rubbed his thumb across her knuckles, more for himself than for her.

"...and in addition to the economic impact, there's a cultural and emotional component," Liz was saying. "Ms. Spencer's proposal for a memorial wall has already drawn interest from families who've lost loved ones. You'll find one such letter at the front of your packets."

Chairs creaked as board members flipped pages.

Hank knew exactly which letter sat on top. He'd watched Bree read it three times last night, tears drying on her cheeks, the laptop glow painting her skin.

"Dr. Charles Bennett," Elaine read aloud, skimming. "Husband of the late Brynna Bennett. He's quite eloquent."

"He's terrifying in academic debates too," Bree muttered, voice thick.

Elaine cleared her throat. "We'll move to public comment," she said. "If you wish to speak, please come to the podium, state your name and address for the record, and keep your remarks to three minutes."

There was a brief, awkward pause, then Lila stood. She smoothed her dress, walked to the podium, and smiled at the board.

"I'm Lila Owens," she said. "I own Harbor Station Café on Main. I'm here because I like it when my morning regulars have somewhere else to walk after they finish their coffee."

A ripple of chuckles moved through the room.

"I've read the packet," Lila went on. "My main concern was parking, and the plan Mayor Harper mentioned covers that. The kind of business these four are proposing is exactly what we've all been saying we want more of, every time we complain about empty buildings. I want more lights on in my neighborhood after dark, not fewer. I want teens and tourists walking between a shop, a café, a marina, not slipping between warehouses. So I'm asking you to say yes."

She stepped back. The marina manager took her place.

"I'm Tom Reyes," he said. "I run the marina. As long as they don't block the ramps or host heavy metal festivals at midnight, I'm fine. If their events bring more people down to see the boats and the water, even better. That's it."

He shrugged, but his signature on the letter had meant something. It said so on Elaine's face as she jotted a note.

A few more speakers followed; the antique shop couple,

talking about foot traffic and mutual benefit. An older man Hank didn't know, who owned a small machine business two streets over, said he liked the idea of another shop that took safety seriously.

Then a woman in a floral blouse stood, expression pinched. "I'm Susan Meyers," she said. "I live on Harbor View Court. I'm not against small businesses. But I remember the microbrewery mess. Cars lined up and down our street, drunk people yelling, trash on the sidewalks. We moved here for quiet. I see 'events' and 'classes,' and I worry we're inviting that nightmare back."

Bree's shoulders tightened next to him.

Liz stepped to the side of the room, hands clasped loosely. Hank could practically feel her waiting to speak, to draw a line between their proposal and the nightmare in Susan's mind.

Susan went on. "And there's the racing," she said. "We all got those bulletins from the track last week. Illegal parts, chemical stuff. That van business. I don't want that element getting a permanent foothold on Bay Street."

Now the room really stilled.

Hank felt Brian's attention sharpen behind him. Colby's breath came a little more slowly, the calm he used when someone on scene started to spiral.

He stood before he could overthink it.

Bree's head jerked toward him. "Hank," she whispered.

"I've got it," he said quietly.

He made his way to the podium, aware of every step. The microphone squeaked when he adjusted it. He cleared his throat.

"I'm Hank James," he said. "Current address is a hotel room on Harbor View, future address, if you'll have us, is

412 Bay and my girlfriend and I have put an offer in on a farmhouse just out of town."

A few soft laughs. Good.

"I'm also the guy in some of those bulletins," he said. "Not the illegal part. The part where I called series officials when we found them."

Susan's mouth pursed. "You race," she said. "You're part of that world."

"Yes, ma'am," he said. "I am. I've also been the one calling next of kin after crashes. I've picked friends up off the asphalt. So when I saw those guys trying to sell dangerous shortcuts at a local test day, I didn't shrug and walk away. I called Sergeant Diaz."

He gestured toward the back of the room. Diaz sat by the door in plainclothes, sunglasses perched on her head, expression steady. She lifted a hand in acknowledgment, but didn't move from her seat.

"I'm not interested in bringing that mess to Copper Moon," Hank said. "Our shop is exactly the opposite. We want to be the place kids bring their bikes when they don't know what they're doing and don't want to die figuring it out. We want to be the ones teaching them there's a difference between fast and stupid." He let that sit for a second. "As for events, you've got our proposed hours. You've got our parking plan. We're talking evening workshops that wrap up by nine, not keg parties. I'm too old for keg parties, and she hates sticky floors."

Bree snorted softly behind him.

"We can't promise nothing bad will ever happen on Bay Street," he said. "Nobody can. But I can promise you we're not coming here to tear it up and move on. We're buying a building. We're under contract on a house. My business partners are looking at real estate listings instead of race calendars. We're in. And if you give us this permit, we'll spend the next twenty years proving you didn't make a mistake."

He looked at the board, at Susan, at the collection of neighbors and officials and friends who'd somehow become part of this life he wanted.

Then he stepped back from the mic.

Diaz rose. "Sergeant Marisol Diaz, Copper Moon PD," she said at the podium. "I'm not here to tell you how to vote. That's your job. I'm here to give you my perspective on what they've already done for this town."

She outlined it simply: their cooperation with the investigation, the way Hank and his crew had made themselves available for questions about the racing world, and the incident at the test day.

"You all know we've had outside actors sniffing around," she said. "People who see small towns as easy pickings. What I need, as your cop, are more locals who pay attention and care, not fewer. These four pay attention. They call when something's wrong. They also talk to the kids I can't always reach in uniform. That matters. From a safety standpoint, a well-run business on a dark block is almost always a net positive."

She stepped back. Public comment closed.

The board retreated into a short deliberation, though it did not feel short. Hank sat again, Bree's hand crushed in his.

"You did good," she whispered. "Even the part about sticky floors."

"Truth is a powerful tool," he murmured.

Colby leaned forward. "You hit the 'we're buying, not renting' line exactly right," he said quietly. "People up there like commitment."

Brian nodded. "Plus, Diaz looked like she wanted to adopt you," he added. "Should play well."

The door to the small side room opened sooner than Hank expected. The board members filed back to their seats.

Elaine cleared her throat. "After reviewing the updated materials and listening to public comment, the board finds that the proposed use is consistent with the comprehensive plan, provided certain conditions are met," she said. "We're prepared to vote on approval of the special use permit with conditions attached."

Bree's fingers froze in his.

"Conditions," Brian muttered. "Here we go."

Elaine read them: adherence to submitted hours, limits on amplified outdoor sound, cooperation with the parking plan Liz had outlined, and coordination with the civic center for overflow lots on event nights. Annual review for the first two years.

Nothing fatal. Nothing they hadn't already planned to do.

"All those in favor?" Elaine asked.

Hands rose around the table. One, two, three. Four.

"All opposed?"

One hand lifted, the board member who'd glared hardest at the word "events" in the packet.

"Motion carries," Elaine said. "Special use permit ZB-24-16 is approved with conditions."

For a second, the words didn't quite penetrate. Then they did.

"Approved."

Bree exhaled like she'd been kicked. Her shoulders sagged, then straightened.

Hank leaned in, pressed his mouth to her temple. "We did it," he whispered.

Her eyes shone. "We did it," she repeated.

Behind them, Brian let out a whoop that he tried to smother into a cough. Colby clapped once, hard, like he was sealing the moment.

Liz slid into the row in front of them, turning to grin. "Welcome to the charmingly bureaucratic side of Copper Moon," she said. "You've got your permit. I'll have the signed copy for you this afternoon."

"Thank you," Bree said, voice shaking.

"Don't thank me," Liz said. "You brought half my talking points with you in person."

Hank's phone buzzed in his pocket. He fished it out, thumbed the screen.

It was a group text from Kara.

Offer accepted. Sellers agreed to your terms with a small roof-repair credit. Congratulations, homeowners. I'll call with details.

He stared at the words.

"Well?" Bree asked, trying to read his expression.

He turned the phone so she could see.

Her hand flew to her mouth. "Oh my God," she breathed.

Brian leaned over their shoulders. "No way," he said. "House and shop in the same day? That's showing off."

Colby whistled low. "You two don't play," he said.

Hank felt lightheaded for a second. Paperwork and permits, two different sets of signatures, and underneath all of it, the simple truth.

They'd just anchored themselves here in two directions at once.

Copper Moon wasn't a pit stop anymore. It was the map.

The celebration was exactly the opposite of fancy and exactly what he'd wanted.

Jason had strung old café patio lights across the front half of the warehouse, cords looped over beams. The bulbs cast a soft, warm glow that turned the bare brick golden and made the exposed ceiling less intimidating.

Someone, probably Lila, had sent over two huge boxes of mixed takeout: sandwiches, salads, and a tray of brownies. A cooler in the corner held beer, sparkling water, and the cheap champagne Brian had insisted on.

They'd dragged in a handful of mismatched chairs from the office area and turned a sheet of plywood on sawhorses into a table. The bay door was rolled up partway, the harbor breeze sweeping in, carrying the distant slap of water against hulls.

Hank stood near the doorway for a moment, taking it all in.

Bree laughed at something Lila said, her head tipped back, paint smudge still on her wrist from earlier. The soft light threaded through her hair, pulling out amber notes. Brian perched on an overturned crate, chopsticks in hand, re-enacting a dramatic moment from the board hearing with too much flair.

"...and then Hank was like, 'I'm too old for keg parties,' and Elaine actually smiled," Brian said. "I thought the fluorescent lights were going to flicker."

"They did," Colby said, leaning against a pillar with a beer. "You didn't see it because you were texting half the firehouse about the drama."

"I was inviting them to our inevitable grand opening," Brian protested. "Marketing never sleeps."

"You texted them a photo of the board," Colby said.

"It was a good angle," Brian said.

Diaz joined them straight from shift, still in her duty boots, badge visible at her belt. She carried a foil-covered tray that smelled like empanadas.

"Don't get used to this," she said, handing it to Bree. "I don't cater for all my informants, just the ones who sign up for lifetime service."

Bree grinned. "We prefer 'partners,'" she said.

Diaz's eyes softened. "You earned that today," she said. "All of you."

"How bad's the hornets' nest?" Hank asked, keeping his voice low as he took a beer from the cooler.

Diaz rolled one shoulder. "Buzzing," she said. "We've got enough to keep the state interested. Our friend from the test day has been encouraged to find employment far from my jurisdiction. It's not over, but the net's tightening. You don't need to carry it around with you."

"We're not," he said. "We've got sheetrock and beams to carry instead."

"Good," she said. "Be the boring business owners who call me when something's wrong. That's the dream."

Lila popped the champagne with more enthusiasm than skill; foam sprayed, everyone laughed, and Hank found himself with a paper cup of cheap bubbles in hand.

Liz raised hers. "To Copper Moon's newest permanent residents," she said. "May your inspections be smooth, your parking lots orderly, and your engines well-tuned."

"Hear, hear," Jason said.

They drank. The champagne was terrible. It tasted perfect.

Conversation bloomed in pockets. Jason and Colby argued cheerfully about the best way to reinforce the mezzanine for both art and office load. Brian and Lila debated flavors for future "Bryn Wall" themed cupcakes. Diaz listened, smiling in that small, fierce way that meant she'd tuck these details away as proof that the town she fought for was worth it.

Hank drifted through the clusters, topping off drinks, grabbing slices of pizza, and fielding questions about house repairs from Jason, who demanded photos of the barn.

He kept finding his gaze returning to Bree.

She moved among their friends with a kind of surprised ease, like she hadn't realized she knew this many people who'd show up for her on a weeknight. Every time she laughed, that tight knot in his chest loosened a little more.

At some point, music appeared, tinny from someone's phone speaker. Not loud enough to violate any conditions, but enough to set a rhythm under the conversation.

Colby dropped down onto the crate beside Hank. "You look like a guy who just realized his entire life pivoted in twelve hours," he said.

"That obvious?" Hank asked.

Colby took a sip of beer. "I've seen that look before," he said. "Usually after a big call. Everything's the same, but you're not."

"You good?" Hank asked, turning the question back on him. "You've been kind of quiet."

Colby's mouth twitched. "Just thinking," he said. "Got a text from my captain this afternoon. There's talk of openings at the station up here. They know I've been looking at Copper Moon. Asked if I wanted an introduction."

"Do you?" Hank asked.

Colby stared at the string lights for a long moment. "I love my crew," he said. "Walking away from that feels like leaving family. But I'm getting tired of sleeping in a city that never shuts up. Tired of watching the same apartment go up in smoke because the landlord ignored all the warnings." He tipped his head toward the warehouse. "This feels like the right kind of work. And if I can run a few calls here while we build this place up, be useful in both directions, it's hard to argue with that."

"You'd make a hell of an asset for this town," Hank said. "Firehouse and shop both."

Colby's smile turned wry. "You just want someone to yell at you about your electrical choices."

"I want someone who knows how many extinguishers we actually need," Hank said. "And who'll tell me if the sprinkler layout sucks."

"Already started that list," Colby said. "Sent it to Jason. He pretended to be offended."

Hank laughed. "Of course he did."

He sobered, nudging Colby's shoulder. "Seriously," he said. "Whatever you decide about the department, you've got a place here. You know that, right? After all, you're one-quarter partner. You can be a silent partner, or you can be the man you are, doing the work you do."

Colby's jaw flexed, eyes going a little bright before he blinked it away. "Same goes for you," he said. "If you ever decide to stop throwing yourself around racetracks at illegal speeds, we'll find you a hobby that doesn't involve broken bones."

"Like woodworking?" Hank asked. "Knitting?"

"Probably not knitting," Colby said. "Those needles are dangerous."

They fell into easy silence for a minute, watching Bree talk with Diaz at the far end of the space. Bree's hands moved as she spoke, sketching imaginary lines in the air.

"This is good," Colby said quietly. "You two. This place. It's... right."

"Yeah," Hank said. "It is."

The night stretched in a warm, looping way. People drifted out slowly. Tom from the marina had an early morning maintenance window. Lila had to prep the café for the breakfast rush. Jason left with promises to be back at dawn to start framing.

Liz hugged them both tightly. "Take fifteen minutes tomorrow to enjoy this before you dive back into forms," she said. "That's an order."

Diaz left last, pausing in the bay door.

"You know how to reach me," she said. "Not just for work. This many big changes at once can knock people sideways. If you need a sounding board who isn't personally invested in your paint choices, my office is open."

"Thanks," Bree said. "We might take you up on that."

When the last car pulled away, and the warehouse settled into a gentler quiet, Hank turned off all but one string of lights. It painted a soft halo over the center of the room.

Bree stood in it, barefoot now, her shoes kicked into a corner, curls escaping her clip.

"Everyone's gone," he said.

"I noticed," she said, smiling.

He walked to her, stopping close enough that their toes nearly touched.

"How's your panic level?" he asked softly.

"Strangely low," she said. "High on the 'holy crap, we just signed our lives to this town' scale. But the panic's... quiet."

He tucked a loose curl behind her ear. "Good," he said. "Because I've got it all scheduled for next week."

She laughed, leaning into his touch. "You realize this is the part where a normal person would say we should get some sleep," she said. "Big day tomorrow. Contractors and realtors and mortgage people."

"Lucky for you, I'm not normal," he said.

"No," she said softly. "You're not."

He kissed her, slow and sure. The taste of cheap champagne and pizza, and something that felt a lot like the future, slipped between them.

The string lights hummed softly overhead. Outside, somewhere beyond the open bay, the harbor whispered against the shore.

Hank rested his forehead against hers when they broke apart.

"We did it," he said again, needing to hear it out loud.

"We did," she said. "And tomorrow we keep doing it."

"Tomorrow," he agreed.

He had no idea exactly how they'd juggle construction schedules, loan payments, racing commitments, and house repairs. There would be arguments and setbacks and nights where this string of lights was replaced by flickering work lamps and exhaustion.

But standing here, in the echoing center of the life they were building, Hank James felt something he hadn't felt in a very long time.

Home was no longer an idea he'd lost in the rearview mirror. It was right here, watching him with green eyes and paint on her wrist, asking him to stay.

He planned to.

TWENTY-FIVE

The morning after the party, the warehouse smelled like leftover pizza, cold concrete, and the faint ozone of overworked fairy lights.

By early afternoon, it smelled like primer and coffee instead.

Bree stood barefoot on a drop cloth in the upstairs space, brush in hand, the light from the big windows stretching long across the floorboards. Someone, probably Jason, had pulled out the last of the old shelving and swept; a fine dust still clung to the corners, but the bones of her future studio were visible now.

In the far corner, a stretched canvas leaned against the wall, the paint on it still drying. Bryn's face emerged there in color and motion, not as Colby's grand mural concept, but as a more intimate study; eyes crinkled in laughter, hair tucked under a sun hat, the suggestion of the track behind her. It wasn't finished, not yet, but it was far enough along that Bree could step back without wanting to tear it in half.

Today, though, was for something else.

Two easels stood in front of the windows. One held a

blank canvas she'd primed last night. The other held the painting she'd started at the hotel weeks ago, in that liminal space between the race and everything that came after.

Hank on the track.

She'd painted him from memory, from slow-motion replay, from the way her chest had clenched watching him lean into those corners like he'd been born there. Then life had rushed in: investigations, permits, meetings, and house tours. The canvas had followed, propped against walls and tucked in corners until it finally found its place here, in the light.

Now she stood in front of it, brush hovering.

The basics were already there. His body tucked low over the bike, the curve of the fairing, the suggestion of the crowd in blurred strokes. But the faceplate of his helmet was still rough, the background too clean. It felt like the painting of a man racing, not of the man she'd come to know off track; the one who triple-checked her locks and teased her into breathing when fear pinched too tight.

She wanted both.

Her phone chimed from the crate she was using as a side table. She ignored it. The outside world could wait.

She dipped her brush in a thin wash of color and met the canvas where the helmet curve framed his gaze. She added depth there, shadows that suggested the intensity that had pulled her in from the beginning. Small strokes, barely there, that hinted at vulnerability under that focus.

She worked in slow layers, stepping back often. The background shifted as she added movement; streaks of color that suggested speed without pinning it down to specific banners or logos. The track became less a place and more a feeling.

After an hour, she set the brush down and circled the easel.

It looked like him. Not in the literal sense, though anyone who followed the series would know who she'd painted. But in the way that mattered.

The risk. The joy. The weight he carried and the defiance with which he kept getting back on the bike anyway.

Her throat tightened.

"Hey," a voice called from downstairs. "Are you planning on letting me in your secret upstairs club, or do I need special clearance?"

She smiled, wiping her hands on the rag draped over her shoulder. "Up here," she called.

Boots thudded on the stairs. Hank appeared a moment later, one hand on the rail, the other carrying two takeout cups of coffee.

He'd shed his jacket somewhere, leaving him in a faded T-shirt and jeans, his hair still damp from a quick shower at the hotel. There was a smudge of something on his forearm, probably grease; she was starting to think it was a permanent feature.

"Delivery," he said, holding out a cup. "Café Lila's finest. She insisted I bring her regards and threatened bodily harm if you don't come by for pie later."

"I'm not sure that's how that works," Bree said, taking it. "But I'm not going to argue with pie."

He stepped beside her, looking around. "It's starting to look like a real place up here," he said. "Less haunted storage, more artist lair."

"That's the goal," she said.

He turned his attention to the easels. His gaze landed first on Bryn's canvas in the corner. He walked over, stopping just short of touching it.

"She's almost here," he said softly.

Bree exhaled. "Yeah," she said. "I kept trying to make it perfect. Then I remembered that's not the point."

"What is?" he asked, still studying the painting.

"That she's more than the worst thing that ever happened to her," Bree said. "That she was a person who laughed and swore and hogged the blankets. Not just a sad story about her last days."

"And this helps," he said.

"It helps me," she said. "I hope it helps other people too."

He nodded, then turned, eyes catching on the second canvas.

When he realized what he was looking at, he stilled.

"Is that... me?" he asked, almost cautiously.

She felt suddenly shy, which was ridiculous. They'd shared beds, showers, a thousand moments more intimate than this. Yet something about showing him how she saw him made her palms sweat.

"Yeah," she said. "It started as a way to keep from spiraling while you were out there. I wanted to catch the way you looked on the track, like it's the one place your brain quiets down."

He stepped closer, mug dangling forgotten from his fingers.

The painted version of him leaned into the corner, background streaked in color. She'd deepened the shadows around his helmet, caught the angle of his shoulders, the way his hands held the bars like they were both weapon and lifeline.

"It's not exact," she rushed on. "I took some liberties. The crowd's just a suggestion, and I left off the sponsor logos because I didn't want to think about contracts. But..."

"Bree," he said quietly.

She shut up.

He set his coffee on the crate beside hers and reached out, hovering his hand over the edge of the frame like he wanted to touch it but didn't quite dare.

"You made me look..." He shook his head, searching for the word. "Whole," he said finally. "Like I'm not just running from something."

"That's because you're not," she said. "Not anymore."

His jaw flexed. His eyes stayed on the painting, but his voice had that rough edge she'd learned meant something important was scraping against his ribs.

"I've seen a lot of photos of myself on bikes," he said. "Video, slow-mo replays, all that. They always look like someone I used to know. Like I'm watching a stranger who happens to have my name."

He swallowed.

"This feels like me," he said. "The me you see. I didn't know how badly I wanted to know what that looked like."

Her chest pulled tight. "I could do another one," she said, half joking. "Something less dramatic. You on a stool in the shop, yelling at Brian about torque specs."

"First of all, I don't yell," he said. "I passionately discuss." He glanced at her. "Second, this is enough. More than."

She stepped closer, close enough that his shoulder brushed hers.

"Good," she said. "Because I planned on hanging this somewhere you can't ignore it."

"Like where?" he asked.

She considered. "House hallway," she said. "Top of the stairs. So every time you leave, you remember who you are.

And every time you come home, you remember what you're walking back to."

His breath hitched. He turned from the painting to her, really looking now.

"You want me in your hallway?" he asked.

She rolled her eyes. "I've already got you on my mortgage," she said. "Kind of hard to walk that back."

Something in his face softened, then set. Resolve, sure as any line he'd taken at ninety miles an hour.

He took a step back, just enough space to move. His hand went into his jeans pocket.

Her heart did something strange.

"Hank?" she asked.

"You remember when we sat in that awful plastic chair waiting for tech inspection," he said. "Before any of this. When I told you I didn't know how to want things that lasted."

She did. It was burned into her memory, the smell of dry erase and gas, the way his voice had gone quiet.

"I remember," she said.

"I've been thinking about that a lot," he said. "Apparently, self-reflection is a side effect of zoning hearings."

She snorted, but her pulse thudded hard against her ribs.

"I used to think wanting things was the dangerous part," he went on. "If you didn't want anything too much, you couldn't lose it. Then you walked in front of me on the racetrack, in this tiny harbor town, and every theory I had went out the window."

He pulled his hand from his pocket.

A small velvet box sat in his palm.

Her mouth went dry. "Hank," she whispered.

He smiled, nervous and a little wild. "I thought about

doing some big speech at the board meeting," he said. "Or down at the harbor, with a sunset and at least three bystanders filming. But that felt wrong. This feels right."

He went down on one knee on the drop cloth, between splatters of primer and coffee rings.

Her world narrowed to him; the curve of his shoulders, the way his fingers tightened around the box, the deep, steady look in his eyes.

"Aubree Spencer," he said. "You're the bravest person I know. You stayed when every part of you wanted to run. You took my chaotic life and somehow made it feel like it points somewhere. I want to spend the rest of my days building things with you. Walls, engines, whatever. I want to wake up in that creaky farmhouse and trip over your paint tubes on the way to the coffee maker."

He opened the box.

The ring inside caught the light; a simple silver band, a round stone that wasn't huge but sparkled like it meant it.

"I don't know what the next race season looks like," he said. "I don't know how many permits we'll have to file or which pipe in the house is going to burst first. But I know I want you there for all of it. Will you marry me?"

Her vision blurred. For a heartbeat, she couldn't see the ring at all, just color and light and the memory of Bryn saying "You deserve a big love too," on some long-ago night.

She'd thought that promise went into the ground with her sister.

Apparently, it had just taken the long way back.

"Yes," she said, the word spilling out before her brain could wrap its arms around it. "Of course, yes."

Relief crashed across his face, chased quickly by joy. He

exhaled a laugh that sounded half disbelieving, half triumphant.

"Okay," he said softly. "Okay."

She held out her hand, fingers shaking. He slid the ring onto her finger, the metal cool against paint-stained skin.

It fit like it had been waiting there all along.

She pulled him up before he could say anything else and kissed him, hands fisted in his shirt. The coffee mugs wobbled on the crate, sloshing a little, but neither of them cared.

He kissed her back with everything he'd just tried to put into words and more besides; promises and apologies and wild, startling hope.

When they finally broke apart, breathing hard, he rested his forehead against hers.

"You sure?" he asked, voice rough.

She laughed through the tears. "Ask me again when I'm trying to match paint colors to your torque wrench collection," she said. "But yeah. I'm sure."

He kissed the corner of her mouth, her cheek, the spot just below her ear that made her knees go unreliable.

"Good," he murmured. "Because I'm not returning that ring."

She pulled back enough to look at him. "Where did you even get it?" she asked, swiping at her face with the back of her wrist.

He winced. "You're going to laugh," he said.

"Try me," she said.

"Harbor Jewelers," he said. "I went in for batteries for my watch and walked out having an intense discussion about settings with a woman named Mabel who's apparently known Liz since kindergarten."

Bree clapped a hand over her mouth. "You went ring

shopping with Mabel," she said, delighted horror and affection twined together.

"Look, she had opinions and pictures," he said. "I panicked."

"You did good," she said, looking at the ring again. "It's perfect."

He relaxed, shoulders dropping. "Mabel will be relieved," he said. "She threatened to hunt me down if you hated it."

"I'm terrified of her, and I've never met her," Bree said.

"You should be," he said.

She laughed, the sound bubbling up, untangled from fear for the first time in what felt like forever.

Her phone chimed again. She sighed, reaching for it.

"Do not be Diaz with an emergency," she muttered. "I am having a moment."

It was Diaz.

She opened the text anyway.

State's filing preliminary charges against the shell company guys. Test day vendor flipped. You two are officially listed as cooperating witnesses, not targets. Keep your heads up and your doors locked. And go live your lives.

Bree's chest softened. She typed back with one hand, the other still curled unconsciously to feel the ring.

We plan to. Thanks for keeping the monsters out of the corners.

A second message buzzed in almost immediately. This one was from Kara.

Inspection scheduled. Sellers are fixing the roof issue. You're on track for closing in four weeks, and they've agreed to let you rent from them immediately so you can get out of the hotel. Hope you like signing your names a lot.

Bree set the phone down.

"Well?" Hank asked.

"Diaz says the net's tightening," Bree said. "We're officially in the 'good guys' column. Kara says the house is moving forward. We can move in right away and pay rent to the owners for the four weeks we're waiting on closing."

"Big day," he said.

"You just proposed," she said. "Understatement of the year."

He grinned. "That too."

She looked around the space; the half-sanded floor, the patched wall where Jason had already started prepping for future hanging rails. Bryn's painting drying in the corner, Colby's projection marks still faint on the far bricks, and the new canvas waiting.

Her gaze fell back to the painting of Hank.

"I want to finish something," she said.

"I thought you just did," he said, glancing at the ring.

"That too," she said. "But I meant this. I want to sign it."

She picked up a thinner brush, dipped it in dark paint, and stepped close to the bottom corner of the canvas. Her hand shook once, then steadied as she wrote her name. Not the careful gallery signature she'd used in the city, the one that tried to sound older and cooler than she felt. Just her real name, in the script her grandmother had taught her as a kid.

Aubree.

She stepped back. The letters looked right there, small but sure.

"There," she said. "First official Copper Moon piece finished."

Hank slipped an arm around her waist, pulling her back

against his chest. "Second," he said, nodding toward Bryn's painting.

"That one's close," she said. "Not quite there."

"It can take its time," he said. "We're not going anywhere."

She leaned into him, feeling the steady beat of his heart against her back.

"What happens now?" she asked quietly.

"Now we get used to calling each other fiancé," he said. "We meet with Jason and Kara and Liz. We start arguing about tile choices and shop signage. Colby freaks out his captain by asking for transfer paperwork. Brian designs at least twenty terrible logo options before we talk him down to five."

"And me?" she asked.

"You," he said, kissing her shoulder, "paint. You teach. You yell at me when I leave greasy handprints on your clean walls. You hang that," he nodded at the canvas, "wherever you want. And when it all feels like too much, you come upstairs and breathe in this light until it doesn't."

She turned, facing him fully. "That sounds like a plan," she said.

"Good," he said. "Because I'm not really capable of subtle ones."

He bent, scooping her up before she could protest. She yelped, arms flying around his neck.

"Hank," she said, laughing. "You're going to throw out your back."

"Rude," he said. "I'm a finely tuned athlete."

"You're a mechanic with good cardio," she said.

"Same thing," he replied.

He carried her the few steps to the sunlit patch by the

windows and set her down gently on the drop cloth, following her down, bracing his weight on his hands.

The kiss that followed was slower, deeper; less about the adrenaline of new decisions and more about the quiet certainty underneath them. His hands slid along her sides, callused palms familiar and grounding. Her fingers curled in his T-shirt, tugging him closer.

Clothes didn't come off all at once, but piece by piece; a shirt tugged over his head, her tank top peeled away, jeans half unzipped. The afternoon light painted them in gold, catching the curve of his shoulder, the rise and fall of his chest.

He moved carefully, giving her space to say no at every point, even now. She didn't. She pulled him closer instead, arching into the heat of him, the ring cool against his skin where her hand slid along his back.

There was nothing frantic in it. No fear they were trying to outrun. Just two people who had chosen each other, again and again, anchoring it in skin and breath.

Later, when they lay tangled on the crinkled drop cloth, the studio smelling faintly of sweat and paint, she traced idle patterns on his chest.

"We're going to need a couch," she murmured.

"For the studio?" he asked, eyes half closed.

"For the house," she said. "I'm not explaining paint stains on the bedroom floor to your insurance agent."

He laughed sleepily. "We'll add it to the list," he said. "Couch, bed frame, and eighteen fire extinguishers to make Colby happy."

"Bridal registry is going to be weird," she said.

"Functional," he corrected. "People will appreciate the clarity."

"I'll need to go home and pack up my stuff. Give notice

to my landlord. Hug my parents. Are you ready to come with me?"

He nodded. "I have to do the same. Let's plan for later this week. We'll need the furniture for the house."

She rolled onto her side, propping her head on her hand. "You know what I'm looking forward to most?" she asked.

"Hot water that isn't timed by the front desk?" he guessed.

"That too," she said. "But I meant this. Waking up in that farmhouse, coming here, climbing these stairs, and seeing work in progress. Not in a guest room in my parents' house, not borrowed, not temporary. Ours."

He reached up, brushing her hair back from her face. "You're really in," he said quietly, as if testing the shape of it one more time.

She looked at the ring on her finger, at the paintings around them, at the dust motes swirling in the light.

"Yeah," she said. "I'm in."

Outside, a gull cried. Somewhere below, the faint sound of the bay door rolling echoed briefly; Jason, probably, coming to grab a tool he'd forgotten. Life, already moving around them.

Bree sat up, pulling her shirt back on, not bothering with the paint streaks. She crossed to Bryn's painting in the corner, touching the edge of the canvas lightly.

"We're going to need more names," she said.

Hank pushed up on his elbows. "You okay?" he asked.

"Yeah," she said. "Just thinking. Bryn won't be the only one. There are so many families out there who never got a place to put their grief down. We should start reaching out when we're ready."

"We will," he said. "One story at a time."

She nodded, then turned back to him.

In a few weeks, this room would be full of easels, tables, and racks. The wall downstairs would start to bloom with color and memory. The farmhouse would creak under the weight of their furniture and their arguments over cabinet handles.

The case Diaz was working on would grind forward. New problems would appear: pipes, engines, permits, and people.

But right now, in this small, bright pocket of time, the future felt less like a cliff and more like a path. Not smooth, not without potholes. Just something they could walk together, one step at a time.

She picked up her brush again, loaded it with color, and turned to the blank canvas waiting on the second easel.

"What are you starting?" Hank asked.

She smiled, feeling the weight of the ring, the steadiness of his presence, the ghosts that felt a little less heavy here.

"Home," she said. "I'm painting home."

Outside the windows, Copper Moon glittered along the harbor. Inside, Bryn's portrait dried in the corner, Hank's finished painting gleamed under the afternoon light, and on Bree's hand, the ring caught every bit of brightness it could.

They'd started. They weren't stopping.

EPILOGUE

The farmhouse looked different on their wedding day. Not just cleaner or dressed up with flowers, but lived in. Owned. Claimed.

Morning light spilled over the front field, laying gold across the grass as if the whole town had decided to bless them at once. The porch had fresh paint, courtesy of Colby and Brian after a "we swear this is a gift, not an intervention" weekend. Strings of white lights looped from the house to the maple trees. Lila's crew had set up tables and chairs under the branches, each one draped in simple white cloths that fluttered in the breeze.

It felt like the place had been waiting its whole life to host a wedding.

Hank stood in the bedroom he shared with Bree, doing the world's worst job of tying his tie. He'd rebuilt engines with fewer curse words.

"You'd think a mechanic would have better fine motor skills," Brian muttered behind him. He leaned against the doorframe, already dressed in a dark shirt and slacks, looking annoyingly put together.

"Engines don't require formal wear," Hank said.

"I'm just saying," Brian replied, strolling over and nudging Hank's hands away. "This is the price of marrying an artist. You have to look like you're capable of attending a gallery opening without embarrassing her."

Hank didn't bother denying that he'd do anything Bree asked today.

Brian finished the knot and stepped back. "There," he said. "Passable."

"I'll take passable."

Down the hall, laughter rolled from the den, where Bree and her mother had taken over the space to do hair and makeup, and what sounded like last-minute crisis management. Something thudded, followed by Bree's voice.

"I'm fine! I swear I'm fine!"

Brian grinned. "Sounds like pre-ceremony panic."

Hank's heart tightened. "She's not having second thoughts."

"No," Brian said, clapping him on the shoulder. "But she's allowed to freak out. You're allowed, too."

He didn't say he already had, alone in the truck fifteen minutes earlier, when the weight of what he was about to commit to had hit him in a way that nearly knocked the breath from his lungs. Not fear. More like awe. The kind that humbled a man.

Colby appeared in the doorway next, hair trimmed, suit pressed, carrying himself with the calm steadiness of someone who'd run more dangerous calls than anyone here knew.

"Your arbor's good to go," Colby said. "Bree's dad helped me reinforce it. The wind won't take it."

"Thanks," Hank said.

Colby leaned a shoulder against the wall. "You ready?"

"Yeah," Hank said. "Surprisingly so."

Colby's mouth tipped into a small, knowing smile. "Good. Because you're about to marry the kind of woman who'll expect you to show up. Every day. Fully."

Hank nodded once. "That's why she's the one."

Colby squeezed his shoulder, then headed downstairs, where guests were beginning to gather.

Hank took one last look at the room. Their room. Clothes in the hamper. A mug with Bree's lipstick mark still sitting on the dresser. A painting she'd done of the farmhouse leaning against the far wall. Life, in actual objects.

He felt that old ache, the one that used to whisper *Don't get attached*. Today, it was silent.

He went downstairs and stepped out onto the lawn.

The ceremony took place beneath the oldest maple on the property. Jason had built a simple arch of reclaimed wood, and Bree had decorated it with white flowers, soft greenery, and a length of ribbon her mother insisted had been in the family for thirty years.

Chairs filled with people who'd become their unlikely Copper Moon circle stretched out in rows. Liz. Diaz. Lila. Tom from the marina. Even the antique shop couple had closed early to attend.

On the far side of the yard, both sets of parents mingled. Hank's mother wiped her eyes every thirty seconds and insisted she wasn't crying. Bree's father kept clasping Hank's shoulder like he wasn't sure if he wanted to hug him or intimidate him into behaving.

Hank straightened his spine when Bree's father approached.

"You ready?" Roland asked.

"I am," Hank said. "More than ready."

Bree's father studied him, then nodded once. "Good. My daughter deserves steady."

"I'll give her steady," Hank said. "Every day."

A slow smile broke across Roland's face. "Then welcome to the family."

Music floated from the speakers Colby had set up. Guests rose to their feet.

Bree stepped out of the farmhouse and onto the porch.

Hank forgot how to breathe.

Her dress wasn't extravagant. It was simple, soft, flowing around her legs like something made to move with the breeze. Her curls were pinned back loosely, a few strands brushing her cheeks. She wore little jewelry. Just the small necklace Bryn used to wear, a gift from Charlie, who stood near the back, blinking furiously.

She looked like every moment of his future.

She looked like home.

Her gaze found his through the rows of people, and the nervousness he'd seen earlier vanished. Her smile grew, slow and certain.

She walked toward him with her mother, Mary, and her father at her side.

Hank swallowed hard.

When she reached him, she slipped her hand into his.

"Hi," she whispered.

"Hi," he whispered back. "You're stunning."

"Your tie's crooked," she murmured.

He laughed softly. "I had help."

The officiant cleared her throat. The ceremony began.

Vows were simple. Honest. No grand speeches, no overblown metaphors. Just two people promising to keep choosing each other, even on the days when choosing felt harder.

When Bree said "I love you", it went into him like a vow she'd carved straight onto his ribs.

When he said it back, her eyes filled.

"You may kiss the bride," the officiant said.

He cupped her cheek, leaned in, and kissed her slowly, with an intimacy he didn't hide from the crowd. This wasn't for show. This wasn't for the photographs. This was the beginning.

The guests cheered. Someone popped the champagne early. Brian shouted something that earned him a fierce elbow from Colby.

Bree laughed into Hank's shoulder.

"Married," she whispered.

"Married," he echoed.

Reception chatter filled the lawn. Tables covered in flowers, plates of food, and the kind of desserts only Lila could produce kept people drifting, eating, and celebrating.

Hank made the rounds, family member to family member. His mom hugged him until he couldn't breathe. His father shook his hand, then surprised him by pulling him into a brief, awkward hug.

"You've done well," his father murmured. "Proud of you, son."

Her parents, niece, nephew, and cousins, laughing, swatting away her father's attempts to interrogate Hank about the house's structural integrity, surrounded Bree.

"He's marrying an inspector," Brian said cheerfully, passing by with a beer. "You'll be fine."

Colby floated between groups with the ease of someone accustomed to managing crowds. Several locals stopped him to ask about the firehouse. He kept answering with the same careful honesty.

"Beginning the transfer process," he'd say. "Copper Moon's been good to me. Feels like the next right step."

Hank didn't miss the way several women eyed him with interest.

Colby pretended not to notice.

Something twisted warmly in Hank's chest. He knew exactly what awaited Colby next spring when tourists came to town, and they'd hopefully get super busy. Copper Moon would have no idea what hit it.

Bree appeared at Hank's side as the sun dipped low.

"You doing okay?" she asked.

"Perfect," he said.

"You sure? Because Brian and Tom are arguing about spark plug brands again."

"That's normal," Hank said. "Let them fight it out."

She smiled, then slid her hand into his. "Come with me," she said.

She led him through the yard, past the barn strung in lights, past the tables where guests lingered over dessert. Up the porch steps and through the house, down the back hall, out the side door.

To the outbuilding.

The shop.

He opened the door for her. The space glowed. They'd strung up lights earlier for the grand opening preview, but he hadn't seen it like this. Soft light fell over the lifted bikes, the polished concrete, the framed paintings Bree hung along the main wall: Hank on the track. Colby at a fire call. Brian covered in paint and grease, holding a wrench like a trophy.

And along the far wall, next to the tool chests, were three framed photographs from the Copper Moon Cup. All of them captured moments he hadn't known she'd seen.

"This is what we're opening tomorrow," she said quietly. "This is what we built."

He stepped closer to her. "Feels like a beginning."

"Feels like everything," she said.

He reached for her hand, but she slid her arms around his waist and pulled him down into a kiss that felt different. Deeper. As if marriage had stripped away some final layer of hesitation, neither of them realized they'd kept.

The door clicked shut behind them.

Heat curled low in his spine.

"Bree," he murmured.

She backed up slowly until her shoulders touched the workbench, pulling him with her. The lights cast a warm glow across her skin. Her wedding dress rustled softly as he set his hands on her hips.

"You look incredible," he said, voice low.

She reached up, fingers slipping beneath his tie, tugging him closer. "I want my husband," she said simply. "Right now."

A bolt of want went through him so sharply, he had to steady himself with one hand on the bench.

"Here?" he asked, voice rough.

"Yes," she whispered. "Here."

He kissed her again, and this time it wasn't soft. It was hungry. Weeks of pressure, fear, hope, triumph, all boiled down into a kiss that went straight through him.

He slid his hands along her waist, drawing her closer, feeling her melt against him. The room smelled like cedar, oil, and the faint sweetness of her perfume. She lifted his shirt from his waistband, fingers skimming under the fabric, nails dragging lightly across his skin. His breath caught.

"Hank," she said, voice low and certain, "touch me."

He did. Carefully. Reverently. Then, with the kind of confidence that came from knowing exactly what made her breath stutter.

She tugged him closer, her dress whispering as she shifted. He lifted her effortlessly onto the workbench, her legs parting to draw him between them. Her hands slid over his shoulders, down his back, then under the hem of his shirt to feel the muscles along his spine.

Heat unfurled fast. Deep.

He kissed her throat, her shoulder, the soft place beneath her jaw that always made her gasp. Her fingers dug into his arms. The lights glowed overhead, painting her in gold as he lowered his forehead to hers.

"You sure?" he murmured.

Her smile was soft, full, devastating. "I married you today," she said. "I'm sure."

The intimacy that followed was slow and deliberate, guided by whispered wants and familiar rhythms. Her dress pooled around her waist. His shirt hit the floor. She wrapped around him, warm and certain, and he moved with her, each breath shared, each touch layering meaning into something already deep.

When release came, it came together, powerful and quiet, her breath catching against his neck, his grip tightening at her waist as the world narrowed to just this moment.

He kissed her gently as they came down, foreheads pressed. Breath mingled. Hearts steadied.

"Married," she murmured again, voice hazy.

"Married," he whispered back.

Later, when they stepped outside, the sky had darkened fully. Music drifted from the backyard. Laughter carried across the lawn.

"Ready to join the party again?" she asked, slipping her hand into his.

"In a second," he said.

He turned, looking at the shop glowing behind them, then at the farmhouse lit with lanterns, and the field full of friends and family who'd chosen to gather around them.

Copper Moon wasn't just where they'd landed.

It was where they'd built something lasting.

She leaned into him, head against his shoulder.

He kissed the top of her head.

"Come on," he said. "Let's get back before they send out a search party."

They walked toward the celebration, hand in hand, lights twinkling, voices rising, the future unfolding itself in front of them like a road they'd finally chosen together.

Tomorrow, they'd open the shop.

Next month, they'd settle deeper into the farmhouse.

Next year, who knew.

But tonight, surrounded by their people, on their land, with the woman he loved, Hank knew one thing with absolute certainty.

They'd started something in Copper Moon.

And they weren't stopping.

WANT one more moment with Hank and Bree?

I've written an exclusive bonus epilogue that gives you a tender, intimate look at what comes next for them in Copper Moon. It's available **only to my newsletter subscribers.**

Sign up today and I'll send it straight to your inbox.

🤍 **Grab your bonus epilogue here:** https://www.pjfiala.com/hank-epilogue/

. . .

IF YOU'RE NOT ready to leave Copper Moon yet... you're in luck.

Hank's best friend, **Colby**, is about to take center stage —and his journey is nothing like he expects. When a resilient woman with a heartbreaking past steps into his life, everything he thinks he knows about control, trust, and love is tested.

Secrets. Healing. Heat.

Everything you love about Copper Moon begins again.

Grab **Colby** and continue the journey. https://geni.us/ColbyEBAll

Or scan the QR Code below.

ENJOY THIS BOOK?
YOU CAN MAKE A
BIG DIFFERENCE

Your Review Matters!

As an independent author, I don't have the big budgets of major publishers for splashy ads or subway posters (not yet, anyway 😊). But what I have is something far more valuable—amazing readers like you.

Your honest review is one of the most powerful ways to help my books reach other readers. If you enjoyed this story, taking just a few minutes to share your thoughts would mean the world to me. Reviews, even short ones, make an enormous difference.

Click below to leave your review and help others discover *Hank*:

🔜 https://geni.us/HankEBAll

Thank you for your support—it means everything! 🤍

ALSO BY PJ FIALA

I'm fortunate to be able to do what I love. It's a blessing.

My list of written works has gotten so long I needed to move it to my website! How's that for blessed?

Anyway, click the link below to see the list of all of my books.

Thank you so much for reading.

https://www.pjfiala.com/bibliography-pj-fiala/

or scan the QR Code below.

"Scan this QR code to view PJ Fiala's complete list of
published romantic suspense books"

MEET PJ

About the Author

Writing has always been my dream, but it wasn't until I found the courage to put pen to paper that my life changed in the most profound way. Creating stories that resonate with readers and bringing to life flawed yet lovable characters brings me endless joy—and I hope my books bring you the same.

When I'm not writing, you'll likely find me enjoying time with my family or hitting the open road with my husband, Gene. We're avid bikers who love exploring new destinations, meeting fascinating people, and soaking in the beauty of this incredible country.

Coming from a proud family of veterans—including my grandfather, father, brother, two sons, and daughter-in-law—I have a deep appreciation for service and the sacrifices that protect our freedoms. Their dedication inspires me every day, and I'm honored to share stories that celebrate resilience, love, and the American spirit.

"QR code linking to USA Today bestselling author PJ Fiala's Linktree hub with direct access to romance novels, signed books, shop, newsletter, and social media for romantic suspense and small-town romance fans."

Copyright © 2016 by P.J. Fiala

All rights reserved. This book or any portion thereof may not be reproduced or used in any manner whatsoever without the express written permission of the publisher except for the use of brief quotations in a book review.

Publisher's note: This is a work of fiction. Names, characters, places, and incidents either are the product of the author's imagination or are used fictitiously. Any resemblance to actual events, locales, or persons, living or dead, is entirely coincidental.

Printed in the United States of America

First published 2016

Fiala, PJ

Hank / PJ Fiala

p. cm.

1. Romance—Fiction. 2. Romance—Suspense. 3. Contemporary

I. Title – Hank

ISBN-13: 978-1-942618-08-9

January 2016 – first edition
March 2019 – second edition
February 2026 – third edition

www.ingramcontent.com/pod-product-compliance
Lightning Source LLC
Chambersburg PA
CBHW071351300726
48976CB00006B/1847